All for Now

a novel

Joseph Di Prisco

All for Now

a novel

Joseph Di Prisco

MACADAM CAGE

MacAdam/Cage
155 Sansome Street, Suite 550
San Francisco, CA 94104

www.macadamcage.com

Library of Congress Cataloging-in-Publication Data

Di Prisco, Joseph, 1950-
All for now / by Joseph Di Prisco.
p. cm.
ISBN 978-1-59692-371-3 (hardcover)
1. Monks—Fiction. 2. Future life—Fiction. 3. Psychological fiction. I. Title.
PS3554.I67A79 2012
813'.54—dc23
2011038148

Publisher's Note: This is a work of fiction. Names, characters, places, and incidents either are the product of the author's imagination or are used fictitiously. Any resemblance to actual events, locales, or persons, living or dead, is entirely coincidental.

Book design by Dorothy Carico Smith.

Printed in the United States of America.

First edition.

10 9 8 7 6 5 4 3 2 1

To my brothers, John, Bobby, and Eddie
in memoriam

THE DEFINITORIUM

Q. 1. Who made the world?
A. God made the world.
                    —The Baltimore Catechism

The summer sky looked milky blue, color of a wonder drug, and everyone was alive for now.

Inside the school building, a man sprawled along a weathered conference table like somebody's lost raincoat. His weary eyes could have been pleading for a wonder drug. His name was Stephen.

Suddenly his head jerked to the side. He seemed startled, as if someone had shouted his name. Though others were nearby, nobody had shouted anything. That was when Stephen noticed the butterfly. It was dancing on the other side of the windowpane, its orange wings framed by those blue depths of sky.

Stephen was the kind of man who registered everything. He never went anywhere without a notepad, and he jotted down details along with observations about—about anything, really. A hawk sighting, a beautiful number, a tricky password, a book somebody recommended, a line of poetry, a social slight, the doctor's appointment, a song he couldn't get out of his head, a chore, anything. Also jokes. Someone who does a lot of public speaking can always use an ice breaker.

Today was different. Reaching for pen and paper was not an option. He had seen his share of butterflies, but this one seemed to constitute a shocking revelation. Not knowing better and seeing his eyes wide open and his mouth agape, you might think a grizzly bear was running straight at him.

It was a memorable moment for Stephen, though he would not be the one to remember it. That fluttering butterfly was not only the most beautiful one he would ever see in his lifetime, it was also the last.

———

It was a Monarch butterfly. Its brilliant campfire-orange wings were striped and bordered jet-black. Everybody knows that if you wish to attract Monarchs, plant some silkweed. Silkweed is sometimes called milkweed or butterfly weed, for one excellent reason: it's the only thing Monarch larvae feast on. In no time, after a few days of metamorphosis, some Monarchs could be putting on a show. Understand that the silkweed plant is poisonous or at least disgusting to all other creatures. Whoever said that the cultivation of beauty was risk-free? As for a Monarch's lifespan, it depends—a few whirlwind weeks to several months.

It was a rosacea-cheeked, sad-eyed, big-shouldered man who noticed the Monarch. Stephen was a member of a Catholic religious order, the Holy Family Brothers. His was an order beleaguered, like many others, by civil lawsuits and criminal investigations, and he was in the thick of every controversy. He was called Brother Stephen and today he was dressed as usual in his plain black robe and white collar. He was fifty-five years old and the butterfly would outlive him. Brother Stephen had one minute left.

Sixty seconds, of course, is an eternity. A minute is an immensity. It takes less time for strangers to lock eyes across a room and in a flash go sick with desire. A poem comes together, a city crumbles, a track record is set, genius flowers on a microscope slide, a melody fills the hall, the sauce attains perfection, the suicide bomber takes down a building, the wine flows across the palate, a baby wails its first rowdy *you-gotta-be-kidding-me* to the world—all in practically no time at all.

The butterfly was dazzling, its painted wings delicate and translucent as a Chinese lantern.

Stephen wondered if anyone else in the gathering of the Definitorium saw the Monarch as it floated near the window, or if he was the only one. If so, he felt sorry for the rest. Brother Ignatius, Brother Gregory, Brother Harold, along with Brother Paulus, who was the Provincial, and Tom Newgarten, ex-officio member and chief legal counsel for the order—together with Brother Stephen they formed the Definitorium, the collective brass of the Western Province of the Holy Family Brothers. The truth was that he often felt sorry for them. He could usually count on their missing something magnificent in plain sight.

The butterfly hovered and bobbed, floated and dipped. The Definitorium had the same attention span as a silkweed-nibbling Monarch.

Then, outside, the excitable lawn sprinklers flipped on. The timer was malfunctioning once again mid-afternoon. The sprinklers stuttered *tsk-tsk-tsk-tsk-tsk*, shooting out slow, mannered, silvery arcs of water. *Tsk-tsk-tsk-tsk-tsk.*

He sensed something strange happening within himself. For a moment he could not name what it was. But—"Oh," he said to himself—then he could. The word for this sensation landed on the tip of his tongue.

A strange thought crossed his mind. He might be *dying*.

"Oh," he said again, this time under his breath.

Brother Provincial overheard him: "Stephen, you say something? Stephen?"

Tsk-tsk-tsk, the sprinklers kept stammering.

Tsk-tsk-tsk.

———

Stephen would never have the opportunity to record the sensation in his neurotic notepad. It would be an experience he would never get over, or, to put it another way, survive.

You only die once, he assumed, so in case he was right, he paid close attention. Then again, he continually paid close attention. Even as a schoolchild his attention hardly flickered. He was well aware of what was going to be covered on Friday's examination. He was prepared. In fact, he was never anything but *over*prepared. If he was instructed to bring a sharpened No. 2 pencil to class, he never failed to arrive with *two*, both of which were sharp as a porcupine quills. If he was assigned memorizing ten question-and-answers from *The Baltimore Catechism*, he would memorize fifteen, or twenty. Not to earn any extra credit. Just because. He did not need *extra* credit.

Speaking of which, *The Baltimore Catechism* loomed in his imagination. That was the slim canonical text possessed once upon a time by every Catholic schoolchild. It comprised the crucial doctrinal questions and the crucial doctrinal answers. It was a compact primer indispensable to a child inclined to ponder the meaning of life and death, this world and the next. A child who would become Brother Stephen didn't want to be caught dead without indispensable information like this:

> Q. 1397. *What does St. Paul say of heaven?*
> A. *St. Paul says of heaven, "That eye hath not seen,*
> *nor ear heard, neither hath it entered into the heart*
> *of man what things God hath prepared for them*
> *that love Him." (I Cor. ii., 9.)*

Stephen had been a brilliant student. That differs from being particularly intellectual or being academically successful, though Brother Stephen—or Stephen, or Stevie, as he was known growing up—was regarded by every one of his teachers as being one if not both. Brilliance is also unrelated to being popular or being a so-called student leader or being a candy-ass brown-nosing suck-up.

For the record, in high school Stevie did not have coarse terms like *candy-ass, brown-nose,* or *suck-up* in his working vocabulary. For one thing, his head was jam-packed with SAT words, like *oscillate* and *adjudicate* and *replicate* and *coruscate*, among the legions of *ates*, including *reprobate*. And let's not forget *mastur-* and so on, which he often wished he could. Come to think of it, it was test prep that originally inspired him to start using the notepad, to record the definitions. Yes, vulgar, derisive expressions such as *suck-up*, etc., did *contaminate* his vocabulary at a later junction, just in time for his service as Auxiliary Provincial. That was when the rarely *sedate* Brother Stephen had occasion to make daily use of such expressions. Let's not get into *celibate* right now.

But being brilliant at school has nothing to do with being happy at school, or *with* school, for that matter. No, Stephen was brilliant at school the way some people are brilliant at walking across a room, or eating an apple on a picnic, or speaking a foreign language at the airport. Everything he did in the unnatural environment of school indicated that this was his habitat and he was an alpha. Yes, Brother Stephen, when he was Stephen the teenager—baby fat, bad skin, cracking voice, and all—was once upon a time the most perfect schoolboy.

Today, as the once and future most perfect schoolboy began to expire, he smelled the fresh pot of coffee brewing in the conference room. He noticed the parched walls pleaded for a new coat of paint. He regretted he would miss the opera. *Madame Butterfly* had earned raves. Was anything as good as a good Puccini? He lamented that the latest voicemail message from the Brother Provincial would go unreturned. Brother Stephen prided himself on responding promptly to voicemails, even if they were the routine bullying communications from his micromanager of a superior, the Brother Provincial.

A scent, a sight, a regret, a lament. That summed up his and perhaps many others' endings. He was not the first to buy the farm, to kick the bucket. Unruly Roman legions in need of discipline were decimated by their commanders: one in ten executed on the spot. Saints were martyred. Others were liquidated, offed, zapped, wasted, rubbed out, eliminated. The dapper, loquacious mobster John Gotti termed an abrupt introduction to mortality getting *whacked* or being *clipped*.

In a blink, Brother Stephen was adjusting to his hasty demise, even if he had been neither whacked nor clipped. He didn't think he had a right to complain, yet it did strike him that a careless mistake was being made somewhere. The wrong button had been pushed. The papers had been mixed up. Maybe everybody felt that way at a time like this. Because of course death was a commonplace. Of course death was universal.

"Not mine," he argued with nobody. "*My* death is not universal, it's personal." All the while, the wings of a butterfly burnished a brighter, glossier shade of orange and the sprinklers stuttered *tsk tsk tsk*.

———

He had been thinking about death as long as he could remember thinking about anything. Not that he was disappointed to discover as much, but so far death was proving to be a little bit on the boring side. After all, his whole life long the Church had been orchestrating for him an overdetermined buildup to the spectacular experience of mortality. Certainly, Catholics were excellent on dying. They all seemed to possess the equivalent of PhDs on the subject.

Maybe that explained why Saint Thomas More famously said this: Nobody on his deathbed regrets being Catholic. Something told Stephen, however, that the same might not be said of some other moments spent in bed.

Really, Catholics think they practically invented the subject. If dying was their specialty, what gave Catholics fits was the subject of living. Being a baseball fanatic, Stephen would concede that going one for two over the course of a season would amount to an unfathomable batting average, .500.

Death was not feeling exactly predictable, but his postmortem *Baltimore-Catechism*ed self would have been shocked if he had not found himself transported somewhere, somehow. So far death had him on the move. Now deceased, there he was, driving along a country road weaving through stands of stately redwoods and underneath spreading pines. It was a two-lane road that curved and twisted, rose and fell, for what felt like miles and miles. And miles.

He remembered when he first got his driver's license, the sense of excitement and liberation, and what his buzz-kill of a dad had advised him on that occasion: "No teenage boy should be allowed to drive a car till they've driven for two years." He wondered if he was going to be bumping into his dad. He wasn't sure he would like that.

While Stephen was not conscious of having to be somewhere soon, he did have the hazy sense he was late. He had read that John Gotti whacked somebody in his crew because he was tardy for sit-downs. The made guy showed no respect for the capo, he had to go. Most gangsters weren't exactly great idea generators, but *The Godfather* he could watch over and over. *Keep your friends close and your enemies closer*, whispered Don Corleone. Brother Stephen took to heart the oil importer, sage, and patriarch's counsel when it came to his dealings with The Definitorium, whose members he kept closer.

Words, images, ideas, memories—they buzzingly bounced about his brain like models of electrons inside one of his gold-medal school science fair exhibits.

"*Doctor*"—why was he recalling this operating room clunker?—"*after surgery, will I be able to ski?*"

"*Certainly.*"

"*That's great, because I never could ski before.*"

A foggy intimation engulfed Stephen, the sense that there was somewhere—somewhere *else*—he was supposed to be. As he drove—

Wait, how did he get behind the wheel of this car? The Prius—should he say *his* Prius?—the Prius was so smooth, so pristine, so quiet, and it had that new-car smell, part spring wildflowers, part embalming fluid. He had only seen the hip hybrid vehicle from a distance before, invariably operated by stylish men and women who conveyed a certain self-conscious, self-congratulatory gravitas.

His car moved briskly, smartly down the road, not that he registered the engineering principles, and not that the odometer registered anything. It was fixed on 00000. It was so eerily quiet he wondered if the engine was in fact running. And he feared deceased pedestrians, expecting the *vroom* of a normal car, might be redundantly mowed down at the next turn by his stealth vehicle. The Prius was indeed comfortable, he had to admit, and featured lots of entertaining gadgets and multi-color gauges. And no ignition key as far as he could determine, which meant one fewer thing for him to lose. The Brothers normally drove utilitarian Ford Tauruses (fleet price courtesy of Joe Valli Motors—"*Go Joe: Get Value with Valli*"). With the Prius, though, Stephen felt an unaccustomed, non-utilitarian pleasure, gazing through the windshield toward the adorable white snout of the sedan, which resembled that of an exotic albino marsupial.

A billboard with red, white, and blue bunting, a billboard big as a bread truck, popped up on the roadside:

COME TO LUNA PARK!

The words were superimposed over a gigantic super-realistic image of a terrifying Ferris wheel, a Breughel knock-off.

Billboard?

NOW MORE THAN EVER!

Yes, a billboard.

Luna Park, It's Luna Park!
Where day is night!
Where black is white!

There had been a distinct shortage of exclamation points during Brother Stephen's lifespan. But if the roadside billboard—

A billboard?

Advertising in the next life?

There was a lot to get used to.

But if the roadside billboard were any indication, there was perhaps going to be a distinct longage of exclamation points in his afterlife.

As he drove, he noted how the light alternated with shade along the road. The brightness shuffled with the darkness as if a Casablanca fan the length and breadth of the whole sky hung beneath the sun and whirled. This development was unwelcome. Specifically, he hoped against hope that that whole phenomenon of light alternating with dark was not supposed to be symbolic, because if it was, he was in for an excruciating afterlife, one not covered in *The Baltimore Catechism*. Symbols: why would anything that had any self-respect bother to stand for something else? If symbolism were going to have its way with him, somebody should just shoot him now. Or whatever the equivalent would be.

He recalled that during class discussion—he had been a high school teacher for over twenty years—his students sometimes liked to complain: "Brother, there you go again, over-interpreting the story!" To which he used to reply: "You think so? OK, your turn. Go ahead, and why don't you under-interpret it for a while?" Since becoming an administrator, he sometimes missed the classroom. Yes, sometimes he missed the classroom the way a dehydrated man wandering in the Mojave misses barbecue.

He did not lust to correct comma splices or coddle whining parents, whose children they presumed others would regard as faultless though they themselves were never so stupid. But that gives a distorted impression of Brother Stephen's career. The truth was different. Ever since being kicked upstairs to the Auxiliary Provincial office, he felt homesick for his gloriously imperfect students.

Brother Stephen observed that teachers were drawn to teach the children whose developmental stage mirrored their own arrested development. He should have concluded, therefore, that he became a high school teacher because, in absolute psychological terms, he was sixteen years old. No wonder a schoolboy like him missed teaching in his advancing years. He missed the things his students told him that he didn't know before that he didn't know. Truth was, he had never taught a single day in which he had not laughed, really laughed, at least once. He even missed his students' complaining, because they weren't complaining at all. That was just teenagers' awkward way of connecting.

This was not his experience as a member of his religious order's hierarchy. There, it was the opposite. There, people complained in order to avoid connecting. Ultimately, death could end up being a disappointment, but if some Brothers marched up to him right now to utter some complaint, he would be delighted. He would love to tell them where they could go.

A priest misses his airline connection, and there he is, stuck in town with no place to stay. He's not wearing his clerical collar, and all his luggage has taken off without him, so he goes to the local Catholic parish and knocks on the rectory door.

He explains to the resident priest what happened and that he needs a room for the night. "I have some identification that identifies me as a priest."

"That's not necessary, Father," says the hospitable pastor, who welcomes him inside. Once he takes a chair, the host asks his visitor if he would like a cocktail.

"No thanks, Father. It's very kind of you, but I don't drink."

"Well, then, could I offer you a nice cigar?"

"Sorry, I don't smoke."

That's when the pastor said: "On second thought, maybe I should see that identification."

Again, a joke? What was with the jokes? This was not the occasion to break any ice—or was it?

Then he got it.

Was this all a big joke?

Not funny.

Maybe a little bit.

No, it wasn't funny at all.

———

Thus far his afterlife experience seemed to consist of driving toward the Northern California coast, or so it felt. There were worse alternatives. At least it was not the New Jersey coast, not that he had anything against The Garden State or its supposed coastline. He was sure it was a very fine state and had a very fine coastline—he just had never had the pleasure. He figured he should not jump to conclusions, though. Based on everything he had seen so far, anything might happen.

He looked at his wristwatch. Talk about an anachronistic reflex. What prompted the unexpected profusion of tears? He did not feel sorry for himself. Or did he? Still, the teardrops blurred the face of the watch, made it seem as though both the big and little hands had been washed away, which perhaps was true. Then, as unexpectedly as they had started, the tears ceased.

In many respects, this ride was like others he had taken to the shore. As before, he braked for white-tailed deer striking Sierra Club poses in the middle of the road. As he passed through a picturesque hamlet, a psychotic dog chased his Prius till it tired, then stood there and barked bon voyage. Cows grazed on hillsides, horses pranced in their fields. A family of skunks waddled single-file along the shoulder of the road. How had he missed that skunks sometimes travelled in a pack in the broad daylight? He had assumed skunks came out only at night, like owls, like dreams, like the clandestine bottle of Old Bushmills Irish Whiskey from the bottom of his desk drawer.

Brother Stephen hunched over the steering wheel, as if he were encumbered by a parachute strapped to his back. He became conscious that he had neglected to attach his seatbelt. That was not at all like the Brother Stephen of old, not to buckle up. He felt no urge to rectify that mistake, where before he would have been mortified. He needed to keep going wherever it was he was going, and he did. He drove, he drove.

———

It was not so long ago that Provincial Brother Paulus had dispatched his Auxiliary, Brother Stephen, to a forced stay in rehab. That was when the Provincial decided there was no alternative but to send away the about-to-crash-any-minute Auxiliary, for the Provincial's own good, if not for the Auxiliary's. Around that time, Brother Stephen had a spirited conversation with someone on a related subject. Though he could not summon up every detail, he vividly recalled the essence of the exchange.

"Brother Stephen, if I were a drunk, I'd want to be a drunk just like you," a Brother was saying to him.

That was direct. It took Brother Stephen a second. "Coming from you, that's high praise, Brother."

"I'm just like the umpire. I call 'em like I see 'em, Stephen."

"You're kind. Join me for a shot? When you stopped in, I was just about to…"

"*I'm* kind? Excuse me, that's merely the way you inspire me to be."

"I never would have said as much, but I suppose I *am* a gentleman of a drunk."

"You are being humble. You are downright courtly, not to mention thoughtful and unassuming."

"I try, I try."

"You're not the type to fall down drunk and cry in your beer. You keep yourself up. No stains on your shirt, no threadbare clothes, no stubble on your chin, no dandruff on your shoulders."

"Not to brag, but my shoelaces are tied, too. And my fingernails are impeccable." Brother Stephen made an ostentatious show of his clean hands.

"What's more, from my point of view, you are a drunk somebody could have a drink with. You're not like other drunks, who after their first cocktail jut their chin out and want to arm-wrestle or shout about dogma or politics or sports."

It was good to be appreciated, Stephen supposed. He remembered the location of the chat, that it took place in his cell.

"Thank you, Brother. I can't tell you how much your words mean to me, I simply cannot."

"You're very welcome, Brother Stephen."

"Bottoms up?" said Brother Stephen, with the tiny chalice of a shot glass raised to the level of his uplifted, bloodshot green eyes. "Confusion to our enemies!"

A drive to the coast had always been Stephen's guilty pleasure. He forced himself to clear his calendar in order to get away from his stressful job, to steal a few precious hours to unwind. The rocky shoreline became his sanctuary. His retreat, the sea, his open-air cloister, where he might be solitary but for the company of birds.

You might assume that being a member of a religious order amounted to living in a goldfish bowl. Actually, he did not require the sea to achieve solitude. In many respects, communal living was the ideal habitat for a recluse or a criminal in Federal Witness Protection. It was a place to hide in plain view.

Ah, that's right. He recalled that conversation now. He had been talking about being a very special drunk that evening with somebody who was very special. Himself. No wonder the conversation rang true.

———

Man goes into a monastery to live a monk's austere life, where he vows to keep the Great Silence twenty-four hours a day.

After five years, he is called into the Abbot's office for a rare exception: to express himself in spoken words.

"Brother," says the Abbot, "is there anything you would like to say?"

"Bed's hard."

Five years later, the Abbot summons him again.

"Brother," he says, "what else would you like to tell me?"

"Food sucks."

Ten years later—after, that is, twenty years of monastic existence— the monk is invited once again to the Abbot's office.

"Brother, is there something else on your mind?"

"Yes, there is. I quit."

"I should have guessed. You've been complaining ever since the day you got here."

———

When the car intercepted the coast highway, Stephen came to a full stop.

He weighed the options presented through the bug-splattered windshield. Right or left. Of course, there were never only two options.

There was always a third and, sometimes, a fourth. He could stay where he was for all eternity, or he could drive straight ahead. Straight ahead led impractically into a redwood tree. He felt a calm descend upon him. Usually, a feeling of calm made him anxious. He liked the calm all right, but did not trust anyone or anything descending upon him.

He studied a gas gauge that had not budged from "F."

He wondered whether he had become a man whose best days were behind him.

He asked himself how he missed them.

Mostly Brother Stephen mulled over how he had become a man who was a dead man mulling. He should have guessed that old habits die hard, especially for the dead.

He had assumed that when the Grim Reaper showed, contrary to conventional assumptions, he would be neither grim nor a reaper. He was correct. Otherwise he had little clue. One thing he never would have counted on was the black velvet gloves.

———

And so it was that one lovely afternoon in the middle of July, Brother Stephen would slip his corporal moorings after he noticed the Monarch butterfly fluttering outside the window. This would take place during an emergency session of the Definitorium, which was the ruling body of his religious order. It was sometimes known as the Board of Inquiry, and he was the chairman.

The august group had been summoned by him in response to the latest in a string of civil lawsuits against the Holy Family Brothers. Very, very few dioceses and religious orders had escaped unscathed the legal gauntlet in the last few decades. But this particular claim blindsided the Definitorium.

This new complaint told a by-now familiar, sleazy tale of alleged sexual misconduct. In this case, the events took place long, long ago, 1969, and revolved around a certain Brother Joel, who had been deceased now for many years (car accident, big rig out of control, tunnel, explosion, fireball) and whose legacy had been minor—until now. The female plaintiff claimed that she had been the victim of Brother Joel's sexual predations. She also detailed the role played by another Brother, in this instance a Brother of venerable standing, Brother Charles. Brother Charles was now retired and creakily stumbling toward eighty years old. He was called Brother Charlie by everybody who wasn't suing him and his religious order for a boatload of cash. Brother Charlie had been the principal of the high school where one spring day this senior came to him with serious allegations pertaining to Brother Joel. At the time the girl was seventeen, close to eighteen, and she supposedly informed the principal that her teacher had pressured her into consummating a sexual relationship. Catholics take advantage of every opportunity to invoke the word "consummate."

As it turned out, nobody in the Definitorium had a clue that such charges had ever been leveled against the late, unlamented Brother Joel, and there was nothing on the record to indicate disciplinary measures had been taken in response to this student's sordid accusation. The principal purportedly urged her to keep this allegation to herself, and not to tell her parents or anyone else. Were she to go public, it would boil down to the adult authority's word versus hers, the principal told the student, and her credibility and her motives would naturally come under scrutiny. The world would not be nice to her. Things could get very messy. For one thing, it would be difficult for her to draw the line between being "pressured" and being "seductive." What would she gain from the embarrassment she would inevitably suffer? Besides, Brother Charlie personally assured her that Brother Joel would leave her alone from now on, just trust him. Beyond that, he counseled her, she had the opportunity to learn from her mistake. She should pray for forgiveness for her own sorry part in this sorry episode, her own lapse in judgment. Furthermore, graduation was only a month away. Incidentally, Brother Charlie was looking forward to hearing her valedictory address, so she said. Any second she would be off to college, starting a new life. Did she really, truly want to risk being remembered for something so unpleasant? Didn't she want sweet memories of high school?

That was, in any event, the tale told by the lawsuit.

If the plaintiff were to be believed, she had kept this secret for thirty-five years until one day something turned for her. She had changed, and she decided enough was enough. She regretted that she had ever trusted Brother Charlie. She had unfinished business to attend to and so did the Holy Family Brothers. She wanted a measure of justice. It wasn't her so-called mistake when she was in high school that nagged at her as an adult. It was the vivid recollection of her teacher's and her principal's exploitation of her. She was done living in denial. She contacted an attorney.

The seedy details were there for all to read, including a dated and detailed catalog of sexual acts initiated by Brother Joel behind closed doors, everything narrated for perpetuity in the public record.

"Welcome back to 1969, Brothers," intoned Brother Stephen. "Her *mistake*," he said over and over again. "Learn from *her* mistake." He shook his head. *What a nightmare*, he was thinking. He had nothing but a fuzzy recollection of Brother Joel. He had a moustache. He wore Birkenstocks. It was that sort of era.

"If she's telling the truth," said Brother Gregory, "it's bad enough that moron Brother Joel crossed the line with the girl, but it's incredible that Charlie swept it under the rug." Brother Gregory (called G to distinguish him from the *other* Brother Gregory, whom nobody much wanted to put on any committees because he ate raw scallions like they were bonbons)—Brother Gregory Called G was the resident intellectual of the Definitorium, and was customarily astute, despite a fondness for mixing those metaphors. It was one thing for a repulsive adult—and a Brother at that—to take advantage of an impressionable teenager, he said through pursed lips while peering over rimless eyeglasses. It was another when the formal response of the principal rendered the whole order morally accountable—and financially exposed.

"Let's not forget, it was a different world back then," said dour Brother Harold, whose twinkling eyes and puckish smile had been sighted about as many times as the Loch Ness Monster. "Why do people insist on dwelling on the past? Ask me, we'd all be a lot better off forgetting a few things."

Brother Ignatius, a pragmatic Brother with great taffied earlobes that trembled when he talked, weighed in: "Maybe Charlie had his reasons. And how do we know she isn't an opportunist, trying to hop on board the Catholic-pedophile-scandal gravy train? When does the cash hemorrhaging stop—when?"

Tom Newgarten stuck a finger into the air as if he were gauging the wind. "Who made Charlie principal?" he asked.

"It doesn't matter," Brother Stephen explained impatiently, "but he was sent back into the classroom not long after. As principal he was a disaster. He couldn't tell the difference between a budget and a bitewing. And how could he manage a staff? He himself was completely unmanageable."

"When he stood in front of a classroom," said Brother Paulus, "he worked miracles." Something in the Provincial's acerbic tone implied that, as far as he was concerned, teachers' working miracles was not all it was cracked up to be.

"In his prime, Charlie was the best teacher there ever was," Brother Stephen testified, and honestly, because he knew. "The best."

All the same, Stephen felt weary and heartbroken. What had happened to his religious order? Why had things gone so terribly awry?

The anticipation of heartbreak was usually more dreadful than its ultimate arrival, or so Brother Stephen had discovered in his own admittedly restricted experience of life. Heartbreak is heartbreak, he had concluded, tautologically and not very memorably. And he had also discovered what he didn't know in advance about heartbreak: awful as it might be, he could survive its depredations. Until, of course, one day—this day, as it turned out—he could not.

Still, when Brother Stephen was served with the papers, he felt mournful, sadder than he might have expected. For one thing, he felt awful for the plaintiff. What an experience for her to have endured—if what she had said was indeed true. And how miserable she must have felt for so long, keeping those secrets and memories to herself. For another thing, however, he found it hard to believe that Charlie had played some conspiratorial part in this repellent matter. The recognition caused him to question everything he had ever thought he knew about his life. If Stephen was so wrong about Brother Charlie, what else could he have gotten wrong in or about the past? How faithfully could his memory recreate it?

Brother Stephen, Auxiliary Provincial of the Holy Family, the number two man in the hierarchy, was also named in the suit. The plaintiff, casting a wide net of institutional liability that included the higher-ups in the order, was pleading for relief to the tune of an unfathomably large number containing a menacing daisy chain of zeroes. This week the Metro section of the local newspaper had carried news of the lawsuit. Brother Stephen himself was quoted. He stated, in response to the reporter's question, "No comment, thank you." The item appeared alongside articles treating assorted felonies and corporate defalcations and car wrecks, as well as obituaries of local philanthropists, community leaders, artists, war heroes, and entertainers.

On this page, two days from now, would appear a pitifully outdated (1979), vaguely inappropriate photograph of him (toothy smile, furrowed brow, hair gelled into a jittery pompadour) alongside this ham-handed header for his obit:

Brother Stephen, 56, Educator:
Leader of Religious Order Beset by Child Abuse Scandal

Only two "facts" in error: age (off by one) and title (he was not the "Leader," merely the "Auxiliary"). And one dubious descriptor: "Educator."

Everyone in the Definitorium presumed that, now that the lawsuit was public, affairs were going to turn nasty. Based on past experience with lawsuits against the order, it was a safe bet. The Brothers' retained public relations firm would soon be gearing up to respond, as it had in the past. Many of the Brothers had given testimony in previous cases, some of them for days at a time, and consequently they knew the dismal drill that awaited them when they were subjected to the lawyers' carving knives during depositions. They would invariably proceed something like this:

"Ready to begin, Brother?"

"One thing I'd like to get straight. You do not answer directly to the Bishop, but to your superior, who is called the Provincial, who is the chief executive officer of the order?"

"I did not mean to imply that the Provincial did not have a spiritual role, not at all. But as you say, you answer both to your Provincial and to the Bishop. We'll come back to this later, because it is a complex matter, as you indicate."

"Something else I want to get clear. There are no priests in your religious order? All brothers, correct?"

"Just brothers, then. Priests say Mass, give out Communion, the other sacraments. You don't do that as brothers. You teach, and so on."

"Wow, that is impressive. I had no idea there were that many brothers working in the Church in all those religious orders. Speaking of brotherly love, are all those religious orders of brothers in as much legal hot water as your order?"

"Fine, no problem, withdrawn."

"Nobody calls you Father or Reverend?"

"So, you might say, you're like male nuns without the wimple."

"No, no, no. No disrespect intended. To nuns. But now that you raise the issue, who enjoys higher status, a priest or a brother?"

"No need to go there, counselor. Let's just get back to the situation that unfortunately brings us together this morning. When you received this complaint, did you ever at any point contact law enforcement?"

"How about County Child Protection Services?"

"And the reason you didn't was…?"

"What does that mean, there was nothing factual to report?"

"Did you alert the new school?"

"Who had that brilliant idea?"

"So what you're saying is, what they don't know won't hurt them?"

"Certainly, if you insist, I can rephrase. Why in the world didn't you alert the new school?"

"You had absolutely no second thoughts, not a one?"

"So what you're implying is, you never for an instant took the charges seriously?"

"Did the higher-ups—your religious superiors, such as the Provincial—instruct you to soft-pedal the charges?"

"Did you really believe these children were lying to your face? Help us understand. What in the world would they have to gain? Never mind, withdrawn."

"Had similar complaints been filed about this brother in the past?"

"What specific measures did you take to protect other innocent children from being victimized?"

"In hindsight, is there anything you wish you had done differently?"

"Nothing? Absolutely nothing at all? You were just thrilled with your expert management of the crime?"

"Fine, fine. I will withdraw 'crime.' How about problem? You OK with a 'problem'?"

"Was there anything in your religious training that prepared you to combat institutionally condoned evil on this magnitude? OK, withdrawn."

"Was there a culture within your order that made possible this widespread abuse of children?"

"Well, why don't you define widespread any way you like."

"Did you yourself ever molest a child?"

"Did anyone ever accuse you of molesting a child?"

"My apologies. I had an obligation to ask, for the record. But here's what I don't get. If you didn't molest a child, taking you at your word, Brother, you must have therefore known it was wrong, and if it was wrong, why didn't you blow the whistle on those Brothers who did molest? Why, Brother, why?"

"I'm not Catholic, though I used to be…"

"What was that?"

"Oh, sure, Brother, I guess somebody like you wouldn't be surprised to hear that somebody like me had left the Church. If I could resume my deposition, if you don't mind, please. Thank you. Anyway, Brother, what I dearly want to know—what I would give anything to understand—is how you could live with yourself, knowing what you damn well knew about a predator you had recklessly unleashed on more unsuspecting children."

"Yes, I actually do have a question. Here it comes. Do any of you guys, in your black clerical suits around this table, have a scintilla of conscience? And here's another. How do you sleep at night?"

That last unabashedly hostile, utterly reasonable and predictable question was usually and smugly posed in one form or another and it was always objected to by the order's counsel and, according to Brother Stephen's recollections, never once formally answered. Brother Stephen did have a reply, however, one which he wished his lawyer would have once permitted him to express during a deposition conducted by one Grand Depositor or another.

"How do I sleep?" he would have replied. "That's what you want to know? Let me see. For starters, my self-righteous friend, that makes two of us. Most nights, I still can't quite manage that trick. Maybe you can give me your secret. How do *you* sleep? How does *anyone*, knowing what we know about the damage the world routinely afflicts on the innocent? On second thought, don't bother. Don't think for a minute you understand me, or my religious order. Because the truth is that when I think about the charges before us today I feel sick to my stomach. And angrier than you will ever know for reasons you cannot possibly appreciate."

———

In the very last moments of life Brother Stephen had turned his attention to Tom Newgarten. Newgarten would have been a leading candidate for his law school's Risk Averse Prize. He was outlining the cautious approach to take with the insurance carriers, as well as a negotiating strategy pertaining to this Shannon Reed, the complainant. Technicalities could be invoked, he suggested. The statute of limitations might very well apply.

Newgarten appeared to be an excellently competent attorney. He even sported a bow tie, apparently at no extra cost to his client, the Holy Family Brothers, Incorporated. This sartorial detail invested him with a certain authority, if not with a swagger that was almost coy. At the same time, tying a bow tie also struck Brother Stephen as excessively complicated. Some of the renunciations of a Brother's existence are known to everybody, but there was one unexpected benefit: probably no conceivable call at any point for a bow tie.

———

It so happened that once upon a time Brother Stephen had been acquainted with the Shannon in question. He and the Shannon In Question had attended Angel of Mercy High School together. Technically, she was a junior when he was a senior. They had been friends. Pretty close friends, it would not be an exaggeration to say. Very close friends, to be frank. He pondered whether or not to disclose this information to the Definitorium. He knew he should, because the information was destined to leak, possibly by the first appearance of The Grand Depositor, but he was hesitant.

Brother Stephen was hesitant because he was less politically sophisticated, and less tactical, than, say, the average bottlenose dolphin. Dolphins have been known in the annals of legend and lore to coalesce around a drowning man in order to buoy him up, or to band together to fend off the voracious advance of a great white shark and rescue a human life in the process. Brothers were different. They were more like the sharks.

Brother Stephen never came to a resolution on the question of full disclosure with regard to one Shannon Reed. Besides, that was one deposition he seemed destined to miss.

Was there a possibility that she was lying? Everyone lies sooner or later, or sometimes. Stephen himself had finessed the truth more times than he would like to admit. And yet, even though he had graduated from high school and she remained to finish her senior year, he had to believe that he would have heard about something of this magnitude happening to Shannon. They were such good friends. Weren't they good friends? Of course, they were. He was therefore a little suspicious. At the same time, he had attended the conferences and the workshops that the diocese and the order had mandated in response to the epidemic of reported abuses. That meant he was aware that charges like the ones Shannon had leveled were usually credible, that people did not normally fabricate out of whole cloth such falsehoods.

So would the real monster please step forward?

Charlie? Joel? Shannon? Come on, you'll feel better.

And now for the fool. Stephen had missed the biggest drama of his and Shannon's high school life—either that, or he had completely misgauged Brother Charlie. If Shannon were telling the truth now, he had failed her when she needed him after being molested by Brother Joel and dismissed by Brother Charlie. And if she were not telling the truth, and if Brother Stephen were unfairly doubting Brother Charlie, he was letting down his fellow Brother when he most needed loyalty and fraternal care. He would fail Brother Charlie at the precise moment when he stood unjustly indicted.

Brother Stephen had had complicated dealings with each of them, certainly, for the two of them had historically been, in their individual ways, the most important people in his past.

As for his adolescent romance, such as it was, with Shannon—well, first of all, by conventional standards, it wasn't, not quite. Movies, burgers, long languorous telephone calls at night, doing homework together—that was it. And that was plenty. Yes, they held hands, and once or twice kissed a little bit. He loved the way her hair smelled. One of her blue-gray eyes was slightly smaller than the other, and one eyelid was a little lower than the other. As a result, she somehow always looked a little bit sleepy. And her eye made it so he had to shift his vision side to side to see her whole. As for school, her grades in math and science were higher than his, and he read her compositions and her stories with amazement. She was incredibly smart. Or maybe just a lot smarter than he was.

She used to tell Stevie that she wanted to be friends with him forever, because they were special friends. Very special friends. He had beautiful soft hands. He listened to her when she told stories. She laughed at his jokes. The night he told her he was going to join the Brothers, she hugged him for a long time and, if she shed any tears, she waited until she was by herself.

Their relationship faded just about the instant he entered the order, right after graduation. Yes, the two of them exchanged letters, and she drove up to see him two or three times during Sunday afternoon visiting hours at the novitiate. Those visits were strained and mutually unsatisfying, and by the time she had begun her final year of high school, the time when she may have been preyed upon by Brother Joel, they had fallen out of touch. At this late date it would be impossible for Stephen to reconstruct the sequence of the disintegration, but the outlines were clear. He could not fault her or himself, given how their future seemed foreclosed, but he fell into a protracted sadness, and he missed her deeply until, one day, he accepted the truth. He tasted resignation, loss. It tasted the way he imagined ashes would taste.

The new information contained in the lawsuit—even if he could not be one hundred percent certain it was reliable—colored his recollections now. And he caught himself enraged anew by Joel. That son of a bitch could have been responsible for destroying his relationship with Shannon.

Nevertheless, Brother Stephen would also concede that every now and again, so many years later, he still found himself nostalgically remembering Shannon, wondering about her, wondering about *them*. It was natural enough, human enough, that, though he had been a celibate Brother for decades, he would still fantasize about a married life. Sometimes he lazily speculated as to what might have been if, say, Shannon and he had somehow, against the laws of probability and in defiance of common sense, had…

Enough of that. On such preposterous ideas he did not allow himself to dwell for too long. He had people to hire and to fire. E-mails to write. Positions to take. Bottles of Bushmills to locate in his desk. Meetings to run, like this one of the Definitorium.

To an outsider, it must seem ridiculous, if not quaint, for someone of Brother Stephen's age and standing to be investing his imagination in such impossibilities for even a passing second. Yet living in a community of men sharing religious vows and a teaching vocation made such speculation possible. Reveling in fantasy was a temptation for a Brother, even for one who was a hard-working, continually sublimating Auxiliary Provincial.

As for Brother Charlie, Stephen's connection with him was perhaps more complicated still. Brother Charlie had been his teacher during high school, and afterward his mentor when he was a young Brother. In due course, they were later assigned to teach in the same school, where they worked side by side for years. Charlie was a legendary teacher who had been of tremendous assistance to him in the classroom. Although this was strange to admit, he became one of those friends Stephen did not always like very much—nor completely trust. The two had had their falling-outs. Charlie's charisma and intensity were not always easy to tolerate. Rifts ensued. Sometimes bitter rifts. It was difficult for two men to make an adjustment in their adult relationship when, at the friendship's beginning, one was so much older than the other—and a former authority figure at that. Temperamentally, too, they were night and day. Charlie was flamboyant. He didn't exactly don a billowy white silk scarf around his neck, didn't stick a silver cigarette holder in his brilliantly white teeth, didn't tie back his long, fine hair in a ponytail—those affectations were proscribed by the order. But he cultivated an aura of someone who did just that. Over time, and not necessarily on the basis of sound reasoning, many of his fellow Brothers arrived at the conclusion that Brother Charlie was homosexual. Perhaps tension between him and Stephen was understandable.

What is wrong with this picture of Shannon and Charlie? Brother Stephen was musing. *Besides everything.* A piece of the puzzle had to be missing. No, it wasn't a piece of the puzzle that was missing. There were three puzzles—Shannon, Charlie, and Stephen—and each of them might have been missing a piece. Was it plausible that each was missing the same piece?

But this lawsuit involving Shannon and Charlie had taken a toll on Stephen, too. Whatever turned out to be true, Stephen's conception of his past life—as well as his conception of his present life—needed to be revised, and radically.

Meanwhile, Stephen steadfastly decided something. He would not permit himself to visualize the graphic pictures the lawsuit had insistently, repetitively, voyeuristically painted, page after page, bullet point after bullet point.

He refused. He refused. He refused. But he could not stop himself.

—

Brother Stephen posed a couple of atypical for him questions to counsel and the entire Definitorium: "What can we do to make everything right for Shannon and for Charlie both?" The questions yielded quizzical looks all around the room. "I mean, how can we minister to them in order to heal their wounds?" He surprised himself when he voiced such naïve-sounding concerns. What he really wanted was the truth. Perhaps that was too much to ask.

Tom Newgarten fell silent, indicating in effect that maybe it was too much to ask. His forehead wrinkled and his mouth curved down, but on him such a countenance looked almost intelligent. Then he admitted that short of going back in a time machine and booting Joel and Charlie out of the order before they had ever crossed Shannon Reed's path, he had no clue.

"But that's assuming," Stephen interrupted him, "that Charlie's culpable. And that's a big assumption."

Tom never appreciated being interrupted. He said of course he did not know for sure if Charlie had done what Shannon had said, true. The way he spoke, however, suggested he had his strong suspicions. He had been studying the documents, he had been speaking to her lawyers, he said. "There's a lot of detail in the accusations, Brother Stephen. A lot of very squalid detail. Her lawyers are top-notch, and my hunch is they're working on a big, fat contingency."

Therefore, Tom advised, after the insurance carrier signed off the tactical response of the Definitorium should probably be the following: genuinely apologize and admit limited liability, once Shannon agreed to the terms of a confidential settlement that would represent just and generous compensation, and tie her up in an airtight non-disclosure agreement. Afterward, they would do their best to control the damage to the order's reputation and openly initiate new institutional practices and processes that would promise better results in the future. Tom got paid to think through such matters, which Brother Stephen knew better than anybody because he signed the checks in payment of the reduced-rate pro bono invoices.

That was the instant when he noticed the Monarch butterfly and how the sky had turned, without warning, milky blue.

"But Tom, does anybody really know," said Brother Stephen, "if we can ever make anything right in life?" He wasn't feeling well. His voice had dropped to a hoarse, strangled whisper. "That's something I wish I knew."

"You feeling OK, Brother?" Newgarten asked with escalating alarm, sensing something uncharacteristic in the injured utterance of Brother Stephen. "You need a glass of water?"

Stephen could not respond, but if he could have, he would have replied that a glass of water was not what he needed. He needed those dolphins. How little the Definitorium knew about him. And now, what difference could that make to them or to him? And was that a triumph or a disappointment? He was a few heartbeats away from a clean getaway.

The butterfly disappeared.

———

Tsk-tsk-tsk. The sprinklers were still going.

A chilly shadow seeped from the tall windows and settled into the middle of the room. Black, blank darkness filled Stephen's eyes, sealed his ears, slid down his throat like a gelid stream of mercury. Brother Stephen—once semi-beloved over-interpreting teacher, harried and second-guessed bureaucrat, quasi-non-recovering alcoholic, formerly rising star Brother of the Holy Family Brotherhood, and baseball junkie—Stephen began to shuffle off his mortal coil.

Who could have known that such shuffling would be so very, very effortless? That it almost seemed to be an activity taking place outside himself?

"Brother, *say* something, would you?"

At the same time, he yearned. Even at the end he yearned and yearned and yearned. Who could have anticipated that such yearning would be so gripping, so satisfying? He yearned to be cradled. He yearned to rest. He yearned to yearn no longer.

More than anything, he yearned for the plaintiff, Shannon Reed. It was shocking and a little bit embarrassing for a fifty-five-year-old Brother to admit as much, but it was true. He yearned to feel what he had once felt for Shannon. He yearned to feel what he once *felt*, period. It had been so long since he had felt anything as powerful, as pure as that.

This is the truth, though it says as much about adolescence as it does about Stephen. There was a time when he would have gladly died for Shannon. That probably sounds histrionic to sensible people. Or to the Brothers of the Definitorium. Nonetheless, it is the case. Once, for instance, on that night in the diner when she reached across the table and placed a finger on his wrist. She wasn't measuring his pulse. If she were, she would have discovered he had the pulse of a hummingbird. That might have been altogether the single best moment in his life.

It undoubtedly surpassed the present.

———

His head pitched forward onto the conference table. Then his body began to slip off the chair and crumple to the floor. He was powerless. Vertigo was a word that might have come to his mind, but words were not readily accessible, as only a remnant of his brain functioned. And that part, incoherently. The very physics of his predicament seemed skewed and defiant, too. He was descending, but with a ripcord-less parachute that was simultaneously free falling and floating.

At some point, he lay face down on the threadbare carpet of the conference room, nose bent and broken, arms raised over his head, as if he were signaling surrender. He caught the scent of damp coffee grounds. The smell was acrid, but a little sweet, too.

He reflected that he had picked a very inopportune time to die, what with such an important item on the agenda before the Definitorium.

"Call 911!"

They flipped him onto his side. They were afraid Stephen might drown in his own blood. It was not easy moving him, considering his girth. Stephen expelled what he knew was to be his very last breath. His eyelids fluttered like the wings of a butterfly, in what promised to be his final sensory experience on earth.

"Who knows CPR!"

"Hang on, Stephen, hang on!"

Hanging on was the one thing he could not do, not anymore. At last he was free to let it all go. Inside his eyelids, the color was changing. It was going orange, bright orange. His head might as well have been filling up with thousands of butterflies.

A siren far away, getting closer.

"OK, Stephen, they're coming! Just a minute more!"

Bye bye, Shannon, bye bye, Charlie, bye bye, Brothers. Bye bye, Definitorium. Bye bye, law suits, meetings, schools. Bye bye, arthritic feet and hands, Old Bushmills, thinning hair, gorgeous operas by Puccini. Doctors' appointments and diagnoses and complaints and night sweats and family and chores and computers and e-mail and overflowing desk and bookcase—bye bye.

He was sneaking in under the checkered flag waving at the finish line.

"Stephen! Brother *Stephen*! Come on, say something!"

At the very end, a first. Somebody was pleading for him to speak up. Stephen proved unable to accommodate the request.

You see, he was unavailable. He was reaching after that Monarch butterfly, which promised, much like his understanding of the life that was departing him, to float always just beyond his grasp.

Tsk-tsk-tsk, he was hearing. *Tsk-tsk-tsk-tsk-tsk-tsk-tsk.*

Tsk.

And the wind picked up all around him.

Then, then, was he gone.

———

Afterward, there was something of him that remained. If some unsuspecting caller had phoned Stephen's office that afternoon or evening, this is what he would have heard:

Hello. You have reached the office of Brother Stephen, Auxiliary Provincial of the Western Province of the Holy Family Brothers. Sorry I was not here to take your call. Please feel free to leave a detailed confidential message, and I'll get back to you as soon as I can. Peace be with you. Goodbye.

Q. 1398. Are the rewards in heaven and the
punishments in hell the same for all who enter into
either of these states?

A. The rewards of heaven and the punishments in
hell are not the same for all who enter into either
of these states, because each one's reward or
punishment is in proportion to the amount of good
or evil he has done in this world....

        — The Baltimore Catechism

ONE

Q. 197. What is a mystery?
A. A mystery is a truth which we cannot fully
  understand.
                                        — *The Baltimore Catechism*

Brother Provincial Paulus; Distinguished Members of the Definitorium, Brother Ignatius, Brother Gregory Called G, Brother Harold, Tom Newgarten; My Fellow Brothers and Colleagues:

Now, where were we, Brothers, when I was so rudely interrupted?

I know at some point I began to drive. That's right. I drove and drove some more. Teenagers and dead men cannot conceive of better alternatives, and, being in a way both, I was no exception. I turned on the radio, something I did not normally do in a car, as you may know. What a marvelous sound system the Prius had.

Of its own volition the car gravitated to a National Public Radio station. The theme music was familiar and jaunty, the kind of tune to which callers, when begged, would respond Pavlovianly with donations. I had wondered if the afterlife would be the one place where fundraising would be an afterthought. I think I had my answer.

———

"Our guest on today's show is the late Brother Stephen."

The interviewer had that distinctively lovely, impish voice I had heard plenty of times on the radio in my room, which is where I used to think a radio made sense, not in a moving vehicle where I had my hands full. Hers was a voice full of crafty intelligence and conducive to the un-inhibited disclosure of intimacies, a voice clued in to pop vicissitudes and high culture verities both. Call me crazy as well as deceased, but I was curious as to what she was going to ask and what I would reply.

"After serving many years as Auxiliary Provincial of the Western Province of the Holy Family Brothers, Brother Stephen died during a meeting he had called to discuss one of several suits filed on behalf of students taught in schools operated by his religious order. Individuals have stepped forward and claimed to have been sexually abused as children and teenagers, in some cases decades ago. He has just published a new best-selling book about his afterlife, titled *Last Call*. He joins us today to talk about the scandal in the Church and to discuss his new book. Brother Stephen, welcome to the show."

"Thanks, Terry. You know in baseball, Terry, they call being called up to the major leagues *going to the show*. I like that expression. I'm really on the radio?"

"Brother Stephen, give us a sense of what it's like, the afterlife. Do our preconceptions do it justice?"

"It's just like high school, Terry. You know, maybe it *is* high school."

"How so, Brother Stephen?"

"Remember the insecurity, the dread, the anxiety, the cramming, the first dates, the proms, the French Club, the Math Club, the Humor Club, the baseball team, the incredible desire to insert your tongue…"

"Brother, it seems that Dante, Orpheus, Odysseus, and Virgil—they all preceded you into the underworld, which you say is a lot like high school for you, and then they all came back with stories to share."

"You should check with the Definitorium, Terry. They would tell you that…"

"Oftentimes, these heroes descended in a search for knowledge, or on a quest to bring somebody back. I'm thinking of Shannon Reed."

"Makes two of us."

"Is she the inspiration for your journey?"

"Somebody published a book I wrote?"

"I mean, were you looking for her, or for something or for someone else in the underworld?"

"You might have something there, Terry. I'll have to get back to you. I am curious, though. Why do you suppose the dead wish to come back to the land of the living? Think nostalgia would make them forget what the world was all about? Not to mention they'd have to die all over again. Believe me, that's no picnic. It's like an all-time giant ice cream headache. The descending dark, which is a frozen thermometer stuck inside your head. The unmanned shuttle that blasts you into the big wherever—not exactly my idea of a good time."

"When did you decide to write *Last Call*, which is about your life, death, and afterlife?"

"I kind of like that title. I myself never thought much about the afterlife, to tell the truth. You don't think it's kind of cheesy, the title *Last Call*?"

— ABOUT THE AUTHOR —

Brother Stephen is the author of zero works of fiction, non-fiction, and poetry. He also was the author, etc. There was an anxiously awaited trilogy, momentarily. But then the trilogy was no more. Isn't that the way with trilogies? They seem like a good idea, and then you have to leave the dinner party, saying: "Oh, my, whatever happened to the time?" You might say he was born. It is conceded. Of parents, what is he supposed to say, if anything? For thirty years he… He divides his time between… Once he wanted a dog, a child, a bicycle, a sports car, a pair of boxing gloves. He taught. He forgot. Prizes? He never got the phone call in the middle of the night with the breaking news from Oslo, if that's what you mean. The only calls that come in the middle of the night led to his getting dressed in the dark and going to a hospital and saying goodbye, usually too late, to those he once loved. Occasionally numbered among these were his mother and father. His website is shut down temporarily for construction, please check back soon.

"That reminds me. There's this moving passage where you write about the *Baltimore Catechism*. Or as you would say, *Ballamore* Catechism."

"Home of Babe Ruth, you know, and of Edgar Allan…"

"Would you read from that section when you had just entered the novitiate, you were eighteen I think, and you learned how to drink with your fellow Brothers after swearing off booze because of your parents, who were both alcoholics—"

"Well, I don't have *Last Call* with me, Terry. I still cannot understand how I wrote a book in the first place. The title has at least a few levels of meaning, whoever titled it, besides the obvious bar and grill connotations. Then you have *last call* as in *last calling*, as in vocation. I suppose that works all right, too. Plus, the *last call* as in last phone call or final communication, or the last call into the night, a lonely voice. You have a fabulous voice, by the way, Terry."

"You recall the account of your own personal battles with alcoholism. Was that difficult for you to do, to be so confessional?"

"Look, being a drunk—the problem with being a drunk is that you can't enjoy a drink. But it's true, I am an alcoholic, to invoke a very crude and imprecise term for the self-serving gentleman drunk that I am. I'm probably a pretty typical alcoholic, always in denial, always deferring changing my life. Possibly I wrote about this experience, if I did, because I knew I never could definitely change my life. Near as I can tell, that's the best thing so far about dying. Your death puts your life in perspective. Now that I think about it, could be the only good thing."

"Another way to ask the question is, does the afterlife live up to your expectations?"

"I'm certainly trying things I never tried when I was alive. Such as being interviewed on the radio by you, Terry. Love your show, by the way."

"As Auxiliary Provincial of your religious order, you personally handled child abuse lawsuits. I imagine that it was a very depressing experience."

"You're right about that. You probably have no idea. Probably nobody does."

"I wonder if you have had any second thoughts about the way you handled those cases. Do you have any regrets about how your order disposed of these suits?"

"All I know is that I've never been so busy on these matters as I am now."

"Have you had a sexual relationship, Brother?"

"Today? No, I haven't."

"Isn't it impossible to understand the effects of sexual molestation upon a child if one hasn't had sex?"

"Depends on your definition of 'isn't,' Terry."

"So what you're implying is, molesting a child is not about sex at all, it's about power and exploitation, and it's a sickness that leads to the commission of a vile crime."

"That's what the psychologists, what the lawyers say. Yes, the men who perpetrated such crimes are dangerous and they are damaged both. You can call them sick if you want, but lots of sick men don't savage the lives of young people, as these men did. Some of them probably spend their afternoons doing crossword puzzles in convalescent homes. I don't comprehend what turns someone who once made idealistic choices into a monster. Something went wrong deep inside. Isn't that obvious?"

"Are you asking for sympathy for these child-abusers?"

"Of course not. Well. Maybe I am, not that I can defend that position. Because at the same time, they must be held accountable. They victimized people who were in no position to defend themselves."

"Are you sorry about any of the decisions you made?"

"Going against advice of counsel, let me say I do not understand the question. And I probably will contradict what I have gone on record saying, by saying I probably regret everything."

"Everything?"

"I regretted being born, Terry."

"But not now? Now you don't regret being born?"

"It is sort of a moot point. You're a quick study, Terry. Can't say the same for myself, of course."

"Anything you wish you could do over?"

"If you don't understand how anybody, anybody in the world, could do such terrible things, you don't understand anything about human beings."

"We all read our Dostoevsky, especially *Crime and Punishment,* when we were sentenced to four years of hard labor in high school, if that's what you're suggesting."

"Dostoevsky, he gets it, no doubt, but he's not the only one. Look, if you cannot see the darkness within your own soul, you won't be able to see the darkness in somebody else's. If you don't think you are capable of snuffing out the innocence of a child, you need therapy, you need religion, you might need both. I can tell you from personal experience that finding the monster within is at the very least, well, humbling."

"Speak about your monster within."

"My monster within? He's a lot like the guy talking with you on the radio, Terry. In fact, he's more like him than any movie monster you can imagine."

"I'd like to follow up with you on another matter, Brother. Do you think there's a direct connection between your journey to the underworld and these lawsuits you were fighting?"

"I can see why you're asking, but it's kind of ridiculous. We weren't fighting the lawsuits, Terry. We were trying to do the right thing. Why do people get this so wrong?"

"Let's stay in the underworld, Brother."

"Like I have a choice."

"As you know, the world above is divided between those who adored *Five People You Meet in Heaven* and those who torched it. You have a pretty special vantage point, I'd say, so where do you stand on that book?"

"Never had the pleasure, Terry. Have you read it?"

"Our show is coming to an end, but I want to know. How was your time on Earth, Brother?"

"You been talking to Brother Paulus?"

"You must have had the chance to reflect now, where you are. What stands out? What, for instance, was the biggest surprise for you, being alive?"

"Looking back, reflecting, as you say, I would say the biggest shock is that I was ever alive, even for a minute. It seems incredible now to have been given a life that one day is no more. You would think life never ends, though everything in your experience proves otherwise. Makes you wonder if the God who made us is cruel or if the God who made us never existed in the first place. And if the latter is true, then our existence must be called into question. Which it most definitely is. When I was alive, in the world, and a friend would die, I could never get over the emptiness, the absence, the loss of that person. Death seemed like such a terrible, terrible idea. How does one really go on after facing the absence of somebody you once loved?"

"Speaking of which. What did it mean to you, being reintroduced to the love of your life, Shannon Reed?"

"I don't know how to talk about that."

"Before we close, Brother, I'm curious. Where you are now, what's the weather like?"

"Cloudy, with a slight chance of late afternoon sunshine."

"I want to thank you, Brother Stephen, for appearing on the show."

"*Last Call*, that's really the title?"

"One final question, Brother Stephen. If we have learned any-thing about predatory clerics, and their effects on future generations… Brother Stephen, you write about this issue with such fire. Were you yourself ever molested?"

"I would answer your question if it mattered to anybody but me."

"Dr. Samuel Inskeep, author of another new..."

"Inskeep? You're kidding me. Samuel Inskeep? That's my loser of a shrink. Anybody ever heard of doctor-patient privilege?"

"Inskeep has gone on record in his new book..."

"That's one book I won't be reading any time soon."

"Funny, he said the same about yours. In any case, thank you very much, Brother Stephen, for talking with us today. Brother Stephen is the author of *Last Call*. He has been speaking to us from his afterlife. Join us tomorrow, when our guest will be author Samuel Inskeep, who joins us from the farthest reaches of Manitoba."

"Son of a bitch."

"You can't say that on the radio. By the way, who's Terry?"

TWO

Q. 793. Is our Confession worthy if, without our fault,
we forget to confess a mortal sin?
A. If without our fault we forget to confess a mortal
sin, our Confession is worthy, and the sin is
forgiven; but it must be told in Confession if it
again comes to our mind.
                        —The Baltimore Catechism

Brothers, did you hear the one about the deceased Auxiliary Provincial?

He knew where all the bodies were buried—except his own.

So, my fine-feathered functionaries, lend me your ears. I have much to recount to you about death and the afterlife.

You might be curious about the fate of your extinguished contemporary. Even if you are not, I feel duty-bound as the former (no kidding) Chairman of the Holy Family's official Board of Inquiry, the Definitorium. I have an amoral obligation to present you my insider findings from the so-called other side. I consider this my first assignment as the recently self-installed Chairman of the Indefinitorium.

As my students might have said about their old teacher Brother Stephen—man, he was so dead. If the crisis called dying isn't enough to get a man's attention, I don't know what would be.

Now, it is well known that the Chinese ideogram for *crisis* contains two characters. Raise your hands, Brothers. Who hasn't received this memo?

One of the Chinese characters: *opportunity*. The other one: *danger*.

If I had ever concocted an ideogram to delineate my experience of *crisis* in my pre-afterlife, it also would have contained two characters:

$$Crisis = Ben + Jerry's.$$

Often as Auxiliary Provincial I was embroiled in nasty little dust-ups that I needed to mull over before muddling through and thoroughly mucking up. That is when I would pry open the refectory freezer door armed with nothing but an unloaded tablespoon. Then I would scoop out sweet, cool comfort and enlightenment from the creamy coffers of a pint of Cherry Garcia, or two. When that didn't do the job, the ideogram metamorphosed into:

$$Crisis = Old + Bushmills.$$

Under current circumstances, I have no expectation of finding a gelato shop open any time soon. But as for the prospect of that bottle of Irish whiskey, that is another story, as you will see. Could it be true what I used to believe? That the only surefire cure for my drinking was death?

Let us get something straight and, not to be hostile about it, but then again, why not? You not so secretly wished to remove me from my seat on the Board, to cut me out of the order's power equation. No wonder you privately feel relieved I am out of your hair. Careful what you wish for, children.

A little teaser: If you stick around, I guarantee there's a funny twist or two in store for you. But don't expect me to become a ghost haunting your deliberations. If I ever do get into the haunting business, it won't conform to your idea of what a ghost does.

These aren't really findings, I should also say off the top—not really and truly. *A trace of lead* is an example of a finding. *Two out of three in a blind taste-test prefer Coke to arsenic,* that is a finding. *130 over 85,* a blood-pressure finding my perennially disappointed doctor would have been pleased to relay to me. Instead, this is simply the account of my personal inquiry into the hereafter. I did not actually find anything I had not already discovered long ago. Or if I did, it found me. So I guess you could say I myself am the finding.

Which encourages me to correct my lead. I have much to recount to you about death and afterlife. How my experience applies to yours would be the sum and substance of your problem. I am still trying to understand how it applies to me.

Excuse me, but I can almost hear your sputtering impatience, which I can testify that you all elevated to a high art. "Executive summary, Brother Stephen," you are snippety-sniping. "Cut to the chase. We have a packed agenda for the Definitorium."

If you insist, here goes. It's a two-part sound bite. *One*: Death is a kingdom, and *Two*: There is no king. Oh, and *Three* (Bless me, Brother, for I have sinned): If I had thought about it in advance, I would have known all along exactly what awaited me.

Nobody will confuse my narrative with Dante's science fiction *The Divine Comedy*. What's more, I would never have the courage to admit that I was ever *Half in love with easeful Death*, and I never would have claimed that *Now more than ever seems it rich to die*, because this is no minor league "Ode to a Nightingale," and John Keats, I don't need to tell you, I most definitoriumly ain't. Even your bad reviews won't kill me the way they killed that genius, because, well, the point is now—as my students liked to opine—mute.

If you are prepared to hang with me, thank you for whatever attention you invest in my account, and please do with it what you will. On one level, your reception is immaterial. On another, I care more than I should. Being dead has made me both less and more sentimental, often in the same instant.

As you can appreciate, I am not in possession of my très cool Power-Point, so I cannot facilitate your deliberations, gentlemen. Afterward—just a humble suggestion, of course—you might consider breaking into small groups and discussing questions like the following:

FOR FURTHER BREAKOUT DISCUSSION
IN THE DEFINITORIUM:

Is Brother Stephen a sympathetic figure? If he isn't, who the hell do you think you are? If he is, what are the chances you just might be out of your mind?

What do you think death will be like for you? Could it possibly be weirder than Brother Stephen's?

Once a chairman, always a chairman.

Where, oh where, does a poor dead boy begin?

———

For openers, check this out for amazing and trivial. Right after I performed my big swan song, I drove for what felt like a long, long while in the California countryside before I came to a stop sign—but the little white Prius! Don't you think that is perfect? Come on, this is *California*—or a version of the Golden State.

Let that other little detail sink in. A stop sign! Doesn't that boggle your bureaucratic mind? Set aside the whole car question, and the California part, too. Who could have presumed my afterlife staked out a position on traffic control? This, you will note, is a theoretical question. Now I had more liberty than before to entertain theoretical questions.

My car idled at the stop sign and my mind raced.

Death will do that to a dead man who finds himself dead and driving a hybrid vehicle. Of course, life will, too.

Hold that thought, would you?

After a while, I swung open my door and stepped out onto the road, leaving the engine running—at least I guessed it was running. Wasting precious fossil fuels and the prohibitive cost of gasoline had been subjects of no urgency to me even before I was in possession of an automobile that laughed in the teeth of the oil company thieves and sheiks who posted their exorbitant prices at the gas pump. To tell the truth—and why shouldn't I tell you the whole unvarnished truth now?—they never had been major issues of concern to me. Now the mystery of my excessive expense receipts that has been eating away at the independent auditor and the CFO can be solved. Chalk one thing up in the Death + column: hybrids rule.

Let's turn to the weather. The wind was constant and gentle, a soft melody adrift. The wind seemed to be coming from all directions, or, rather, it seemed to come from one direction and then another, in quick, shifting succession. Almost more significant than the feel of the warm breeze was the sound, the steady susurration. I love that word, *susurration*. Like the endless rustle of pages. The sleepy drone of a distant twin-engine plane on a spring afternoon. The whisper in the bestirred leaves. The water burbling in a fountain. Yes, I put *susurration* in my notepad.

I faced the wind and my Brother's robes flapped in the salty air. For some reason I cannot rationally defend, I walked around to the back of the Prius. Something about the car made me want to pet it, but I resisted. Then I popped open the hatchback. I had no idea what to expect, but inside the trunk, there was…

———

Yes, none other than our very own Brother Charlie.

Who else would be in the trunk of my afterlife-mobile? Keep your friends close and Brother Charlie *closer*.

In his rumpled, bunched-up robe, legs pulled up to his chest, fetal-like and cramped in the small trunk, my former friend resembled a pile of freshly cleaned laundry. I should probably mention that the besmirched and guilty-till-proven-innocent Charlie was bound hand and foot. And he was wearing, as I always imagined he was wont to do, a black cashmere scarf rakishly and ostentatiously drooping around his neck. That was the perfect look for the artistic director of the spring musical production, though as to whether or not his services in that department would be called upon under the present circumstances remained at the very least unclear.

"Charlie?" I asked irrelevantly. As Chairman of the Definitorium, irrelevance was my specialty, as you all know from long and painful experience. But I digress once more. Get used to it. My afterlife sometimes feels like a French art house movie: one long drawn-out, subtitled digression.

"You'll never get away with this, Stephen," he complained, lifting up his head from its resting place. "Never."

The combative tone was a shocker. Of course, I think I can now say with some assurance that positively everything was proving a shocker. And I replied, "I'm not too worried at this juncture, but are you positive?"

"OK, good question. No, I'm not."

"Incidentally, how'd you get here?"

"Same way you did. In this so-called car."

"I mean, what are you doing tied up in the trunk?"

"Like you don't know."

"You died? What an amazing coincidence."

"Don't be condescending, Stephen. You're not half as good at it as I am."

I caught myself staring at him, the way you might when you pick somebody up at the airport gate and greet him upon his return from a long journey, and you sense he has been altered in some fairly ridiculous way. Now he has a silly tan the shade of an orange peel, or a sketchy goatee or ponytail, or he is wearing a goofy hat or an *I'm with Stupid* t-shirt or some floppy sandals. In other words, I was probably making Charlie feel uncomfortable. Good.

"*What?* What are you looking at, Stephen? You find it amusing, me being in the trunk? You should see how you look from my perspective, standing up there, lording it over me." His voice trailed away.

The question finally dawned on me. "Charlie?"

"Go on, I know what you're going to say—go on."

"Are you still *you*, Charlie?"

"What a dummy you are. Unfortunately, I am still me. Who else would I want to be? But how about you? Are you? Are *you* still you?"

"I think I am, but how would I know if I weren't?"

"You would be the last to know, true, Stephen."

Then, as if we were wordlessly cueing each other, we both looked at the black leather messenger bag draped over my shoulder. I had not been conscious of the bag and I had no idea where it came from. It did not look like the sort of bag that would have belonged to me.

"What you got in there, Stephen?"

I wasn't sure I wanted to know.

"Go on, take a look. Won't kill you." His afterlife wisecracks might prove tiresome.

I unzipped it and rummaged inside. Not much there beyond the predictable. Some notepads and, oh, a fifth of Old Bushmills. I zipped it back up.

"Anything good in there you want to share with a monster like me?"

"Not really." Besides, I had another line of questioning to pursue. "Hey, are we really in hell, Charlie?"

"Let's change places, you can tell me."

I gave that suggestion the consideration it merited. A new thought occurred. "You know what Jean Paul Sartre said?"

"I *thought* I heard you talking with somebody in the front seat."

"That was the radio."

I reached into my robe pocket for my trusty notepad and flipped through the pages. "Ah," I said, "here it is. Sartre said, *Hell is other people.*"

"Very profound, Brother Stephen. And all along I thought that old frog ball Sartre spoke French."

"That's *my* dumb joke, Charlie."

"You stole everything from me, and don't forget it."

That wasn't even remotely true. I tucked away the notepad. The reason I quoted Sartre then and there was that I used to think the Galloise-puffing, mossy-toothed, bed-hopping existentialist was probably right about that one part, the demographic slice of the population that would inhabit the Inferno. Yet I acknowledge that it left certain other problems on the table. If hell is other people, is heaven destined to be just me? That would rule out celestial bingo and cocktail parties and pick-up basketball and religious orders. If my life was any indication, being alone was not necessarily a cure-all.

Of course, Sartre also proceeded to screw up the so-called God problem by positing Him out of existence, and by implying that the end is already written, when everything we experience in our lifetime screams otherwise, insofar as incompleteness is the complete meaning of our life (as well as my death, so far, too). Sartre stupidly left blank the page where God is supposed to explain *His* failures of imagination.

"About dying, Charlie. I have to say I expected it to feel kind of different. That it would feel like the equivalent of the warm glow in your brain the instant the blue Valium eagle swoops down from the heights and your eyes go gauzy and your lungs fill with helium and the room goes golden."

"I love Valium, too, Stephen. Me, I would have thought I could sit up there in heaven and watch and, being dead, comment on everybody's atrocious fashion decisions and their disastrous little escapades."

"Isn't it strange, when you remember being alive, going to funerals, giving eulogies, how the dead always seem to be at your mercy? They are pitied. They are mourned. They are understood. They are interpreted. They are accommodated. Their work is appreciated. I hope nobody *appreciated* me at my funeral."

"I could not comment. I didn't have the pleasure of attending yours, but I think you were probably pretty safe in the appreciation department, Stephen. Brother Paulus delivered your send-off, I bet." He laughed out loud, clearly amused by the prospect of old Paulus wheezing his way through a litany of insincerities as he gave his valediction for his old untrusty sidekick, me. "But tell me all about it. The wishes of the dead can be overridden. Their hopes can be put into context. God, I hate putting anything into context. It's just a way of making things safe. I was born out of context, lived my whole life out of context, too. And I'm proud of it. Anyway, the old ideas of the dead can be rejected out of hand, their grand designs revised. We recycle their book collections, their out-of-date clothes, their music, their cheap little photo reproductions of Cezanne and Matisse picnics that hung on their little walls. If the living only knew. If they only knew!"

Charlie was making sense, as much as I hated to acknowledge. "Pretty sad," I said, "isn't it? Spare us your sorrow, people. Mourn for your own lives, not for the dead."

"Still," Charlie said, "what a revelation when everybody discovers exactly how the world really does revolve around them."

I was relieved, I confess. "I *knew* it. I always knew it."

He shook his head and said with the insecure scorn of an untenured assistant professor of English: "You have a whole lot to learn, Stephen."

"You would know, I guess. You were my mentor, after all. There is something in particular I would like to learn. It might be strange, even beside the point, but what I would really like to learn is what happened between you and Shannon Reed and how you got away with it for so long."

"Oh, Stephen, Stephen, Stephen. You are such a romantic, *Stephen.*"

"I am going to find out sooner or later."

"Don't stay stuck in the past, Stephen. You have to try to move on with your…"

"Are you absolutely sure you are dead, Charlie?"

"I thought so, but now that you mention it, it's not crystal clear. Why do you ask?"

"Because right now, with each passing moment in your orbit it sounds more and more like a good idea."

I never could skewer the invulnerable Charlie when I was alive, and in the aftermath I had acquired no new arrows for my quiver or my black bag, so he appeared supremely nonchalant for somebody trussed up in the trunk of my car, and he asked, "You ever watch women's figure skating, Stephen?"

"God, you are gay as a parade through the Castro." It is strange to say, perhaps, but I had never before used the g-word to his face.

"Maybe everybody is."

"Don't start with that again, Charlie."

"But I'll take that as a yes, that you've watched these gorgeous, intense young women flashing in circles wearing their sequins and spandex, their lithe, powerful, anorexic bodies racing around the rink to the music of Wagner or some other German on the verge of well-deserved self-annihilation, all the while doing these tricky figures and jumps, the triple axel and the triple klutz."

"Lutz. Triple *Lutz*, Charlie."

"You do watch figure skating. I knew it, I just *knew* it."

"And you're sharing this fascinating information with me why?"

"Hang on, I'm getting there. At the end of their performances, these skaters go sit in some box while the TV cameras chew on them like a pack of hyenas. Usually their faces are ruined, their makeup is sliding, their eyes are going sideways with disappointment and self-castigation, they are crushed by the recollection of something that wasn't quite right, and they await the rulings of the judges, who give them the scores they have to live with forever. They take off points for perceived improper execution, not just the ass-flops on the ice, not just the unscheduled plowing into walls. And here's why I'm talking about this. Lots of times, these performances look perfect to me. Lots of times, I cannot see anything they did to deserve a demerit. All I am is cheered up by something so beautiful and so sweet and so silly and so difficult. And yet! And yet the judges deduct a point for this technical problem, a point for that artistic lapse. But me? I didn't see anything. From my vantage point, it was pure perfection.

"Here's what concerns me, Stephen. Say we are like those figure skaters. Is our judge judging us the way somebody like me might judge the figure skaters, or is he judging us like one of those experts? Taking off points when we least expect it, and cutting us down to size?"

"Charlie, there's one big flaw in your thinking."

"I know: Living your life is not like figure skating and the world is not like an ice rink and no score is kept."

"No, for all we know that might not be a bad analogy. When it comes to life, as with figure skating, it all comes down to the degree of difficulty. Anyway, the big flaw in your thinking is that you are the big flaw thinking it."

"Don't you English teachers call that an ad hominem argument?"

"And don't you ever shut up?"

I unzipped the bag and pulled out the Irish whiskey. I took a long, lingering swig. It tasted like the heady stuff I had given myself over to for many years, it certainly did. I waited for the kick to, well, kick in. I waited for the glow to drain from the tap in my forehead and seep down like lava from the volcano top to my chest to my belly and zoom all the way down to my knees, the way I could always count on this potion doing. This time, nothing happened.

I took another death-defying drink. More of the same nothing. Now what was I supposed to do?

Not funny, Omniscient and Omnipotent God—you're not All-side-splitting after all. Which reminds me of how when we were kids we took delight in the theological dilemmas. If God is All-Powerful could He create a rock that He Himself could not pick up? If God is All-Knowing could He make up a math test He Himself couldn't pass?

"Charlie, I have a question."

"You always have a question. Shoot."

"Does the wind ever stop?"

"What wind?"

"You don't feel the wind? It's warm and it never stops."

"You got me, Stephen. There's a warm breeze, you say?"

"What am I doing here talking to you?"

"I can't help you there. But it's like what they say. It's not the heat, it's the humility."

~

REMARKS FOR THE GRAND DEPOSITOR

I have to confess that it is fathomable—call me cynical, I don't care—it is completely fathomable that somebody with whom I have lived in religious community, worshipped and taught alongside, would be capable of doing such damage to a young person—as Charlie and Joel have been accused. And they are both equally guilty. Joel for what he did to Shannon. Charlie for what he did not do on her behalf. They were cut from the same cloth. The spectacle of innocence makes many men go purely nuts. Maybe all men, given the right set of circumstances, will find themselves one day driven to harm somebody this way. It is not about the sexual release—that is something I cannot believe. Men have routinely thrown their lives away due to the madness that is erotic desire. But these offenders aren't about desire. If you don't know that, man, you don't know anything. It is more pathetic and more dangerous than that. And yet, and yet, it seems to be the case that I have lived alongside such dangerous and pathetic men in my time as a Brother and I am required to assume a measure of responsibility. I could not see this coming and I could do nothing to stop them ahead of time. Life is full of such mysteries and abominations, and I should have taken the lead. Sometimes I wonder what went wrong with these men, but not often, to tell the truth, because if I chew on this story long enough, I might find an undigested morsel of sympathy stuck inside the pocket of my moral molar, and I don't have any sympathy to spare. And that is a grievous fault of mine. My faith tells me that these are men worthy of redemption, though my common sense tells me that they are certainly not worthy of teaching a child ever again, or of ever being in their vicinity. I think of the twelve disciples of Jesus and how they must have felt when they realized that one of their own, Judas, had sold out Jesus to Pilate and to death on a cross. But you know what Judas's great sin was, don't you? You are the Grand Depositor, so of course you know. It wasn't betraying Jesus, selling him out for thirty pieces of silver. Recall that finally Judas cannot even pocket the silver. He is so haunted that he goes back to the temple to return the deposit on his guilt-ridden mortality and says to the chief priests, "I have sinned by betraying innocent blood." But they can't accept his blood money, either. You can read about this in the Gospel According to Matthew, but why? We discussed this problem at length in Religion class when we were in Catholic school. The subject was covered in The Baltimore Catechism, *which we all read and where all possible bases are covered, where all questions are answered. The Judas question remains the great eye-opener for budding little Catholics. You see, finally, Judas is profoundly ordinary and sleazy, even you might say uninteresting as a man. The only respect in which he was interesting whatsoever was with regard to his real sin. His real sin was despair, theologically speaking, the despair that forced him to hang himself. Jesus would have forgiven him, don't you see? We human beings cannot forgive him, perhaps, but that's only because we are not Jesus. Jesus spent all his life telling anybody who would listen that it's OK, I forgive your sorry miserable worthless dumb ass. He would have forgiven Judas for anything, even betrayal unto death, but he could never forgive him for not trusting in his love for him—which mistrust Judas evidenced by hanging himself. That's what condemns Judas. Which takes us back to the origins of my sadness today in this deposition. Along with all my fellow Brothers, I am one with a man who has violated our trust and who has, more importantly, violated the trust of a child. In case you have missed positively everything, let me tell you once and for all: every man has his price, every man is riddled with sin, and every man—should he be unfortunate to live long enough—will one day contemplate slipping a noose around his neck, like Judas, and stepping out for a little stroll along the avenue of the empty air. And some of us will have the necessary courage and cowardice to do just that.*

THREE

Q. 2. Who is God?
A. God is the Creator of heaven and earth,
   and of all things.
                              —The Baltimore Catechism

Before we go too far down the road, Brothers, I need to get something off my chest. It was a little embarrassing to die with bystanders making mental notes about preferable death venues and about how not to perish in the future. Good luck, pilgrims. Word of advice. Next time you witness somebody's expiration, please, a little more sensitivity, thank you.

Montaigne, the sixteenth-century essayist, wise guy, and my hero, had it right. He wrote, "I want death to find me planting cabbages." Yes, he wrote that in French, Charlie. I often pondered this wish of his long before, *mes petits choux,* I was on the verge of being planted by cabbage-heads like you.

Apropos of just about everything, one of the most beautiful words in the language is *revenant* in my opinion. See? The word's right here, in my notepad. Means somebody who returns after a long absence. Also means somebody who returns after death. *Revenant.* So pleasurable to articulate this word. Try it, go ahead. Revenant. Let it roll around in your mouth like an excellent 1997 California Cabernet.

But why, you may be asking yourself, why in the world does the revenant Brother Stephen yank on our sleeves, poke us in the eye, and insist upon our attention now? What happened to the congenitally reticent and self-absorbed man with whom we rubbed shoulders for what felt like centuries? The man who was so discreet that he could be trusted with the order's deepest, darkest secrets. The man whose personal views with regard to just about anything you would be hard-pressed to identify. Cat or dog? Bach or Beethoven? Thanksgiving—white meat or dark meat? Yankees or Red Sox?

Answers, in case they matter: a) dog, obviously dog; b) Puccini, maybe Mozart; c) stuffing; d) just for the sheer fun factor, some time may both these teams finish in a dead heat for last place.

I offer a couple of inadequate explanations for a deracinated dead man's imminent self-disclosure—along with a confession. One: though not well understood, death will do wonders loosening even a Parisian street mime's tongue. Those pesky inhibitions begin to seem downright quaint. And two: to my everlasting surprise, it turns out that we are not finished, you and I, not by a long shot and not yet.

But first, come on. Where *do* you suppose the dead go? It is tough to give you anything that resembles a cogent account, but I do have a clue or two as to where I have gone and where I am. As of this moment, for instance, I can testify that I am right *here*. You can't shake me, Brothers, try as you might. And the corollary is, I can't shake you, either. You see, the living and the dead are both less and more involved with each other than ever before.

True, one moment the living are suddenly—and it is always suddenly for some reason—not living. In time bodies will pass into chemical compounds, eventually becoming one with the earth. As the priests say on Ash Wednesday, while smudging your forehead, "Dust thou art, and to dust thou shalt return."

~

A FREQUENTLY UNASKED QUESTION:

But what of dead souls? Assuming souls exist, and only fools would not make that assumption, don't they linger somewhere?

They do linger. In your bones, you know they linger. That's what the moonlight and the eaves and the lengthening afternoon shadows are for, to shelter them. That's what waking up in the middle of the night is all about, so they can remind you. That's what daydreams are for and why the seasons change, to get your attention. That's why the trees shimmer, why the lakes ripple, why the hair stands up on the back of your neck. It's why you remember things that happened twenty years ago as if they occurred this morning. That invisible tap on your shoulder? Guess who. The dead fill your ears with incessant whispering, much like leaves lashed by last night's windstorm. Sometimes, they drift along the lilting melody of a trilling songbird. Of course the dead remain. Since they must abide, where else should they abide, if not among and inside you?

At the same time, we deceased are uninvolved in your mortal affairs. There are sound reasons. For one thing, the dead have more important things to do than meddling in your trivial problems. We have our own trivial problems. In other words, don't count on us popping out of your midnight medicine cabinet with a banshee screech or rattling chains or slamming doors down the hall when you're trying to get a good night's sleep in preparation for the big day tomorrow.

These are all matters I will help you gradually understand, Brothers, and with any luck at all, eventually misunderstand. I have much to recount to you about death and the afterlife. It may well prove to be information you will find useful. Besides, who doesn't enjoy a sneak preview? And forewarned is forearmed, as I always say in my classroom.

Or I always used to say, till one day, when I was going on and on and on about some upcoming test I was giving. I was giving my students the skinny on what to expect and how to prepare, finishing with, "And so, as I have often told you before, forewarned is…"

"Foreskinned." So popped off a student named Jimmy. It was almost gratifying to note that he had been swayed by a topic treated in health class.

〜

THE GRAND DEPOSITOR

"Call no one happy till he is dead," said the Athenian statesman Solon, though the provocative saying has also been attributed to Aeschylus and sometimes Sophocles, as well as being rashly attributed (by that rash attributor, me) to my grouch of a grandfather, who might have said it and who died from a spider-bite reaction at the age of ninety-three and was miserable, family legend has it, every miserable day of his miserable life. My grandpa was also famous for saying, "Only the good die young"— though, in his case, boy, was that old man on target.

What is forgotten, however, is how he completed the thought. Not my grandfather. He was incapable of completing any thought more complex and extended than Scotch AND soda. Talking about Solon. The Solon fellow who said: "Call no one happy till he is dead...for you know not what changes may pass upon him in life." I myself think that the great Solon should have cashed in his chips when he was ahead. He was playing with the house's money and he had the chance to say something radically true, and only messed it up with a rhetorical sentimentality. Being dead, I have to say that I find the thought of happiness hardly crosses my mind at all. Happiness was not the goal of life, and it certainly doesn't seem to be the goal of the afterlife, either. What is your view, Grand Depositor? Would you agree with this update: Call no one unhappy till he is dead?

———

To resume my own personal Travels with Charlie:

"It's never too late to change, Brother Stephen," Charlie offered. "And never forget, only you can change you."

Charlie smiled. He possessed a smile that would make Mother Teresa herself hold off and slap him. Old as he was, he still possessed a pink, fleshy, jowly baby face that would have responded very nicely to a crisp smack from a saint's cupped paw. Don't you agree that Brothers and other longtime teachers of children seem to have a disconcertingly youthful appearance, doomed as they are to pass from class to class with a perennially buoyant step in their redundantly named walking shoes? It is a career benefit taken for granted, unfortunately for labor negotiators, though it is more precious than any other perk available to them, including those extended summer vacations. Brothers, please play this card with the Teachers' Union during upcoming contract negotiations.

Still, baby-faced Charlie had an altogether impossible and infuriating smile. His smile had its own smile, you might say, as if it smiled at itself. His smile had a way of making you regret smiling in reply, which was the emotional equivalent of extortion. White teeth, opened mouth, crinkled nose, creased forehead, sparkling eyes—all were working in concert. His smile was reckless and contrived, dangerous and inert as a work of art or a remote-controlled detonation device. It was an audience participation smile. It was an embossed invitation with your name on it. Maybe to a party, a party you weren't sure you ought to attend.

One other point I ought to make, and it might as well be right now: I could never get over how pedophiles could manage to be so charming at times. Were they different people when they weren't molesting? Or did we just miss this aspect? Or were they both charming and false?

"Only you can change you?" I repeated the Oracle of the Trunk's opinion, with a little edge in my voice. "I *must* be in hell, getting self-help advice from you, Charlie."

"Don't mention it. And that's pretty nasty on your part, calling somebody a pedophile."

"When did I say anybody was a pedophile?"

"You didn't have to, you were thinking it."

"It's part of my job, or used to be, thinking about pedophiles. And then, there is that lawsuit. If there is merit to Shannon's claims, you and Joel might belong in hell."

"God, my boy, you *are* naïve. That's the last, flimsiest vestige of hope we hold onto here. Besides, people throw around that word *pedophilia* these days. Remember when everybody believed in recovered memory, that other boondoggle? Sure, some Brothers and priests are guilty of sex with teenagers, sometimes with children, but they have exploited their charges at no greater rate than rabbis and pediatricians and…"

"What the fuck difference does that make! You disgust me!"

"You always were a man of discrimination, Stephen."

"There you go again, not being helpful. Come to think of it, you never were."

"You're getting pretty worked up there, Stephen."

"Shut up already."

"Calm down. You will never grasp what happened. It will always remain a mystery. No point in raising your blood pressure—sorry for mentioning your health concern. Remember what Philo of Alexandria wrote? 'Be kind, for everyone you meet is fighting a great battle.' But why should I be helpful? Dear Lately Departed, I'm trying to put death behind me."

"You would. And what is your Waterloo, Charlie, and what are you fighting about?"

"You got it wrong, Stephen. It's not what we're fighting about that matters. It's only what we are fighting *for*."

I'd had enough and I reached up to shut the hatchback, but stopped when I noticed a book lying beside him.

"Catching up on your reading, Charlie?"

"It's not mine. Never cracked it open." He was defiant. People are like that when they feel threatened and exposed, aren't they, Brothers?

"*Left Behind*, huh?" I jotted down the book title for future reference, assuming that there was a future to my seemingly defunct present. "Doing research?"

"Aren't you late, Stephen?"

"Got enough leg room, Charlie?"

I slammed the trunk with such extreme prejudice I wanted to apologize—to my Prius.

—

Back in the driver's seat, I reviewed the facts, such as they appeared to me. Hell, purgatory, heaven—where exactly was I? I didn't count on a posted admonition similar to Dante's *Abandon All Hope, Ye Who Enter Here*, or on hearing chanting choirs of angels, but a clue or two would have been considerate. Say this *was* hell—and Charlie's noxious presence could have been a reliable indicator that it was. Fire and brimstone, gargoyles and bubbling cauldrons, gobs of human flesh hanging from the Italian poet's blood-spurting trees, and those surfers skimming the surface of simmering fecal pools—what was all that? A fairy tale?

Minus a map—either of hell or of California, assuming there to be a difference—and without the benefit of knowing how to operate the underworld equivalent of a Navigation Positioning System in the Prius, I nonetheless determined I must be looking for a certain destination. I just didn't happen to know which particular certain destination. So I was operating the vehicle with a sense of purposelessness that passed for a purpose. You might say that I was driving under the influence— the influence of the idea of not giving a damn one way or another.

Brothers, I turned right. What the hell, reasoned I.

As soon as I did so I instantly wished I had turned left. I also knew that had I turned left I would have wished to have turned right. Even though Brother Stephen's life was over, it was still exhausting being me. You are no doubt nodding your heads, because this is something you have always known about yours truly.

Which brings up a related subject. When people speak about death, they euphemistically refer to it as being a state of "eternal rest." Which is somehow even worse than nattering about some supposed "bet- ter place." The natterers even helpfully encourage the dead to "rest in peace." Thanks, Breathers. And you Brothers, too. But I'm here to say something on that subject: No way, Saint José. Death was busy, busy, busy. Always something to do. If I had been trained to use my official, recently-dispensed-by-the-tech-nerds Blackberry, or kept my own per- sonal afterlife blog or Twitter account, or had places where you could friend me, I would be keeping you posted in excruciatingly minute detail about what I did not have for lunch. If I were you, and maybe I am, now that I think about it, this is the place where I would give thanks for Brother Stephen's technological limitations.

I stepped on the gas pedal and sped down the road. Nothing would stop me now.

Until, as you will see, it would.

∽

THE GRAND DEPOSITOR

Stop me if you've heard this one.

A man goes to church. He's feeling sorrowful and guilty over his failings and his sins, so he drops to his knees and humbly prays to God for forgiveness. Afterward, he feels pretty good about himself, satisfied with his confession. But then after a while, alone in his pew, another, disturbing thought intrudes. He contemplates all the problems in the world, the wars and the suffering and the poverty and the hunger, his personal suffering, the tragedies and the pain all around. He grows angrier and angrier. Next thing he knows, he is addressing God very differently.

"You know, you have a lot of nerve making ME beg for forgiveness. I say YOU have a lot of explaining to do! What kind of life is this?! What kind of a car wreck of a world have you created?! You should be on your knees begging me to forgive you!"

Fed up and righteous, he storms outside, where he immediately runs into the meek, elderly pastor. He cannot stop himself. He blurts out to the priest what has just taken place.

The pious man listens with a stupefied and mortified look, and then gently inquires: "You told God that He had a lot of explaining to do?"

"Yes, Father."

"You told God He should ask you for forgiveness?"

"Yes, I did, and that's when I left."

"That's when you left, my son? You took off right when you had Him by the balls?"

———

Brother Paulus, I don't think the public speaking coach you retained for me would have approved of my summoning up that last ice-breaker I employed with the Grand Depositor. I can imagine your displeasure to read the expression of such blasphemous views. Please understand that I am being sincere when I say that anticipating your irritation makes my precious heart skip a little beat. I think my HMO doctors would call such rhapsody *atrial fibrillation*: A-Fib, for short. But if you think I am in the wrong here, Brother, just remember I am dead. You know what that means, don't you?

OK, I don't, either. But one thing it probably means is I know more than you do.

At least I think I do.

Here's a curious aspect about my mind-state: I am absolutely sure about, say, X, but in the same instant I am absolutely mystified about X. Psychoanalysts have a term for that condition: *ambivalence*. Which means not that you sort of want X or you sort of also want Y, though this is what people mistakenly take for ambivalence. Instead, it means you really want X and you really want Y. So far, in my afterlife, I have yet to run into a shrink. Maybe this is accidental, and maybe I haven't got around to every place I need to go, and maybe these health professionals were never ambivalent enough to join me here.

THE GRAND DEPOSITOR

A few questions:

Is there a chance that crackpot Sartre is right about hell being other people? Or does this observation apply only to French shopkeepers and barricade-storming academics?

Do you expect to meet five people in heaven? What makes

you so sure you will be there to take the census?

Think you have a story or memoir inside you waiting to be busted out? Are you the kind of guy who's aching for a desk and a computer monitor and some all-about-me alone-time? Man, do I have a deal for you. Where's a Jim Jones when you need one? Tincture the teapot for your writers' group, pour, and enjoy. You can see for yourself just how well it worked for me.

FOUR

*Q. 198. Is every truth which we cannot understand a
mystery?*
*A. Every truth which we cannot understand is not a
mystery; but every revealed truth which no one can
understand is a mystery.*
                                    —*The Baltimore Catechism*

I know what you are thinking. You are thinking, hey, the afterlife must be a kind of dream. That's not bad for a rookie. What did that genius Baseball Hall of Fame catcher and existentialist philosopher Yogi Berra once say? After a bad loss, he explained to reporters the problem with the game: "We made too many of the wrong mistakes." Yogi's insight gets better the more you think about it, and it leads to the following profound conclusion: You need to start making the right mistakes. Those are words I wish I had almost always lived by.

Truth is, you aren't completely off, Brothers. There are resemblances. I refer to the dreamlike logic. The fluidity. The lack of inhibition. The coherent incoherence. Or maybe that's the incoherent coherence.

Ever find yourself walking in a strange city—not to drop place names, but I'm thinking of Venice, the one in Italy, wise guys, not Muscle Beach in Southern California. And in no time, practically the first corner you turn, you're so hopelessly lost that you look around to see if anybody will notice if you start laughing out loud? And you get the premonition that somehow you're *supposed* to be lost? And that wherever you find yourself (piazza, church, ristorante, gondola, crypt, brothel, ballroom), it is full of surprises that, upon further examination, are not surprises? The sort of place where getting lost is the surefire avenue anywhere?

It's more like that, the afterlife. I was never much of a world traveler, as you know. I was never even much of a hemisphere traveler. For God's sake, I was forced to borrow your luggage, Brother Gregory Called G, for my one and only European jaunt, which gave me a new apprecia-tion for pasta as well as the idea to name-drop Venice in this report to the Definitorium. (Sorry about busting the zipper on your suitcase, G.)

Now I understand why I felt so at home the one and only time I was in Venice. It's a city of water and therefore reflection. It's a city of cut glass and therefore radiance. Most of all it is a city of gorgeous decay and therefore it's a city of the dead. If reincarnation actually happens, in this next life maybe I should become a travel agent. The thing I need to say about Venice is that I felt every bit as at home there as I feel at home here and now, and for the same reasons. I wouldn't be surprised in my afterlife if I came upon a suspension bridge of sighs. The bridge of sighs: that's where somebody like me would feel perfectly at home.

The chief difference between the afterlife and dreaming is that, in a dream, you get to wake up. But that's not the important difference. The important difference is that in a dream you are alone. You feel alone. Sure, your delectable raven-haired first cousin or the tax man or the president of the United States pops in from time to time to make a cameo appearance, to do dreamlike stuff, such as taking flight off the Golden Gate Bridge or surfing off Maverick Beach or strumming a gui-tar, often while dressed in unforeseen (or minimalist) clothes.

In death, it's different. You feel strangely unalone. In death, the oth-ers are *in* your life—I mean in your afterlife. Witness Charlie, whom I found in my eternal combustion hybrid gasoline electric chariot, keep-ing company with the spare tire and the lug nuts and the defiantly un-read and left behind book in the trunk. But here's the point: I had the sense that Charlie wasn't merely, or simply, my psychic projection. He was also *Charlie*, distinct from me, and independent. Which meant, from his side, I might not be merely his psychic projection. Tell you what. I promise next time I bump into a functional electronic magnetic resonance imaging machine, I will attach electrodes to my forehead, push the correct buttons, and print out the results.

My old SAT scores might encourage you to think otherwise, but actually I am not smart enough to understand all this, much less explain. Here's what I just scrawled in my increasingly inconsequential notepad:

What if dying made it possible for people to coexist within the same dream? Was it ever different in life?

Death also makes me believe dreams can be shared. They say when you're in love, you and the beloved dream a double dream. Could that be true in death, too? And with people you also hate?

Furthermore, do all dreams take place, and do all dreamers dream, along parallel planes?

Post job-opening: AUXILIARY PROVINCIAL, Holy Family Brothers. Compensation, questionable. Benefits, dubious.

———

The sun was shining as I drove my slippery car down the slick road, and I pondered the chances that I might find myself sooner or later at the seashore. It *would* be a lovely day to go the beach. That was what I was thinking. I was always drawn to the water, and the salt air streaming into my face through the opened car window testified that I could not be far away. I always counted on the turbulence and the scope of the ocean to make sense of my idiosyncrasies and fill me in my emptiness. Though it never lived up to my hopes, not once, I counted on it. Why not? At the very least, it was the sea.

Another roadside billboard popped up—for guess what?

LUNA PARK!
CLOSER THAN YOU KNOW!

And yet another one.

LUNA PARK, IT'S LUNA PARK!
Where day is dark!
Where joy's a quark!

That last rhyme was a stretch.

What wasn't a stretch now?

I was not destined to reach either the sea or Luna Park. Not yet, anyway. Nonetheless, Luna Park was rousing my ever-increasing curiosity. I considered paying a visit. Only, now something else occupied my attention. Something outrageous materialized. I slowed the car down to a crawl to look more closely.

I could not believe it. Yet it seemed to be true. By the way, I say *I could not believe it*, but don't believe me. I believe everything nowadays. And you should believe me, too, even if you do not believe *in* me. Remember what The Yogi said and don't make the wrong mistakes.

Brothers, there it was, in all its Catholic-hormone-drenched glory: my alma mater, Angel of Mercy High School. Please cue the marching band.

———

Yes, my old high school campus seemed to have been transported to its new location in my afterlife lock, stock, and unadorned three-story-tall white wooden crucifix.

How convenient for Angel of Mercy, I marveled—and how diabolical.

I used to doubt it when people assumed their whole life would flash before their eyes in the moment of death. I was finding out that that cliché might indeed have some validity—I mean, check it out: my high school! The only proviso I would make is that that flash goes on and on and, so far for me anyway, on some more.

I turned off the road, after signaling smartly with my directional, of course, just as the California State Driver's Guide required of me, and drove into the parking lot. In my position, you would have done the very same thing, Brothers.

Off in the distance, the recognizable HOME OF THE IRISH scoreboard loomed large over the baseball diamond, scene of numerous lopsided defeats at the hands of our hated rivals, defeats in which I played—I can admit with no false modesty whatsoever—no small role. All I can say is that there was never much competition for playing time on the team, so I must have looked in my baseball uniform as if I belonged on the field, at least as much as anybody else. Remember this was a long time ago and schools and kids seemed far different from today. That will explain the forthcoming literary allusion.

I was an infielder and my teammates, like me, all over-interpreted to the brink of extinction the famous poem "The Rime of the Ancient Mariner." You might recall that that venerable, insane, and great poem begins with some "greybeard loon" jumping out of the shadows to accost three unsuspecting mooks all spiffed up to attend some wedding. He has an amazing story to tell anybody he can get his mitts on (albatross, zombies, etc.), and he fingers the perfect fall guy for his story. The poem opens this way:

It is an Ancient Mariner
And he stoppeth one of three.

That stoppethed listener's tongue-twister of a life will be lispingly changed.

My teammates used to say that I, an infielder never to be confused with the likes of Luis Aparicio, Brooks Robinson, Ozzie Smith, or Derek Jeter, "stoppeth one of three." It was a different time, wasn't it, when we went to school and studied poetry and occasionally made wise-ass poetic allusions outside the confines of the classroom? Still, it is true that when I took the field I had the range, speed, and agility of a turtle, and my arm rocketed the baseball across the diamond with the accuracy and pop of a deflated beach ball.

Excuse me for the nostalgia. I know you should want to, Brothers. The word "nostalgia" comes from the Greek, meaning "homecoming," which is what this belatedly was for me, wasn't it? Besides, if we have learned anything from attending funerals all our lives, we are generously disposed to being tolerant of the foibles of the dead. Why, entering the parking lot, for old time's sake I even nostalgically hit the same friendly pothole that had never been repaired in all my years at school. The car rattled like a runaway roller coaster shimmying over the boardwalk. I fondly recalled how this pothole jarred my incisors driving over it every single morning as a high school senior with driving privileges and a precious parking sticker. To judge by the yelp coming from the back, now Charlie would possess fond memories all his own.

I should admit the obvious, having nothing left to lose. Filming me behind the wheel of a car would not have produced an award-winning cautionary video to be played for the benefit of novice drivers and futilely titled "How to Be a Safely Hormonal Teenage Driver Behind the Wheel of Your Old Man's Automobile." I had the thought in retrospect that my father, who once paid through the nose for car insurance and also to repair the damages I inflicted on many an unsuspecting tire and fender, may have been onto something about not driving till you had driven for two years. Now, if he had been right about that, he would have established a new standard, for him, of correctness: once in a row. But that, my fellow Brothers, is a whole other story. And he can tell it, if he cares to. I can give him a few tips, though. Starting with, "Dad, leave me out of your story." Ending with, "It's a little bit late, don't you think?"

I discovered that there was no available parking space anywhere to be had, which was another aspect of my experience that was consistent with the high school of my past. What was not consistent was that every space in the lot seemed to be filled with a brand-new white Prius.

So I parked my personal Prius illegally beside the fire hydrant near the red curb and the zero-tolerance posted sign that mercilessly vowed to tow any illegally parked hybrid. Disobedience never tasted so delicious. Besides, what did I have to fear? If I had the great good luck to get the thing towed, perhaps to be shoved into a giant trash compactor, I would at a minimum be done with Charlie once and for all.

The schoolboy I had once been understood intuitively what he should be doing now that he found himself back at old Angel of Mercy. I needed to cross the patch of green grass—and, as invariably happened in my previous lifetime, the instant my feet hit the lawn, as if the ground were mined with sensors, the sprinklers flipped on. I ran through the manmade rain for the front door, and when I arrived my face was wet and my robe drenched.

Once I got up the brick stairs and went through the entrance, I passed into the vestibule, where a precious handful of trophies were invited to be admired, sealed and asphyxiated behind locked glass—a few mummified memories of triumph. Framed rosters of past classes appeared on the walls, as they always had. I looked for my graduating class, naturally, and quickly located the plaque. I put my finger next to my name, which was printed there along with those of the other 123 seniors. Along with my classmates I had gone forth bright-eyed on a mission to save the world right after the culmination of commencement exercises, with a brief stopover at the night's big kegger at adorable Sissie Stearns'. It felt like graduation had happened a minute ago. Of course, being dead, everything happened what could have been a minute ago.

Looking back from my privileged present vantage point, I reflected: So what if we hadn't accomplished saving the big old stupid world? So far Jesus himself did not seem to have pulled off that deliverance trick. Besides, what made anybody think the world deserved saving?

Commencement. What a grand finale to my high school career. That was when, as valedictorian, I slouched at the podium and spoke without invoking an ice breaker of a joke. I did helpfully remind everybody as a public service that high school had been "the best four years of our lives." Please, give me at least partial credit. At least I didn't articulate the original thought that *Commencement signifies not only an ending but a beginning,* that chestnut roasted by every other commencement speaker since the dawn of time. I also had a glimmering, even then, that that was at best a partial truth. Fortunately, Shannon Reed had helped me with the speech the night before, when she typed it out for me at her kitchen table. I stole one of her ideas, and that was why I went on to brilliantly remind everybody that high school had also been the *worst* four years of our lives. I wish I could have heard her valedictory address. I missed a lot.

By the way, yes, all you wise-guy editors-slash-pseudo-grammarians out there, the revised afterlife edition of *Strunk & White*, which was probably still selling briskly in this other realm, requires you to bravely split every single one of your damned infinitives. All my former students would have cheered at being vindicated. In fact, the injunction not to ever split an infinitive wasn't anything but a nonsensical "rule" in the first place, one not canonized by Messrs. Strunk and White (though they did have a curious, quasi-pathological aversion to the innocuous phrase *in fact*), and one generated by a gross misunderstanding of linguistics, of Latin, and of English—as well as a gross misunderstanding of grammar, language, culture, authority, correctness, and reality. The red ink we wasted on the futile, pedantic chore! I digress, but I am one who has put the *die* in *digress*.

Meanwhile, I was beginning to appreciate more and more that it was no wonder my afterlife would have the bright idea to take me back to high school. That was the instant when I, to tediously invoke the tedious expression tediously invoked in my mortal lifetime, *did the math*:

Best Years ÷ Worst Years = Stephen's Afterlife.

I knew why I had been deposited here. For better or worse, I was the perfect schoolboy returning to the proverbial scene of the crime. Perhaps there was also an opportunity to reprise my role of valedictorian, the formally designated articulator of goodbye and other nonsense. Now that I thought about it, there were important things I had left out of my twelve-minute-long speech, things that I later came to understand to be true. And maybe high school redux would be my opportunity to get it right in my report to you. Just a hunch? Don't think so. Take it to the bank, Brothers.

Meanwhile, the plummy, hummy, gummy silence that engulfed me seemed to indicate that the building might as well be empty— which conflicted with the recognition that the parking lot outside was jammed. All the doors along the fluorescent-lit vacant corridor were shut, too. Nonetheless, I caught myself wondering what period it was and what class I was supposed to be attending.

I walked down the main hallway, which seemed as imposing as a five-star hotel's, the corridor much longer and wider and higher than I remembered. It stretched far into the distance, like some object watched through the end of an observatory telescope. The lockers were where they always had been, though. And the greenish smell of bathroom cleanser mixed with bleachy chalk dust permeated the air, as I recalled it always had.

For some reason I determined to open the door to Room 101. I have so far neglected to divulge that all the doors to all the rooms were identically numbered 101. I cracked open the door made of heavy-leaded amber glass and peeked inside. I was not surprised to see about a dozen students gathered in a half-circle of desks.

Once I entered, I sheepishly assumed my place in the seat of a va-cated desk, as if this was indeed where I belonged. My appearance did not cause the slightest stir. When I turned my attention to the front of the room, there was another surprise in store for me. There, sitting in a desk before the blackboard facing the other students and me, was none other than the plaintiff, Shannon Reed.

You're not going to understand the next part, but I will not fault you, because I myself cannot, either. Yes, I was sad to be dead. What's not to be down about? So many missed opportunities to contemplate and mourn. So many losses and miscalculations and mistakes that would now never be salvaged, corrected, rectified. So many sweet memories made sweeter and more poignant by virtue of their being memories. Sometimes, death can feel like a refrigerator strapped onto your back, it's so heavy and awkward and what's inside is so cold.

Put off dying as long as you can, Brothers. That's my unimpeachable position.

Yet I can also testify that it was worth dying for me to see Shannon once again.

FIVE

Q. 482. Can a person merit any supernatural reward
for good deeds performed while he is in mortal sin?
A. A person cannot merit any supernatural reward
for good deeds performed while he is in mortal
sin; nevertheless, God rewards such good deeds by
giving the grace of repentance; and, therefore, all
persons, even those in mortal sin, should ever strive
to do good.
                                        —The Baltimore Catechism

Brothers, you heard me. Shannon Reed, her own self. She was wearing a cute red beret tilted a jaunty angle above her right eyebrow. Her legs were crossed and her thighs draped with a red and blue plaid skirt, her red cardigan sweater was enwrapped by her folded arms, and her lovely white shoe pulsed in the air like a pretty metronome on a music teacher's uptight piano. *Upright* piano.

In an instant, thirty-eight years vanished, flying away like so many birds taking off from the quivering branches of a sycamore. For all I felt, I could have been in my old letterman jacket instead of the robes in which I found myself.

Seeing her made me feel delirious, or maybe a little bit drunk. Something crazy told me that she and I could have been planning to get together after the ball game. We would be talking later about going to college someday. We might soon be laughing about our inef-

fectual parents, spreading rumors about the personal lives of our inef-
fectual teachers. We could maybe go to a movie, and afterward get a
hamburger, holding hands above the table when the spirit moved us
and nobody else was around to see.

I pulled out my notepad and wrote down what I was thinking, the
gist of which was this: In my afterlife, memory was just as inscrutable
and cruel and moving as it was elsewhere and before.

Shannon looked at me—I don't know what the word was for how
she looked at me. Maybe it was *calmly*. Or maybe *confidentially*. Perhaps *conspiratorially*. All I know is that it definitely began with a *c* and
it wasn't *clinically*. She certainly did not appear to be acting *confusedly*,
which was how I must have appeared. Her sparkling eyes laughed a
little around the edges, as if this were some inside joke being told at my
expense. I studied the way she was regarding me, and I saw myself as
she wanted me to be seen, as she used to see me. How did she do that?
I don't know now and I didn't know back when we were together in
high school. More than anything, I was so very happy to be in the same
room with her, even now, under these pretty extreme circumstances.
And for the first time, these extreme circumstances gradually seemed
less extreme, more mundane, though in a delightful way. You see, she
was just Shannon Reed, the high school girlfriend of the boyfriend
who became Brother Stephen—same glow behind her eyes, same tilt of
her head, same drawl in her shoulders, same musical lift of the slightly
slanted eyebrows. It was the glittery blue eyes that always got to me, the
blue that in certain lighting sometimes turned gray, sometimes almost
green. And her complexion glowed rich amber. In any available light
whatsoever, since the day I first laid eyes on her, Shannon never failed
to look backlit. Love has that effect, don't you think?

Yet it was curious. It was as if there were two Shannons present at the
same time. There was the high school Shannon, in plain view in her regulation plaid skirt and white shoes. And there was also the adult Shannon, who was therefore almost as old as I was now, or I guess I should
say as old as I was before I died. It was strange, though—when I looked

around the room at the other bright and shiny faces, the same could not be said about everyone else. They all looked like high school kids.

Now I am duty-bound, and slightly distressed, to report that it was at this precise moment that she ruined the abject reverie of this revenant.

———

"Stevie," she said, pointing at me in my water-soaked robe, "did you run through the stupid sprinklers again?"

I shrugged with accompanying sound effects: "Tsk tsk tsk."

"Silly, silly, silly Stevie," she uttered in petulant sing-song. "About time you showed."

As you might imagine, that was not the warm and welcoming reception a dead man propelled back to his own high school and into the metaphorical arms of his high school sweetheart might have hoped for. All I could utter was, "Sorry I'm late."

That came out wrong, I instantly realized, but I could not erase the tape.

"That's all right. This is your underworld, Stevie, we're all the rest of us just playing our little parts in it."

I wondered if she was right about that, and what that would imply.

"Said I'm sorry, Shannon. For everything." And I meant it, too, for that was when I made the awkward, obvious connection to the lawsuit I was studying the instant I died. Here was teenage Shannon Reed who claimed, as adult Shannon Reed, both of whom were here, to have been molested while in high school by one Brother Joel.

"Whatever, Stevie. OK. Maybe now we can begin, if nobody minds."

There was consensus. Nobody did mind.

I sighed.

"You do that a lot, Stevie, the sighing."

"I know. I try to stop myself, but I don't seem…" I could not finish. I could not explain. I wished I knew why I sighed as much as I did. It seemed to be beyond my control when I was alive.

"I always like it when somebody sighs. Means they desire something. Anyway, where was I?"

As it turned out, Brother Stephen was not the only Brother in the room. Brother Charlie was also in attendance, also dressed in his black robe. Also wearing a red beret to match Shannon's. As I looked around the room I realized that I was the only red-beret-bereft individual.

Shannon called the meeting to order. "We have a lot of business today. First, big thanks to Brother Charlie, who has volunteered to be the moderator of the Drama Club. Merci beaucoup, Brother Charlie." I always was a sucker for her when she was cute like that.

Everybody chirped their boo-koos of appreciation and Charlie gave a papal-hand wave to acknowledge them. I looked hard at him. His returning glance conveyed that he himself did not comprehend how he had liberated himself from the car trunk and, at the same time, he was not so sure that moderating an extracurricular constituted an advance over his previous state of bondage and incarceration. In my past life I would have testified that most moderators would identify with mixed feelings on such a scale.

At the same time I had an uneasy feeling observing Shannon and Charlie cast into the same room again. That wasn't right, considering the claims she had made about him and what he had done. It also wasn't right that Shannon didn't seem to mind that he was present. And if I was here to play a role in that unfolding drama, I did not understand yet what it could be.

∿

THE GRAND DEPOSITOR

What is the role you are meant to play in the Shannon Reed drama? Come on—like the Brothers of the Definitorium, you have a role to play. Step right up. And make no mistake. You will play a part in the future, whether you like it or not, because you have already played a part in the past. Do I make myself clear? No? Excellent!

"We need to plan our activities for the spring," said Shannon. "Any ideas? Don't be shy."

Discussion centered on various fundraising schemes. The predictable suspects assumed their place in the police line-up: the old-faithful car wash and the bankable bake sale and the can't-lose raffle.

"I got it," said one of the club members. "We sell stuff at lunch, OK? Only this time it's, like, *French* food?"

"Brilliant."

"It just might work."

"How about French fries?"

Shannon was miffed, or maybe I should say *meeft*. "What does *French* have to do with the Drama Club, anyway—and besides, French fries are not really *French*, people."

"Oh yeah, Shannon? Why do they call them French fries, then?" asked the first representative of the avant-garde thespians.

"Yeah, and why do the French eat French fries with mayonnaise?" asked the second trenchantly.

Shannon grew adamant: "We are not selling French fries! Over my dead body! But we could bake French bread, or maybe *clafoutis*. That's French." A shadow fell across her features when she added somewhat disconsolately, "Though it's not a French word, unfortunately."

Another club member—a very enticing teenager with flowing black hair resisting the imposition of her beret, which somehow did not fit on her head, a girl with the flashing eyes of an Argentine tango queen—had an interesting proposition. Final exams were coming up, she reminded us. (Incidentally, this was cheery news to me, since, weird as it must sound to normal people, I loved taking final examinations, and I figured we were finally *getting* somewhere.) And then she added that therefore we would have a week without regular classes in order to prepare. That was the period of time set aside in the school calendar otherwise known as Dead Week.

My afterlife's sense of humor was growing on me, if not on you, Brothers.

"OK," said the intense girl, "what's the coolest thing about Shakespeare?" She waited for a response, which was not to be forthcoming, so she leaped. "Exactly. The coolest thing about Shakespeare is the big death scenes. People don't just tip over, like a cow on the hillside. They talk, they go on and on, they feel things, they say things."

"Yes," said Shannon, leading her on. "So?"

"So during Dead Week," the girl seethed, "let's put on lunchtime performances of Shakespeare death scenes and charge admission—and sell French fries, too, or *clafoutis*, whatever the heck that is. Though it sounds weird."

"*Clafoutis* involves eggs and cherries," somebody helpfully explained. "But in a good way."

"Serena," Shannon marveled, "you could be onto something."

Charlie, who was also our drama coach back when we were in high school, thrilled to Serena's idea, too. He thrilled easily, as you know, Brothers. He took the floor and rattled on about the Greatest Hits performance possibilities of *Othello, Hamlet, Antony and Cleopatra, King Lear, Macbeth, Henry IV, Julius Caesar*, and so on.

"Put out the light," he intoned, "and put out the light."

That cheery utility-cost-cutting recommendation, uttered by Shakespeare's romantic murderer and five-star general, was met with silence, so he ventured a follow-up: "Then must you speak of one that loved not wisely, but too well."

Another lead balloon. "*Othello*, children?" he prompted them. "*Othello?* About a great and flawed man with unrealistic expectations about himself and about his celebrity-stalking wife and mostly about the power of love, a man who brings destruction upon his beloved and eventually himself?"

I could not help raising my hand. Shannon called on me, barely disguising her knowing smile, but she spoke first:

"Stevie, maybe you and I could do the famous tomb scene in *Romeo and Juliet?*"

All right, Shannon always was a little bit of a wise-ass. But I was going in a different direction, and besides, I despise that ridiculous play, which I was a little bit stunned she did not appreciate.

"Think about it," she implored me, "would you, Stevie?"

Finally, I asked my question. "Shannon, what exactly are we raising money for?"

Yeah, yeah, yeah. Once a chairman…

"For the field trip, naturally, don't be silly."

"Field trip where?" The question died on the vine, which was an answer in itself. Didn't matter where! It was a field trip out of school! Duh. "No wonder I feel so at home in high school," I concluded.

Somebody else had a question for Shannon. "Everything ready for tomorrow tonight?"

"I hope so! I'm nervous as a cat," she said, laughing. "Thanks for asking. I just happen to have the flyers." She passed them around. "You're all going to be there, right?" She turned in my direction.

"Break a leg, Shannon," somebody said.

I took a look at the pink flyer. One night only! Angel of Mercy Theatre! Presented by the Drama Club! *Shut Up It's My Life: You Call This a Comedy When Nobody's Laughing?* A New One-Act Play in Approx. Five Acts, by Shannon Reed! Directed by Brother Charlie! Starring Shannon Reed, among others! Admission Free!

I had a couple of questions I would keep to myself: Did I really want to see her play and did I have a choice?

"Where you going, Stevie?" she asked when I pushed back my desk and rose to my feet.

"I forgot. I'm late for Calculus Club."

"You never took calc."

"That should stop me?"

"Stevie?" She put a closed fist up to her ear and mouthed *Call me.*

I gave her a look that said *fine*, we would talk later, and she appeared satisfied for now. There was a lot for the two of us to catch up on. Eventually I'd figure out how telecommunications systems functioned in the afterlife.

Once back out into the hallway, on the other side of one of those 101 rooms, I looked both ways and stood there. I did not like that Brother Charlie was there at Angel of Mercy and persisted hanging around in my afterlife. *I* was the chief revenant, not Charlie—wasn't I? Besides, he had caused enough trouble for me and everybody else he came in contact with the first time we had all gone through high school.

———

I detected in the distance, from a distant part of the building, the heavy, jackbooted tread of those ominously, methodically coming my way.

They rounded the corner and approached me. Let us call them The Longcoats. They were three haggard, pasty-faced, defiant boys dressed in long black greatcoats, and they were clearly out of class and probably without the required hall pass. They were wearing sunglasses, as well, chalking up what used to be yet another school handbook violation. They stomped right up to me in their big black laced-up boots, their hands jammed into the pockets of their greatcoats, big woolen garments they were wearing on a temperate sunny day. I could not see their eyes, but it did not matter, as we seemed to recognize each other.

"The big day's coming," said the obvious leader to all of them, and then he addressed me pointedly: "Stevie, you got everything ready you're supposed to get ready?"

"Sure I do." I was always prepared, you know. A charged pause followed before I said, "Ready for what?"

"Time's coming near when we give everybody exactly what they deserve, the lousy parasites. School will never be the same when we're done. We'll show them once and for all."

"The losers," said one of the others.

"The snivelers," said the third.

"Yes, I can tell you think it's about time you all put your foot down," I added to the chorus of assent. "Tell me again, though, what is it that the snivelers are sniveling about and exactly what is it that they deserve for sniveling the way they do?"

They ignored the question. It must have been apparent what parasites all deserved. Meanwhile, they had another idea.

"Stevie, be there tonight. The Hanging Gardens."

～

THE GRAND DEPOSITOR

If you had to live your life over, what would you do differently? And why is it you don't make those changes right now?

Is Shannon Reed portrayed the way you might have expected? Brother Stephen seems to be much taken by her. Are you similarly attracted?

What would you have done, spying Charlie in the classroom with Shannon? Was I showing admirable restraint by not throttling him? If you could win for everybody a moment's relief from the pain Charlie caused by tearing him to pieces, would you do it? Should you do it? Then what about me? Should I?

About the play, "Shut Up It's My Life," shall I get tickets? I bet Tom Newgarten will be getting an injunction, so no time to waste.

SIX

Q. 3. What is man?
A. Man is a creature composed of body and soul, and
  made to the image and likeness of God.
                              —The Baltimore Catechism

Shannon rushed out of Room 101, her red-and-blue pleated skirt atwirl, like a spirally old-school spinning top. Then the carnival colors stopped swirling, and she herself halted when she turned in the direction of the receding forms of the Longcoats as they retreated down the hall.

"Don't talk to them, Stevie."

The hall was transformed into a flurry of to-and-fro-ing, here-and-there-ing on the part of dozens, seemingly hundreds, of forms. *Give me back my lunch. I'll see you there, I'll see you then. Love your shoes, hate your shirt, where'd you get that jacket? I told my Dad stick it. I know I know I know. My mom finds out, she'll kill me. He is such a dick. She is such a fox. They are dead meat. What's for homework? Who cares? Call me. I don't care. Just call me! Give me back my lunch already!*

For my part, I was double-concentrating on the scene around me as well as on the little red ball of woven wool on the top of Shannon's red beret, the cherry on a sundae.

"What did those lunatic morons want with you?" she asked.

Talk about an unanswerable question under the circumstances. I was speechless. Come on, Brothers—Shannon Reed was talking to me.

There was such a hum of activity in the corridor. Like what being inside a beehive must feel like, surrounded by so many fellow creatures caught up in a sense of shared purpose and industry. But I found I could shut out everything and everyone else and just listen to Shannon's voice. I could do that for hours on end in the past, you know. Maybe I could do that again and again.

But before I could rally my faculties, she said, "Stevie, we have a lot to do, don't be wasting your time with the Longcoats. They're losers."

I nodded in stupefied amazement, not quite understanding exactly what we had to do, but having the sense I would be illuminated.

"Just follow my lead, Stevie, and you'll be all right."

When she touched me on the arm, I trusted I'd be all right. I knew that for a fact thirty-eight years ago, when I was in my own crazy way crazy in love with her and she gave me confidence in myself that I lacked—and still lack to this day. But I had to find out something.

"Did Brother Charlie and Brother Joel do what you said they did?"

"Nice seeing you again, too, Stephen. You don't waste any time, do you?"

"Just tell me. I need to know, Shannon."

"Sure you do, sure. For now, we play along with him. For now. That's why I was being nice to Brother Charlie in Drama Club. Don't you see that?"

"Wasn't that the exact approach that got everybody in trouble the first time?"

I don't believe she liked that turn of thought, but she continued, "You have a point, fair enough. But there has to be a reason why we are together again."

"Presuming," I said, "there had to be a reason why we were thrown together in the past."

"We weren't thrown together in the past, Stevie. We found each other because we had to. We were meant to be together then, and we are meant to be together now."

"So what you're saying, Shannon, is that I'm here to save you."

OK, that was a leap, wasn't it? Which I regretted when I heard her response.

She cracked up.

Which hurt.

So I said, "What do we do now?"

"We are looking for the right opening. Just wait for your cue."

With pleasure, I thought. *With more than pleasure.*

"It makes me happy to see you, Stevie. It hasn't been the same without you."

I closed my eyes. Did I want to kiss her? Right then and there in the open corridor with everybody around? You'd think anybody in my position would know the answer to that question, wouldn't you, Brothers?

"Call me," she said.

I opened my eyes. "What's your number, Shannon?"

"Just call me. Or text."

"How do I do that?"

"You'll figure it out."

Did I have a choice?

"No," she said, "you sort of don't."

That is when Brother Charlie and Serena danced through the door into the hallway. She was doing big-time teenage glum and defiant, moody and impassioned, all at the same time. He was doing all-out kindly authority figure being avuncular and considerate. Together they amounted to the predictable. They walked off down the hall, shoulder to shoulder, speaking to each other softly in words I could not hear.

"OK, Stevie," Shannon said. "You see what I see? Can the situation be any clearer?"

"I have been hearing a lot about this place called Luna Park. What's it like?"

She opened up—it was like a curtain pulled back from in front of her eyes—and her voice filled with awe. "It's a very lifelike experience. If you can remember what that was like."

"Do you want to go to Luna Park, Shannon?"

"Are you asking me out on a date?"

Such a crude term, but that was the general idea. "You ever been there before?"

"Who hasn't been to Luna Park?"

"Me, for one." Just go with the "me," Brothers, and don't get all Dr. Strunkenwhitestein again. And then I got into the spirit: "*Luna Park, Luna Park.*"

She followed the bouncing ball: "*Time bends back!*"

And I went: "*And loss is a lark!*"

"Oh, *that* Luna Park. Love to. When do you want to go, Stephen?"

I saw my opportunity and I grabbed it. "Call me."

"OK, Luna Park, fine, it's a date. But first you gotta come to my play. You'll find it interesting."

That was what I was worried about.

SEVEN

*Q. 199. Should we believe truths which we cannot
understand?*
*A. We should and often do believe truths which we
cannot understand when we have proof of their
existence.*
                                    —The Baltimore Catechism

In the moment before I was a goner at that Definitorium meeting, I
felt one particularly keen regret. I wished I had spent more time in
the office. That is not the sort of sentiment you are supposed to plant
on your tombstone. Actually, speaking of headstones, if I had the right
of first refusal, I would dictate the following for mine:

WHAT ARE YOU LOOKING AT?

Let me back up.

When non-Catholics become tourists in Catholic World, they may
hear passing reference to something known as "a good death." A good
death seems to be connected to the condition of releasing oneself to
meet one's Maker, to the inescapable recognition that death is part of
one's life, an essential aspect of the so-called human condition. It must
appear strange to doubters of the concept that nobody gives equal time
to the "good root canal," the "good tire blowout," the "good 7.1 earth-
quake," the "good bronchial discharge."

Do not go gentle into that good night, penned the alcoholic poet Dylan

Thomas. *Rage, rage against the dying of the light,* he continued, and if I know anything about drinking, he should know. I will ask him for supporting documentation if our paths should cross. The continually inebriated, intermittently great poet was closer to the sobering truth, in my opinion, than the good death apologists. Resignation has its consolations—at some point, who isn't tired of fighting the onslaught of decrepitude, sickness, and suffering? But which one is the great illusion: that death will not come knocking, or that health is assured? I do not regard my death as meeting all the stipulated requirements of a good death, and I can't imagine any of you in the Definitorium saying so, either. In the interests of full disclosure, I have yet to run across anybody who happens to be dead advancing the good death concept.

Now, you're going to really, really, really hate the next thing I have to say. Which is this: Just about everything you assume to be true about life and work is wrong.

Calm down, Brothers. Take a deep breath. Don't go sputtering yourself stupid.

What do people say upon getting word that somebody has died unexpectedly?

Don't waste another second. Life is precious, seize the day, carpe the frickin diem. Time goes by so fast and before you know it...hello, Mister Funeral Director?

People are right, I grant, to make such resolutions—up to a point, that is. But only up to a point. Then some people give themselves permission to go sticking their proboscises into blameless, unsuspecting roses. As experienced gardeners would warn them, this can be a risky proposition—yellow jackets, thorns, slugs, the list goes on and on. Fresh from the insight that life is transitory, some resolve to take up knitting or the dulcimer or to quit their day jobs in order to start raising sheep, or some other environmentally correct, sustainable creature.

Despite what you think of me and this report I am spinning into your ear, dying does not make you crazy. Maybe it is just the opposite, in fact. Besides, I was never all that crazy. I had gone to Catholic schools all my life. Before I memorized my multiplication tables and my *Baltimore Catechism* I understood there was no getting around I was going to die. I just didn't know if I was going to stay permanently dead.

Here is the reason I wish I had spent more time in my office. All along I should have been working harder on a plan to address the roots of those sexual abuse cases. The failure of my religious order to anticipate these problems was not only an institutional failure, it was also my personal failure. We should have separated out the nutcases and the clammy-skinned reptilian predators well in advance. Let's not kid ourselves, Brothers. We all knew who they were. But we always got hung up on their personal rights. We were always distracted by the idea of forgiveness and Christian understanding. What crap.

It was on me, as I heard more than a few times during my delightful inquisitions. *Depositions*, I mean.

On this score, I have to give you highest marks, Brother Provincial. As my boss, you never took to heart, as far as I could tell, those expensive positive-management-reinforcement training seminars at tony hotels to which you arranged to have carried your monogrammed golf clubs. Naturally, therefore, you found it incumbent upon yourself to point out regularly my deficiencies in your characteristically gracious manner.

"Can't believe you dropped the damn ball," you often remarked to me. "It's all on you, Stephen. You should have seen it coming. We've got to do right by these people who have been damaged on your watch."

"Damaged on *my* Auxiliary Provincial watch, Provincial?"

"And we have to protect our corporate assets."

"*Nice trick, if we can pull it off,*" I thought—and did not tell Brother Paulus.

"Let's keep our insurance carriers in the loop," the Provincial reminded me. "But not completely in the loop."

"That's why we pay the huge premiums, Brother."

"And let's get these Brothers the help they need. And since most of them can't be helped—well, you know what you need to do. These perverts can't take us all down. We'll be two steps away from bankruptcy if you're not smart about it."

"Are we in communication with the diocese, Brother Paulus? I don't think we want to surprise his Excellency, the Bishop."

"His Excellency is my problem, Brother, not yours. Just do your job, Brother Stephen. I will do mine."

———

So many surprises that were not surprising upon reflection. Besides the frenetic pace of activity in my afterlife, and the Prius, and Shannon, and Charlie, who once was in my trunk, returning to high school was a major one. Here was another big one. I didn't *feel* remotely dead, whatever that was supposed to feel like. On the other hand, I was a rank amateur when it came to the hereafter.

Speaking of Dante, about whom, I would wager, nobody besides me was even thinking, his famous poem was never far from my mind ever since the Definitorium ended somewhat abruptly. The poet enjoyed the benefit of a wise and knowing guide through the rings of the early stages of the afterlife. And as for me?

From the looks of things, this Brother Stephen had only one Virgil candidate he could call up from the minors. But what a Virgil my Virgil was. Brother Charlie? Now that he was out of the trunk and apparently on the loose like some grizzled lifer escaped from his prison work detail, I was provisionally on my own again. So perhaps the illustrious example of the master Dante, who wanders through the underworld while still alive, was not going to prove useful for my purposes. To refresh your recollection of the poem, Brothers, this is how it opens:

The Italian: strolls.

Mood: bleak.

Way: lost.

Middle of life: turning.

Wood: dark.

What he sees: drear.

Language: fails.

Death could not be worse, says he, than what his life has become.
How delivered there: who knows?
True Way: detour.
Thus from the outset the poet sketches the details so memorably. My
particular circumstances, however, could be summarized briefly thus:
Monarch: flutters.
Board of Inquiry: inquires.
Auxiliary Provincial: fin—splat—adios—ciao.
Stephen: high school redux.
In this moment of bedimmed reflection, contemplating the com-
paratives as I was, and while still reeling a little from the incarnation of
the Longcoats and the vision of Charlie strolling along with the lovely
and vivacious Serena, I noticed a supposedly thought-provoking sign
posted on the official FIGHTING IRISH BULLETIN BOARD near the unpopulated main office:

Q. 150. WHY DID GOD MAKE YOU?

"Why did He make me do what?" I wanted to ask, but I probably
shouldn't push my luck, such as it was, because I can't avoid being in
places where nobody likes a wise guy.

Honestly, I was ecstatic because I happened to know the correct answer to that big question #150 as to why God caused me all this trouble
by creating me in the first place, which answer I recited to myself as if
I were a game show contestant vying for the washing machine/dryer
combo or an all-expenses-paid trip to Disneyland of the Dead: *"God
made me to know Him, to love Him, and to serve Him in this world, and
to be happy with Him forever in heaven."* I had memorized the Q as
well as the A from my tattered-from-overuse grammar school *Baltimore Catechism.*

As you are all too well aware, Brothers, this particular book is not
the definitive study of the soft-shell-crab-worshipping Chesapeake
Bay city in Maryland. *Ballamore* (as locals mumble the name, making it practically one syllable, certainly no more than a syllable and a

half)—*Ballamore* is the birthplace of Babe Ruth and of Edgar Allan Poe, though, if murder statistics are reliable, not the ideal location to set up shop dealing crack and smack. Of course, Baltimore is also the home of the venerable baseball team known as the Orioles. Long ago, the team used to play in an old stadium whose infield was so rock-hard that an otherwise routine grounder would sometimes shoot up off the turf and leap up high as a geyser, enabling hitters to reach base before the play could be made to retire them at first. That sort of hit came to be known throughout the baseball world as The Baltimore Chop.

As for baseball, I wondered, being dead and therefore freed up for such activities, if I would be able to enjoy even more the exquisitely interminable game. I was also worried about Internet access, without my laptop—how else might I be able to keep track of the latest scores and standings? And speaking of things I would miss, I regretted I would never see another live baseball game. I loved everything about the game, from the singing of the "Star-Spangled Banner"—even when some singers transformed the anthem into the Star-Strangled Banner—to the "No Pepper" signs to the crack of the bat to the smell of the grass to the… well, I loved everything.

Although I was a lifelong Catholic—a leading member of a religious order, too, as my obit writer would, I guess, be compelled by statute to deferentially opine—I had not been in the habit of reflecting much on the afterlife. That was one thing that was not my problem, thank you very much. You might be shocked to hear as much. You might think that someone in my position would have been hard-wired. Yet despite the liturgical and canonical allusions to the afterlife I intoned daily, sometimes hourly, the afterlife was somehow just not front-burner, certainly not as it had been during my prolonged, agonized childhood. That was the stage when heaven and purgatory and hell were subjects etched on my soul by means of the congenial typeface employed in my handy *Baltimore Catechism.*

Insofar as I wasn't feeling so grand and insofar as God was still keeping a low profile, I was tentatively drawing the conclusion that perhaps I might not be in the place I might have imagined and called heaven. Of course, in my earthly experience, God's middle and last names might as well have been Gone Fishing. Logically speaking, if God's pattern of behavior continued into the afterlife (and why wouldn't it?), I might indeed be in heaven after all. If God had a penchant for being elsewhere, even here, who was lowly Brother Stephen to question divine design?

I took a stab at understanding. I was where I was, wherever that could be. A theological Baltimore Chop. Life after death, I had many times said to myself, was simply not my management challenge. If the catechism was clear on any subject, it was clear on that. The problem was, although the afterlife may not have been my problem before, it had definitely become a very big problem for me.

A melody unexpectedly popped into my head—words, too. *On a dark desert highway...Cool wind in my hair...Up ahead in the distance, I saw a shimmering light...This could be heaven, this could be hell...Welcome to the Hotel California...*

Perhaps the afterlife of Brother Stephen was stuck in the '70s, like an Eagles song, complete with the wind in what was left of my hair? That was not the eeriest part. I was conscious of the absurd illusion that I remained somehow mortal, something to which I clung as desperately as an aging rock star clings to his old platinum records, despite the mountain of evidence that that train has left the station. Call the Figure of Speech Police, Brothers: I mix my metaphors with a relish now more than ever. Death, the Mother of Metaphors, may be a virgin and may be a whore, but she is not a metaphor, not anytime soon in this afterlife of mine. Still, I had to admire what a priceless punishment that illusion of mortality would be to visit upon the deceased. At the same time, this illusion was not unconnected to the delusion I enjoyed while alive, that I would never perish, that the world was inconceivable without yours truly: *c'est moi.*

In other words, I was feeling the same restlessness and confusion that had been the hallmarks of my school years and—to tell the truth—all the years following. I would have assumed that the one sure thing about death was that all earthly business was finished, and if not all earthly business, then, my God, at least high school. How ironic that such a trivial consolation was denied. I still felt the press of unfinished business. Then again, name somebody who does not die with business to finish.

And actually, it so happens that I had a long to-do list inscribed inside my notepad. Conveniently, every item was the same:

1. SHANNON REED
2. SHANNON REED
3. SHANNON REED
4. SHANNON REED
5. SHANNON REED
6. SHANNON REED
7. SHANNON REED
8. SHANNON REED
9. SHANNON REED
10. SHANNON REED

———

Don't you see it now? I do. My current to-do list was indistinguishable from the to-do list that could have been inscribed on the last day of what turned out to be my alleged life. Which explained everything. But even so, that's why I was where I was, wherever that was. Could be heaven, could be hell, could be anywhere in between.

Given the way my luck was going, or not going, it was more likely anywhere in between. Besides, I had things to do, and the list to prove it. My life remains unfinished, just like yours, Brothers.

First, though, I had a game to play.

EIGHT

Q. 140. What do the words "will never die" mean?
A. By the words "will never die" we mean that the
soul, when once created, will never cease to exist,
whatever be its condition in the next world.
Hence we say the soul is immortal or gifted with
immortality.
                           —The Baltimore Catechism

I was gazing up at the scorching sun high in the midday sky, tugging down on the bill of my sweaty baseball cap. I was standing on the infield, right in the middle of a game in which, everything seemed to suggest, I was a participant. Before this moment, I had not been aware that it was baseball season and that there was a game. In my personal afterlife, of course, why wouldn't it always be baseball season? I took stock of the ever-present, ever-changeable wind, which now was blowing out, favoring the hitter. No, now it was blowing in, favoring the pitcher. Wait, it was blowing in and out, favoring neither, if not favoring both.

For some reason, despite its being baseball season, I was depressed.

Despair is usually listed as one of those Seven So-called Deadly Sins, and I could almost justify my gloomy disposition, Brothers, when I imagine trying to explain to you how I got from place to place in the afterlife, here to there, now to then, or how time (which was not even close to being the right word) seemed to flow, morning to afternoon to night, though not quite always in that exact sequence. Then again, my consolation is that, back when I was in your shoes in the world you all take for granted, I would have had similar difficulty.

On this score, I will never forget, Brother Ignatius, when I once asked you a simple question: "Are we here now?" You replied, being the star physics instructor that you are, that all you could assert for certain was, "Probably." How right you would eventually turn out to be, 'Natius, you have no idea. Trust me. Or is your response to that exhortation of mine also "Probably"?

You see, "time" was pretty fluid, and "space" was a permeable boundary, too—which was an awful lot like the original experience of high school, I have to say. And seasons? Talk about another mystery. The afterlife had a certain season, I would have hazarded a guess, but it was the season of all seasons, or the essence of seasonality, which unfortunately for me and my shaky command of the language better describes menu-planning and produce-shopping, and not what I mean at all. But I need to put "season" in quotation marks. Then again, I would also need to write school "day," and "night," and "time," and "space," but if I keep doing that, you will go "batty."

Besides, I remember those annoying e-mails I would receive from one particular Brother, somebody you all know, love, and futilely try every year to send to the Brothers' equivalent of Siberia, Brother Genesius. He was fond of his quotation marks. I mean "quotation" marks, which he liberally employed to suggest I-have-no-idea-what beyond a subtlety that escaped my Scarecrow's absentee brain. He was almost as fond of them as he was of his abbrevs. E.g, this is an e-mail from him:

> Steph:
> I have a "problem" with the decision you and the Definit. made. Don't "shoot the messenger", but I think almost everybody would agree with me when I say "hold your horses". Anyway, that's my "two cents".
> Gen.

You start using quotation marks and abbreviations like this, playing keep-away with words, you probably can't stop. For sure, you will not be able to stop me from wanting to "kill" you.

The fluidity and porousness of seeming time and space—well, that is consistent with all the brain research we are in possession of these days and to which we did not have access when our teachers failed to teach us in high school. Right brain, left brain, hormones, DNA, and so on. We were all adrift in a boiling, bubbling sea of disconnects. Which was what here and now felt like, with tantalizing illusions of connectedness that cried out for the application of a giant neurological soldering gun. And which goes back to another thing *un peu Français*, Rimbaud's "Season in Hell," composed by the precocious French surrealist teenager (quadruple redundancy!).

But come on. Who couldn't really use another helpful vision of early damnation? Raise your hands, Brothers. Better dust off the old books.

On balance, then, I felt pretty unbalanced. What I mean is that there were many more things that I did not now know. In fact there were more things now that I did not know than there were things I did not know when I was first a cocky-slash-insecure teenager walking down the hallways—poor posture, bad complexion, self-doubt and all—of Angel of Mercy High School.

——

So, as I say, there I was on the baseball diamond.

Cool, no?

It would have been nice to have some shades, or some eye-black, but I had neither. That's the sort of thing that makes you look like you belong on the team. My cap was heavy with perspiration. My black robe was soaking wet. I appeared to be playing shortstop, the highest-status position on the field, the most physically demanding and most intellectually interesting, and the bases were loaded.

I put my baseball glove up to my face and breathed in. The soft leather smelled how I imagined a farm might smell: like bales of hay with traces of horse and cornmeal and burnt toast. It smelled the way it always did, in other words. I kicked at the infield dirt ritualistically, right foot, left foot, making half-circles before myself.

Then as the pitcher put his toe on the slab, preparing to make his pitch, I settled into my defensive crouch, butt over heels, and leaned over slightly while keeping on my toes, loose-limbed, shoulders relaxed, glove upright and extended near my knee, head up.

You may be interested to know that everybody on my team was dressed in a Brother's black robes. Everybody on the opposite team was also dressed in a Brother's black robes. In fact, everybody in the stands was dressed the same way, too.

Meanwhile, we infielders were yackety-yacking. That's one of our jobs in the infield, to yackety-yack.

"No batter no batter no batter."

I made some infield chatter myself. That's what you have to do when you're an infielder, you know. "It is what it is," chattered the field-general shortstop, I.

The third baseman looked at me dubiously. "No way."

"Way," demurred the second baseman.

Third: "All evidence runs counter. It is not what it is."

Second: "Rationally speaking, we cannot speak rationally at all. Certainly, not being what it is is exactly what it is."

Short: "Let me rephrase."

Second: "Please don't."

Third: "You've caused enough trouble."

They were right. I never should have said a word.

"Hit it to me, sucker," I chattered some more.

Our southpaw pitcher wound up, raised his right leg, reared back with his left hand, and let the ball fly. When he landed he was squared up to the plate in perfect fielding posture, his position right out of the coaches' textbooks.

Oh, by the way, the batter took a mighty swing and missed.

The *Home of the Fighting Irish* went berserk and cheered.

My teammates exhaled. They looked serious, but like they were nice guys, too. They were a team, we were a team, and who knows how and who knows why people are ultimately thrown together. Just stay with me, let's keep going.

I had a question, though, which was more like a sense of questioning. I couldn't pin it down for a second, but then I realized: Hey, what was the score? And did it matter anyway? I searched the HOME OF THE FIGHTING IRISH scoreboard for answers. 7-7. Two outs, top of the seventh, the last inning. This was getting exciting.

Black-robed Shannon was standing behind the meshed chain-link backstop, and she cupped her hands before her mouth and shouted encouragement across the diamond. "Stevie, be ready."

On the baseball diamond, *come on*, Stevie was never anything other than ready. I winked and tipped my chin toward her—just like in high school when she came to the games and cheered for her boyfriend. A weird thought—all right, if you insist, another one—coursed through my brain: She looked pretty cute in the Brother's robes.

The pitcher wound up again, and the ball spun off his fingers. Remember how I said that time was fluid? Well, my Brother Einsteins, for this pitch time slowed…all…the…way…down…

—

The ball in flight looked big and brilliant as a full moon in miniature, and it moved more slowly than the moon does across the night sky. I counted the stitches one by one as the ball made its deliberate way to the plate. The raised red yarn on the white rawhide was positively glowing. I was up to seventeen stitches, so I had a long way to go till I counted all one hundred and eight.

Sometime, eventually, the ball would begin to break—no doubt it was destined to become the optical illusion called a curve, the Deuce, Captain Hook, Uncle Charlie, Lord Charles, the Local, the Yellow Hammer.

Meanwhile, the sky took on the purpled hue of a bruise. Storm clouds gathered low over the field and burst, and the rain cascaded down, a torrential downpour. I had never traveled to Asia, but I had read a few books and the monsoon concept occurred to me.

The pitch had not yet reached the halfway point to the plate. The ball hung like a luminous piece of tropical fruit from an invisible tree. It was fixed and it was in transit.

Just like me, I thought.

I took off my cap and let the heavy straight rain fall down upon the just and the unjust alike, both of whom were now playing shortstop. I turned up my head and closed my eyes and reflected.

You want to know the weirdest part about death? Even now, by all accounts pretty much deceased, I have to tell you that I remained more afraid of dying than ever before.

No, wait—I was afraid, but I don't think I have captured the essence of the fear I felt.

You know how sometimes we wonder what would have happened if we had made some different choices? Gone to that college and not the other one, for instance. Had a different roommate, took a class from a different professor, and so on. Walked down one tree-lined street and not the other, taken the train uptown instead of down. These are banal reflections, but they still hold sway over somebody as banal as I am. Reason I mention all this is that I wasn't nostalgic for a life that did not come my way. I was nostalgic about the life that did. I wondered if I had managed to live the life that either I had chosen or, depending upon how you look at it, the one that was chosen for me. Did my life happen to somebody else, who had similarities to me, perhaps, but who was not me? That was what terrified me, whoever I, or possibly he, was now.

Meanwhile, it rained and it rained and it rained.

Then, as abruptly as it started, the rain halted. There is no way to explain the afterlife's weather patterns, because there were no patterns I could discern—except for that wind, of course, the constant wind.

Just as quickly, the skies cleared and the sun beat down once more on my sweaty, sopping cap. The crowd surged forward with palpable expectation in their places in the bleachers. I strolled across the diamond to the dugout on the third base side of the field. I took a bottle of water and greedily drank from it. Thirst slaked, I sauntered back to position.

In the meantime, the pitch was still in progress, a white gleaming hummingbird frozen and not frozen. Then the ball made its gradual approach to the plate and began to make its break downward, the classic direction of a curve. But the batter's eyes opened wider and wider. He was on top of it as the ball initiated a downward swerve into the bottom left corner of the plate.

The right-handed batter coiled and tensed, and his knees bent as he was getting ready to swing. I could sense that the batter believed that this was his pitch. He swung.

The bat moved as fast as the ball, and the batter slowly connected, and solidly. The ball was returned into the field of play, and it became a low line drive heading in slow motion in the direction of left field, between second and third, the area the shortstop is supposed to patrol. I could hear the leather of the ball *whortle whortle whortle* toward me.

Sometimes on the baseball field, my life used to pass before my eyes, just as the saying goes. It did so again now. I walked further into the hole between second and third base, that is, to my right, and there I planted myself and waited and waited and waited. When the ball approached me, I raised up the glove to chin-level, and the ball landed softly as a robin's egg into a nest.

Deafening cheers. Out number three.

And the third baseman called out, "Stephen stoppeth one of three!"

Then I ran off with my teammates into the dugout, my black robes coated with dust.

———

Brother Charlie, evidently my coach, called out, "Brother Stephen, you're up."

I put on a batter's helmet and selected an aluminum bat, which gleamed like a silver spike in my hands. This must seem anachronistic, insofar as back when I was in high school we didn't use aluminum bats.

My afterlife is supposed to be linear?

Moving right along—to employ the cherished transitional phrase that appeared in my students' compositions—

Moving right along, I strode to the plate.

Strode is a vinegary word, but so be it, and besides, that's a big baseball term: batters never walk to the plate, they stride.

I assumed my place in the batter's box and swung the bat a few times, readying myself, timing my swing. Then I stepped out of the box to analyze the situation. I looked out across the field. The defense was lined up conventionally, with the outfield backed up toward the fences, playing me deep as if I were the power hitter I had never actually been in my inglorious high school playing days.

"Batter up," cried the umpire, and he pointed at me and toward the pitcher in successive gestures.

"No batter no batter no batter," chanted the infielders.

"Let's have some chatter out here."

"Look alive."

My team exhorted me, too, from the dugout. So did the hometown crowd.

"Stevie, you're the man," Shannon called out, in case I might have forgotten.

It was a beautiful day for a baseball game. Any day is a beautiful day for a baseball game, as far as I am concerned. The score was tied. I loved baseball. Baseball was not really a metaphor for life, after all. Life was never quite so pure and rarefied as baseball.

I gazed in the direction of the pitcher and the pitcher wound up and threw the ball. At least I hypothesized that he threw the ball, because when I heard the pop of the catcher's mitt, I realized I had not seen a trace of the pitch.

"Strike one!" cried the ump.

As I never saw the ball, I had no grounds upon which to contest the call. So I readied myself for the next pitch. Which was soon on its way, and with what would be very similar results. I couldn't see it this time either.

"Strike two!"

This was getting serious.

I had to get the bat off my shoulder. I wasn't going to strike out. Not this time. Not with the game on the line, bottom of the seventh, not with the team counting on me to come through.

Charlie yelled as he jogged out of the dugout, "Time out, blue," and the umpire raised both his arms, signifying time out.

Charlie and I huddled off to the side, along the base path, Charlie placing both his hands on my shoulders. I kicked at the white chalk lines with my cleats because it felt eerie when he touched me. But then we locked eyes. There was a big bulge in Charlie's cheek and a brown-ish trickle running down his chin. The disgusting stuff also stained the front of his black robe.

"You're embarrassing me, Charlie. What the hell are you doing out here?"

"I got something to tell you, sunshine."

"By the way, I'm curious, when did you start chewing tobacco?" I grimaced. "Reason I ask, it looks really appetizing."

"Listen to me, hotshot."

"Hotshot, sunshine, where do you get these goofy names? Is there a book?"

"You can't find everything you need to know in a book, meat. So listen up, meat. Tension. Tension, it's the enemy." He spit out a septic stream of tobacco juice.

"Whose?"

"Your tension, Stephen."

"No, whose enemy?"

"You know what somebody once said? You can't hit and think at the same time. Full head, empty bat. That's what a great baseball man said.

Full head, empty bat."

"Full head, empty bat? That's the wisdom of the ages?"

"Precisely."

"I think I can safely say I have no idea what you're talking about, Charlie."

"No idea, great. That's a start, rook."

"That's what you came out of the dugout to tell me? Thanks a lot. But right now, I gotta get back in the box and strike out."

Charlie frowned. "That's a defeatist attitude."

"Didn't you hear today's National Sarcasm Day?"

"Time to take stock, Stephen. Analyze the conditions."

I licked my finger and held it up to the wind. "OK, the breeze is blowing to left field."

"So you need to turn on the inside pitch and pull it."

"But now it's blowing to right."

"So you need to go with the outside pitch the opposite way, and drive it."

I put my finger down. "Why does the wind never stop, Charlie, why?"

"Visualize success, Stephen. What does success look like for you?"

"Do you ever know what you're talking about, Charlie?"

"Empty yourself, Stephen. Be the bat. Be the ball. Don't think."

"Finally you're making sense. But I have one question. I cannot see the ball."

"That's not a question." Charlie spit again, a rivulet of sepia spattering on the dirt.

"Here comes the question. How can I hit the ball if I can't see the ball?"

"Perfect. Now you've got everything you need, Stephen. Trust me."

Charlie had crossed the line, and I told him so: "I'll never trust you again, Charlie. But I do want to know what chewing tobacco tastes like."

"A lot like disappointment. You'd like it."

"Speaking of disappointment. Joel put his hands on Shannon, and you, you son of a bitch, you let him get away with it."

"Stephen, you don't know what you are talking about."

"I do know what I am talking about. And you know that I know."

"Don't think for a second you can understand what it's like to be anybody else."

"Don't you have any shame?"

"Funny thing for somebody like you to be asking me, Stephen."

The umpire grew impatient. "Play ball, fellas," he cried out. "Batter up."

Charlie tapped me on my helmet and I took my place in the batter's box again.

Maybe Charlie was right. I would be the bat. I would be the ball. I would not think. Besides, had thinking ever helped me a lick? Moving right along…

The pitcher went into his windup and I only wished it was Charlie's head being served up on a platter for me to meet with the barrel of my bat.

And then came the next pitch presumably hurtling toward the catcher, and, despite once again not seeing it, I—not seeing it? why should that stop me now?—my head vacant, my bat pregnant—I swung.

I hit the ball on the sweet spot of the bat—at least I think I did, for that gloriously hollowed-out sound resounded across the diamond, a sound halfway between ping and knock: *pong*. Thus it was that for once I did become the bat, I did become the ball. It was such a glorious feeling, hitting a baseball like that, because even if I could not feel making contact with a baseball I could not see, I could hear the echoing *pong* of the aluminum bat, I could sense that the ball was traveling high and deep toward center field, arcing higher and deeper, and deeper and higher still, until I saw the center fielder leap up with his glove reaching over the top of the fence and in a second come down to the ground, where he collapsed in a heap. He opened his glove to see if he had succeeded, but he hadn't. His glove contained nothing but emptiness. I could relate to the concept.

My teammates rushed, cheering and shouting, from the confines of the dugout as the opposing team began to walk disconsolately off the field of play, the game by all conventional measures over.

I had hit a home run. A walk-off home run, as they say on the sports shows. I, Brother Stephen, had single-handedly won the game, which was something nobody had ever said on a sports show. My life had never been as clear as that, not once, not ever. Maybe death wasn't so awful after all.

Hold that thought.

I started my regal prance of a trot, the whippets and Airedales and the Afghan hounds starring at the Westminster Dog Show having nothing on this Brother. Of course, a regal prance was not so simple as it sounds, given the limitations imposed by a Brother's restrictive robes.

In no time I had turned the corner at first base and was headed toward second.

At this point I recalled my parents sitting around, lit up in the vicinity of a similarly lit-up Christmas tree. There they are smoking cigarettes and I am unwrapping presents enveloped in cloudlets of blue smoke. The signs indicate this must be Christmas Eve. A little boat, a little blue boat, appears inside a little box. A butterscotch moon spreads across the sky outside the picture window. A thimble, a pile of knitting, an ashtray, a bottle of whiskey on the coffee table. A book of fairy tales, pages spread open, glowing before the blazing fireplace.

"He doesn't act like a real boy, that's all I'm saying. Just an observation."

I rounded second.

"What are you saying? That's not an observation a dad makes about his son, that's a punch in the nose."

A birthday cake and a pony. A guitar on the bedroom floor. A monster living in the closet, coming out when the lights are turned off, scampering back into the darkness faster than the speed of a desk light being turned on. A baton twirling. A squirrel praying over a walnut. A television set. A 45-rpm record. A dog giving birth to seven puppies. A swimming pool. A radio.

"What's with that dreamy look in his eye? He is not right in the head, not right."

On my way into third base. A 1951 Ford. The wool upholstery that scratched my legs. A tub of popcorn. A hot dog. A drive-in movie. Jesus dying for my sins. Jesus dead for my sins. Jesus resurrecting himself for my sins. Angels and devils. A map on the wall. Cleo, my dog, lying on the rug, her long, looping body in the shape of a question mark.

"He's a lovely child, a sweet child. Why do you pick on him day after day?"

Rounding third base. A little problem I didn't care to talk about. I had a little tiny problem that I didn't know how to talk about. Sitting in the front seat of the black limousine to the cemetery. Cream puffs on the kitchen counter. A couch and a nap. The caw of a crow. Cowboy boots and a lasso and a toy six-shooter.

"What was he doing in your closet, trying on your shoes?"

"What the hell are you—?"

"You telling me that's normal?"

"He was doing no such thing. You are out of your mind. What kind of father…"

"Stop kidding yourself. Face facts—your boy's a weirdo."

I was coming closer and closer. Almost there. Honeysuckle drifted in the air. A carnival accordion melody played in the distance. A boy drawing a red balloon. A woman in a blue dress, getting ready to go out for the night. A man with a moustache, a glass of booze in his hand. Somewhere I supposed some flowers bloomed, but oh, they had to be so very very far away.

"Just let the boy be, he's just amusing himself."

"With your goddamn shoes, amusing himself? In your goddamn closet?"

"Just let Stephen be Stephen, would you? He's five years old. And he was not trying on my shoes."

I approached home plate.

"That's not what a normal boy does, is all I'm saying."

Home plate: that was where the entire team had gathered to pile on, prepared to celebrate victory. That was where I saw the surging wave of blackness—a churning sea of billowy black robes. And that was also where Shannon was awaiting my arrival, her arms opened wide.

She would let me be. Shannon would always let me be.

Each footfall, each stride should have brought me closer to them, closer to her, closer to anything or anyone. But it did not work that way. Instead, it was more like that terrible dream we all recall. I kept running and running and running and running, and I never would touch home, never.

———

There is one conviction—one conclusion—I keep leaving out of this narrative, I think I must concede intentionally. I have left it unstated, it occurs to me, not to spare you, Brothers, because you do not deserve the sort of protection somebody in my position might provide. Maybe nobody deserves such protection or maybe everybody does, but the problem is nobody can be protected.

No, I do it to spare myself.

But there is no longer any reason to believe we are spared, any of us, so here goes:

Death is very sad, Brothers, far sadder than any of your vain imaginings can suggest, but the thing that is far, far sadder than being dead, as you will come to know exactly too late to do anything about it, if you're like me, is recalling where and how and that you were once alive. I don't care what *The Baltimore Catechism* says. This is what it should say:

Q. What will you miss being dead?

A. Meat, this is easy. Listen up, sunshine. Amazing the sorts of things you will now find, being dead, that you miss, rook. The sandwiches. A child's song from somewhere down the darkened street. The night-blooming jasmine. The peel of an orange. Reading a new book in the shade garden. The sunlight pouring through the chapel window. A student's smile for no reason at all from across the aisle. Catching a green light. A good song that comes on the radio. The first autumn chill on a clear day. Beads of rain on the branch. A spider's web. The moon. The cicadas, the cicadas. The loved one's voice, crying out your name on the other side of the—I don't know, let's say the meadow. A picture of you by the seaside. A bird stealing a crumb of bread from the picnic blanket. The instant you notice the explosion of cherry blossoms. The time somebody put a napkin with a telephone number on your windshield and a note saying, "Love your smile." Isn't it obvious? I mean, it isn't obvious, not in the least, but still. Life is a million meaningless moments that amount to everything. Which I bet you think you knew all along. But guess what, Brothers? You have no idea that you have no idea that you have no idea that you have no idea. And that's the only thing you can possibly know for certain. That, and the song of the cicada, hotshot.

~

THE GRAND DEPOSITOR

Do you believe that they play baseball in the afterlife?

"I believe because it is absurd," said the Church Father Tertullian. "Credo quia absurdum est" for you Latin Lovers, ay caramba.

Bear in mind Tertullian said that while alive.

The Church Brother Stephen asked, in contrast, "Am I absurd because I believe?"

Considering such factors as these, what position on the baseball field are you trying out for?

Brother Stephen unaccountably plays a top-notch shortstop and hits a game-winning home run while wearing his robes. Do you find any of that remotely credible? Even the part about the robes?

What are your secrets? Come on, give them up. Don't go all Opus Dei Mel Gibson on me, please. Look how secrecy works for them. It's just us here, you and me, so what do you have to lose?

NINE

Q. 779. What is to be done when persons must make
their confession and cannot find a priest who
understands their language?
A. Persons who must make their confession and
who cannot find a priest who understands their
language, must confess as best they can by some
signs, showing what sins they wish to confess and
how they are sorry for them.
                                   —The Baltimore Catechism

About a year before my ungainly header of a death I was banished
to The House. The House was a misfit's perfect paradise. What
else would you call such a boutique congregation of boozers and
pill-poppers, manic-depressives and passive-aggressives, sadists and
masochists, game-players and manipulators and substance-abusers?

It was a garden-variety rehabilitation operation in most respects,
save perhaps one: here in The House we were all Brothers—that is,
members of our Roman Catholic religious order. Our mission as Brothers had been to teach children and teenagers in our schools. Barred
from the classroom or, in my case, the administrative offices—temporarily, we all hoped and some of us also prayed—we were exiled to a
place known ominously and plainly enough as The House.

Yes, you got me, Brothers. Do you actually enjoy the taste of blood
or is that an occupational hazard for those in the Definitorium? I felt

humiliated. At the same time, I knew The House was where I was meant to be. Though you will excuse me for not quite appreciating as much at the time, The House turned out to be a pretty fair prelude to my after-life. Could it possibly be true that everything that had ever happened to me was a pretty fair prelude? Hold that thought.

It seems like only last night that I was standing in The House's communal kitchen, pouring myself a hot cup of Nirvana green tea. The raccoons had tipped over the garbage can again a few minutes earlier, and in so doing kept their standing dining invitation, as they had every evening I had been there. "Why do we even bother with the garbage can?" I could not stop myself from uttering aloud. "Why don't we just throw the scraps out the window so the raccoons can save their energy?"

Brother Nils, a devotedly timid man who was at that moment passing down the hallway, glanced into the kitchen, and seeing nobody there besides me, drew a blank. True, he drew blanks as prolifically as Picasso drew skewed nudes. So Brother Nils just backed away slowly into the receding darkness. Yet who was I to blame him? Were I a better man and a better Brother, I would have invited him to join me for a nightcap.

———

In The House there was a full counseling program in addition to regular worship and individual psychotherapy: holistic health sessions, nutrition classes, literature seminars, daily exercise classes (cardio workouts and weight training), tai chi and yoga and qigong, in addition to creative visualization. Despite the best efforts I expended in this regard, I could not successfully creatively visualize being exempt, however, from the mandatory Anger Management Workshop. Though I honestly learned something valuable in every aspect of the House program, Ang/Man was the toughest to endure. It probably means that I was not fully in control of my anger. But what would you do with a typical moment like this?

"Gene, you are a total horse's ass," opined Brother Nick. "I know it's you using my goddamn deodorant."

The group leader intervened: "Brother Nick, you know the ground rules of Ang/Man. You're supposed to make I-statements, Brother Nick."

"You're making a You-statement telling me to make I-statements in Ang/Man?"

"Come on, Brother Nick, that's another You-statement."

"OK. *I feel* Brother Gene was a horse's ass when he used my goddamn deodorant."

"Brother Gene," said the exasperated group leader, giving up. "Response?"

"Respond to Nick the Prick? No, thanks," he replied. "I'll take a pass. Except to state the obvious. When he walks through The House, the scent of the onions he keeps under his armpits arrives a good ten seconds before he does. Man, somebody should use that deodorant of his, as long as he's not going to."

The leader tried to save the day: "Well, your brutal honesty is something we can work with."

Brother Gene had something meaty for him to work with. "I was merely trying to be rude."

Brother Nick wanted the last word. "You are a very funny guy, Brother Hy-Gene."

He would never get the last word, at least not in the Ang/Man workshop.

"Nick," said Brother Gene, soulfully, "I am sorry."

The group leader, caught off guard, congratulated Brother Gene once again, and pronounced the opinion that contrition constituted an excellent start. He was a few thousand hours short of supervised clinical experience to determine that it really wasn't remotely an excellent start. For Brother Gene continued, once he sensed Nick's softening and astonishment: "I'm very sorry you're a prick and I have to live next door to you."

Why a lion-tamer's whip was not pressed into service by somebody at some time remained a minor mystery. Reflecting on the psychic makeup of The House's denizens, I am positive at least one could have been unearthed in the back of a dark closet upstairs.

Notwithstanding the routine of The House, I was indeed an alco-holic—however one defined the term. I myself defined the term as my inability—should I term it my unwillingness?—to stop drinking till I stopped drinking. But—and I never failed to quickly add the follow-up proposition—I was a high-functioning alcoholic, by any applied stan-dard of functional. I showed up for work and for services and kept my professional agreements. I was capable of running meetings hung over and bleary-eyed and bone-aching, and nobody seemed to notice, or so I believed till remanded to The House. I answered e-mails minutes after receiving them. I could draft a position paper in my sleep. No, really. Sometimes I would wake up from my two or three hours of restless slumber and the whole work had formed overnight in my head, ready for transcription upon the waiting laptop. I circled back to people who needed to be kept in the know and circled back to them quicker than any self-respecting border collie. My robes and clerical suits were always clean and pressed. I got regular haircuts for my increasingly diminished head of hair and took two showers a day. And I was drinking all the while, Brothers.

As a result, after a while I almost welcomed having been relegated to The House, having already begun to resign myself to making a very bad end of things. There comes a point in the life of a teacher and a Brother when he has done and seen it all. He has achieved a kind of reputation that cannot be bettered. He may be a sage and a leader and a beacon. In a flash, he is past tense. And he knows it. It's all downhill in a greased toboggan. He realizes that he can only quote himself. That he is competing ultimately with the image he has sculpted in others' minds. The delights of self-sabotage should not be underrated. Brothers, give it a try.

———

The "invitation" to move to The House took this form. One evening, after dinner, Brother Paulus summoned me into his office. I was under the impression that we were about to have one of our routine weekly debriefing meetings. These are the kinds of meetings during which I would tell him all the good news I could muster, couched in a way that he could construe it to be bad. Then I reported the bad news, which he proceeded to interpret as good. A minuet our professional relationship was not. Maybe a tango, more like, though I am just guessing.

This meeting certainly started out in predictable fashion. Insofar as we were always concerned about the potential financial impact of the lawsuits, we examined the order's various holdings with a view toward their liquidity. Cash is king, the Provincial commented, as he did at least once every meeting, incisively if not originally.

"We can't sell any of the schools," he observed. "That would compromise our mission as the Holy Family. And we can't borrow against them anymore, either. We're way too heavily leveraged as is."

I agreed, but noted how these settlements in the child abuse cases were taking their toll on the financial statements. And I proposed that the hour was probably coming when we needed to consider selling off The House, which was such a valuable piece of residential property. The Brothers owned it free and clear and we might be able to make a nice profit by flipping it. Besides, I didn't bother adding, those nutcases did not deserve palatial digs.

"Not so fast," said Brother Paulus. "The order needs The House. We need someplace where we can minister to our own."

Then, the Provincial took a completely different tack: "Speaking of The House, Stephen, and taking care of our own." He folded his hands across his enormous belly, leaned back recklessly in his creaky leather chair in the dimly lit mahogany-appointed office, and, reeking of bourbon, wheezed in my direction, "I have made a decision, Stephen. I'm going to give you one last chance. You can take your bags home on a Greyhound bus, or you can take them to The House. Your choice."

"Oh. I didn't think we were going to have one of your come-to-Jesus meetings."

"Jesus came not to bring peace but the sword."

"I heard that rumor."

"And you are not fooling anybody. You have a drinking problem. So what is your pleasure? House or home?"

"May I think about it?"

"Of course, you can, Brother Stephen," he said, his voice not really dripping with compassion. "Take your time." He selected a strand of white lint off his robe and contemplated it for a millisecond. "Time's up."

I went with Door Number Two. It was a relatively easy choice to make under the circumstances because there was no Door Number One for me anymore.

"Stephen, someday you'll thank me."

"I'll thank you right now. Oh, how the mighty have fallen."

"Don't think of it that way. Besides, it's the oldest story in the book."

"But you're sure you want me to go now—while all these cases are still in process?"

"The abused and the abusers we will always have with us, Stephen. But we're going to lose you forever unless you clean up."

"Anything else, Brother?"

"Yes. I'll pray for you, Stephen."

"I appreciate that. I'll pray for you, too, Brother. It's the very least I can do."

∽

THE GRAND DEPOSITOR

Brother Stephen appears to be quite condescending to his fellow Brothers in The House. Brother Harold, for instance, has kept his alcoholism a secret for a decade at least. Would you, too, be condescending if you were assigned to The House? And can you explain why Brother Paulus spared everyone else?

—

Late at night if you were a Brother, and if you had found yourself wandering through the halls of The House, and if you kept your head down, you would have bumped into Brother Stephen eventually. They say that sperm whales can swim the seven seas their whole life long and never run into another sperm whale. Can somebody please explain how scientists gather the raw data to support such findings? Sometimes one has the sense that half the things believed to have been proven are hypotheses run amok, or jokes the literal-minded take—how else?—literally. Not to mention, how do you go about proving a negative?

Still, sperm whales were not normally swimming around in my pod, and in any event, Brother Stephen would just be the advanced-middle-aged man padding around The House in slippers older than his self-pity, talking to himself in sentence fragments, and doing nothing other than watching the clock drain while being very, very busy with his newest, full-time assignment: cleaning up. You would be naturally wary, the way you are of unleashed crotch-curious Dobermans or of dubious-cause solicitors—or of the Ancient Mariner. The latter in the instance you found yourself projected into that great poem by S.T. Coleridge, the poet who was famously addicted to opium and was a lifelong liar and world-class plagiarist.

But look who's talking. I used to be an English teacher. And like the depressing old geezer in that drug addict Coleridge's poem, I would be reeking of a desire to be anywhere as long as it was far, far away from here. Certainly, my sperm whale homey, you would not send up a frothy *How are you?* through the blow hole on top of your blubbery head. Which is good, because Brother Stephen would be busy mulling.

To return to those garbage wars. Because the Brothers resided on the border of a state park teeming with standard-issue urban forest wildlife, they aspired to live in a spirit of environmental sensitivity, with a commitment to ecological balance. But the raccoons' relentless assault on the garbage caused me to reassess these assumptions. Tipping over garbage cans must have been the principal raccoonological raison-d'être. It required an effort of the will to resist my reflex desires to track down the trusty .22. Besides, I exaggerate. Just to be clear, I have never used a firearm in my life, and would have no clue as to how to operate a weapon of destruction more technologically advanced than a catapult or my mouth. Nonetheless, the raccoons provided anyone this side of Gandhi adequate occasion to question a pacifist resolve.

At first I used to go outside every night to commit an intervention in the wooly mammal nuclear family. I did so in an environmentally appropriate way, shooing them off, hosing them down, banging on a kettle with a soup spoon. I must have struck these eyeliner freaks as being every bit the idiot I considered myself. The raccoons would be preoccupied clawing open the trash bags, feasting on their delicious debris, and therefore quite disinclined to attend to the voice of reason. Or to mine. Such an exquisite exercise in futility. This is a feeling familiar to anyone who lives in the vicinity of raccoons or of higher-ups in the Catholic Church.

Supposedly, some people find these nocturnal, flea-encrusted, snarling carnivores endearing. To be unambiguous, I am referring not to the Catholic brass, but to the raccoons. They are very cunning and resourceful, and they have high IQs—possibly even higher than some of those higher-ups I mentioned. All that I would concede. The most adorable use I could imagine for these critters, though, is the headgear Daniel Boone fashioned from their pelts.

On most nights I was the last one awake in the makeshift community of drying-out misfits that was the semi-safe haven of me and my fellow broken-down Brothers. At one point or another they had removed us all from teaching or administrative jobs in one of the many Catholic schools run by the order. The idea was to rescue us before we hit bottom—or before we hit bottom again. The timing was not always expert. Brother Renaldo, for instance, might have been sent packing well before he was discovered one spring dawn weeping at the base of the cross in the center of campus, wearing his sandals—and nothing else.

All of us were in theory dedicated to the project of cleaning up the town that was thus far our miserable lives, and this was our OK Corral, this ten-bedroom house tucked away, as the realtors would candy-coat it, in a quiet cul de sac nestled high in the hills. Some prized friend of the order had bequeathed us the real estate when she passed to her eternal reward. Probably nobody in a Brother's robe perused the fine print about the late philanthropist's freeloading cohabitants, the raccoons.

At first, the Brothers were embraced by the residential community (also by the deer, the possums, the voles, the field rats and mice, the occasional mountain lion, and you know what else). In fact, the neighbors more than tolerated us. We were solid citizens, we band of brothers, we precious few. We threw Fourth of July parties, complete with egg toss, sack race, and hot dogs. We were open-minded enough to put the neighbors' beer on ice and served them their fill. We put up Christmas decorations that delighted the children and took down the decorations faithfully (unlike many of the residents) on New Year's Day, when the neighbors were making pained resolutions to swear off alcohol while combating their hangovers, something I could still remember feeling to this day. In addition, we furnished sugar and eggs and flour to whoever was in need.

The day would come, however, in the very immediate future, when the neighbors would begin to feel uneasy about having us Brothers living next door to their children. Once the press got ahold of a story about the latest lawsuit, and the case earned headlines, the neighbors from that point forward squinted their eyes in the Brothers' direction and gave us wide berth. They did not know for a fact that any of these Brothers were child molesters, but that was a distinction too fine for them to make and a risk that none of them wished to take.

TEN

Q. 202. Why does God require us to believe mysteries?
A. God requires us to believe mysteries that we may
submit our understanding to Him.
—The Baltimore Catechism

The houselights dimmed, luring the small and willing assemblage into the deepening shadows.

"You nervous, Shannon?" I leaned over and asked the side of her neck. She giggled and shivered. I did not know that I could have such effect on someone.

"I just hope people like *Shut Up It's My Life*," she whispered. "Now"— she put her finger to her lips—"shhhh."

The curtain parted. Instantly, I got my bearings. It was simple to do. Onstage was our old high school and Shannon and I were in the front row, spectators as usual.

———

SCENE

High school corridor fiercely illuminated by fluorescent light. Two girls at their lockers, side by side, rummaging around. They ignore each other at first, then one of them begins humming a tune.

"Hey! You!" yells one girl, who turns toward the other girl, playing

"Shannon." Her gaze is mean and narrow and self-assured. "Do you even know you're humming, you skuzzy little twit?"

"Shannon" is supposed to seem like the polar opposite of the cool girl who is on her case.

"It's kind of sad, Reed, kind of pathetic. Standing by your locker, humming like the star of the show you think you are, reminding every-body you're the stupid lead in the stupid high school musical. I'd call that pretty pathetic."

I remembered that type all too well. Who doesn't?

"You know what I call pathetic, Kathy?" says "Shannon" brightly. (I think I will now, with your permission, stop using the " " marks around Shannon, now that you get the idea that somebody was playing her and now that we have established you aren't Brother Genesius of quotation-mark fame. You aren't, are you?)

"Don't use my name, Reed. I've warned you before about getting permission in advance." Kathy Chinn's perfect little sculpted protrusion of jutting cartilage called a nose lifted up and her tiny nostrils flared with indignation while her long black ponytail swung side to side like a pendulum. The older of the scary Chinn Sisters, Kathy Chinn stared at Shannon. No, she stared *into* her, as if she were taking an X-ray. She was the kind of girl who would make even the tough boys want to stick their heads under a lead apron when she was releasing her radioactive charisma.

"My *lunch*," says Shannon. "Which is chicken salad. That's what I call totally pathetic."

Now Kathy's verbal claws slowly extend. "You think you're clever, Reed, don't you? I don't know why you think so."

"I have a question for you."

"I can't wait."

"How do you get away with putting on that eyeliner and lip gloss every day? How come Mrs. Arechiga doesn't bust you?"

"Nosy bitch dean knows better." And Kathy looks like she believes that is true. Then she takes off. She should have hissed.

(At Angel of Mercy the school uniform for boys was simple: any pants but blue jeans, any shirt as long as it was white and had buttons and a collar, and no jackets that were black or constructed of leather. For girls, however, it was more involved: white bucks, white folded-down ankle socks, white collared blouse, red cardigan, and blue-red plaid skirt. School regulations stipulated that the hem of a girl's uniform skirt fall genteelly to the genteel bottom of the concealed kneecap. I could tell that Shannon's onstage skirt was hitched above her slatternly dimpled kneecap—that is, at least a solid three inches above regulation. It was common for the girls to roll up their skirts at the waistline, and in so doing their uniforms could achieve an alternative if transitory risqué effect—which effect had been produced on Shannon.)

She turns back to her opened locker and stares at the textbooks and clothes and pictures and other conclusive evidence of her being nothing but a teenager. In one fluid motion, she tosses her books into the locker, gathers up her cardigan across her chest, and turns back to face the glaring and self-satisfied countenance of—who else?—one Mrs. Arechiga, Dean of Discipline and personal nemesis, who is jamming a finger into her sternum.

"Detention, Reed," the dean declares, and hands her a pink slip of paper.

Shannon studies the sheet and shakes her head. "Shit."

"I didn't catch that, Reed. What did you say?"

"My name is Shannon."

"That will be *two* days of detention, Reed, starting today. See you after school."

"I have spring musical rehearsal, Mrs. Arechiga."

"Should have thought of that before you rolled up your skirt. Anything else?"

"How come you enjoy picking on me?"

"*Three* days."

Shannon slams her locker shut.

"*Four* days. Shall we go for a whole week's worth? Now, go to the little girls' room, and when you come out I want to see your uniform conforms to school rules. No girl is above the rules, not even a starlet like you, Reed." She points offstage, the darkness where the girls' lavatory has to be, where she can adjust her skirt out of public view. "Now," she decrees. "I'll be waiting for you." Banished, Shannon heads off as commanded.

Curtain.

SCENE

Girls' bathroom.

Shannon enters. It is as crowded as a movie theater girls' bathroom on a Friday night. (My hunch was—and I was to be proved right— she had walked into an impromptu meeting of the Killers, which was the cruelest, most exclusive, unofficial school organization, and one to which she most definitely did not belong.)

Kathy and Debbie, the Chinn Sisters and the prime movers of the Killers, are sharing a suspension-deserving cigarette as they position themselves before the opened window that faces out onto what you are supposed to imagine is the school courtyard. In addition, neither of them is busy readjusting the hem of their foreshortened skirts to conform to handbook regulations.

"Hey, look, it's Barbra Streisand," says Kathy to Debbie, pointing at Shannon.

"She's a funny girl, that Reed," Debbie replies.

The battle with Arechiga seems to have left Shannon feeling beleaguered and, strangely enough, emboldened.

"Why do you two hate me? I never did anything to you."

Debbie has eyes green and gleaming as a Christmas wreath, and she is smoldering and glowing like the tip of her smoldering, glowing cigarette. (As I recall, when she signed her name, Debbie did not sketch a little heart over the "i," but a bull's eye.)

"You know, Kathy, Shannon is right. We should give her a chance," Debbie says, her singed eyebrows flickering.

"Sure, why not?" Kathy agrees, wicked-stepsisterly.

"Want to become a Killer, Shannon?" Debbie asks.

Shannon understands what they are up to. She is no fool. "Who do I have to kill?"

"See," Kathy addresses Debbie, "I told you. Reed *is* funny."

"All it takes to be a Killer," Debbie says, "is that you have to trust us no matter what. We gotta count on each other, that's it. You trust us?"

"Why should I?"

"That's the whole question," Kathy says.

Then, as if the gesture were choreographed, Kathy hands Shannon the cigarette, which for some reason Shannon thinks it only fitting for her to accept. I could understand it all. Her motivation was understandable. She was so tired of always being on the outside of everything. In a way, then, she accepted being for an instant something she wasn't, a fool.

"Go ahead, take a good drag," says Kathy.

"I don't smoke."

"Me, either, Reed. That's not the point."

"Then what's the point if you don't smoke—while you are smoking?"

"I'm smoking in the girls' room, *that's* the point. Get it?"

Shannon puts the cigarette to her lips and sucks in the smoke and holds it in her lungs for a second…until she lets it go. Bad idea. The Chinn Sister Killers are amused at the results. Her eyes seem to cross, her head seems to swivel on her neck.

At which point Mrs. Arechiga barges into the scene, and Shannon drops the cigarette to the floor and rushes toward the nearest stall. Kathy and Debbie glide over to the sinks and the mirrors eager to be of service to their public reflections.

The dean walks over to pick up the evidence that is the cigarette. "Reed! My office. Now!"

The wretching noises streaming from inside Shannon's stall cause the Killers to chuckle.

"You getting sick in there, Reed?" asks Mrs. Arechiga with mock solicitude.

Shannon mumbles.

"Serves you right. Office. Now, Reed. NOW."

Curtain.

SCENE

Theater. Rehearsal is ending, the cast packing up, preparing to leave. A young Brother is taking a seat on the piano bench.

"Shannon," Brother calls out, "very nice job today. You are really improving."

"Thanks to you, Brother Joel. Thanks to *you*."

"If you've got a few minutes, maybe you could stick around for a bit, would you, please, after everybody leaves?"

"Sure, Brother. Something wrong?"

"No. Brother Charlie and I were talking, and he wanted me to work with you some more on your big number. OK?"

"Sure, Brother," she says, and smiles.

Darkness. Curtain.

SCENE

Novitiate visiting day. It is Sunday, springtime. A tree is in bloom. Shannon is walking with Stephen, novice Brother Stephen in his robes, along the road that is outside what appears to be a chapel. The two are laughing, walking a discreet distance apart.

"You didn't!" says "Stephen." (OK. You get the idea.)

"No, I did. I told Mrs. Arechiga that my mom worshipped the devil."

"And she bought it?"

"Who cares? Probably not. But Brother Joel did, and he went to bat for me, and somehow got me out of detention."

"So, how'd the musical go?"

"I could have done better, but people applauded and…whatever. I'm glad it's over."

They say nothing for a long time.

"You haven't visited me for a while."

"I know, Stevie."

"Did I do something wrong?"

"I guess having a monk for a boyfriend is not doing wonders for my self-esteem. Do you like living here?" She makes a sweeping gesture with both her arms to indicate the whole novitiate, somehow the entire vocation. "Or are you still thinking about leaving?"

"I'm always thinking about leaving. But I'm always thinking about staying, too. I look at my life, and see nothing but hard choices. I really care for you…"

Shannon stops in her tracks and shakes her head. Seconds pass. A look of worry crosses Stephen's face.

"That's all I needed to hear," she says. "I guess we should stop seeing each other. What do you think?"

Slowly, mournfully, he says: "I would understand."

"That makes one of us."

"Is that why you came up today? To break up with me?"

"I can't break up with you! You broke up with me when you became a Brother!"

"I didn't break up with you. I became a Brother, though. This is crazy."

"I wasn't sure till I heard you say you really care for me."

"What's wrong with saying that I care for you?"

"Nothing. Everything. You really care for me. But see? The difference is, I love you. We are not speaking the same language."

"I'd really miss you."

"For a while you would, maybe for a while."

"How about you? Would you miss me?"

"What if I said forever?"

"Big word, forever."

"That's why I used it."

Darkness. Curtain.

SCENE

Empty classroom, end of the school day. Brother Joel is standing by a window, looking out, appearing forlorn, and there is a knock on an invisible door.

"Come in," Brother Joel says to the window.

"Brother?" says Shannon, entering.

"Shannon, thanks for coming by. Close the door." She does so. "I've been thinking about you all day and I wondered if you would ever forgive me."

"No need to worry, Brother." Big smile. "I'll never forgive you." Triumphant. She takes a seat in a little chair as if she were colonizing a small country.

"I wish I could undo the past," Brother says. Almost candidly.

"Really? OK. Why don't you try?"

"What can I do to get you to stop hating me?"

"Why don't you just die? That would be a start."

"Come on, Shannon. We both made a mistake."

"A mistake." She shakes her head. "We *both* made a mistake?"

"Yes. A mistake," he says experimentally.

"A mistake is what you make on a trig exam. A mistake is wearing the wrong shade of lipstick. What you did was not some slip-up. You made a decision, you thought it through."

"You make me feel like a disgusting old man."

"No, you're a disgusting young man. What if you got me pregnant?"

His shoulders slump. "That would be, well, physiologically impossible."

"I mean, what would have stopped you from taking the next step?"

"You would have stopped me."

"It's my job to stop you? Since when? I used to think about you every night. I used to love to hear what you had to say in class. I can't believe what's happening between us."

"I loved you a little too much, Shannon. Is that so bad?"

"Loving me is not so bad. I was loving you and that was not so bad, either. What you did had nothing to do with loving me, it had to do with loving yourself."

"You're right to be angry with me. I'll never be able to make it right to you, I know that."

"Let's see if you are correct. Come here, Joel."

He crosses the room and approaches her.

"Get down on your knees."

He complies.

"Beg for forgiveness."

He puts his head into her lap, and she strokes his hair. Seconds slowly pass.

Her voice drops. "I want you to do something for me, Joel."

He raises up his head. Obediently. "Anything."

"Kiss me," she says sternly.

He stares at her a long time.

"Really?"

"Yes, kiss me like your life depends on it."

They do not kiss.

The lights go down. Curtain.

SCENE

Principal's office. "Brother Charlie" presiding.

"What is going on with you, Shannon?" Very animated. Big gestures. "You've totally gone off the rails. One minute you're the star of the show, you're named the valedictorian of your graduating class—next thing I know you are getting suspended for…what the heck are you doing bringing a six-pack to school?"

"It's been a tough semester."

"Tell me about it, Shannon."

"My boyfriend broke up with me, for starters."

"I didn't know you had a boyfriend."

"Stevie."

"Well, Shannon, Stephen is a novice Brother now. He's one of us."

"Like that means anything."

"What does *that* mean?"

"Nothing."

"Then you egged Mrs. Arechiga's car."

"That was Kathy's idea. Things got out of control when the dean gave Debbie detention for wearing eye makeup."

"This is not you, Shannon. I thought you were a student body leader. Your teachers all loved you."

"Especially one of them."

"What are you talking about?"

"Brother Joel."

"He is a wonderful teacher, what are you talking about?"

"Yes, he is, but I am having trouble with him ever since we had sex."

"Ever since *what?*"

"You can talk to him, I don't want to explain. Just keep him away from me."

Charlie looks dumbfounded, uncertain what to do. He knows he has to say something after that bombshell.

"I am going to be calling your parents in a minute. Get a grip on yourself. Such wild accusations."

"So you don't believe me, Brother Charlie?" says Shannon.

"Let's slow down. Are you telling me the truth?"

"Joel—"

"Brother Joel."

"Brother Joel is in love with me. That's what he says. But it's all wrong."

They look at each other. Time seems to slow down. They look at each other some more. This could go on for a while.

"Do you realize what you are saying?" says Brother Charlie.

"We covered the sex subject in health class, if that's what you're asking. But you don't believe me, do you?"

"Did you tell your mother?"

Shannon looks at him in a way that suggests she knows a trick question when she hears one.

"Does Stephen know?"

"Does Stephen know? Why would I want to hurt him like that?"

"OK, good. Tell me more."

"You want pictures?"

He glares at her.

"You don't believe me, do you?"

He studies her for a long time. "I need to talk to Brother Joel."

"He's ready—what did he say? He's ready to fall on his sword. The things guys say, unbelievable. Maybe they do have swords. But you won't believe me."

"Maybe I do believe you. Maybe *I* believe you. Maybe I *believe* you. It's the world that won't believe you. Given what happened—if what you say is true."

"What happened, Brother?"

"Did he force himself upon you?"

"That's one way to put it."

"This is a very sad development, Shannon."

"It's your job to figure out what to do. Aren't you the principal?"

Darkness. Curtain.

THE GRAND DEPOSITOR

Brother Stephen was deeply disturbed in his lifetime about those sexual abuse claims made by former students in the Brothers' schools. Does his attitude seem appropriate to you? Which creature would symbolize the approach of the Brothers: a) ostrich; b) pit bull; c) jackal; d) pussy cat; e) dinosaur.

What is your definition of childhood?

ELEVEN

Q. 141. Why then do we say a soul is dead while in a
state of mortal sin?
A. We say a soul is dead while in a state of mortal sin,
because in that state it is as helpless as a dead body,
and can merit nothing for itself.
—The Baltimore Catechism

I cannot put off this next part any longer. You should know everything about the instant I accepted my calling to the Brothers. As it happens, Brother Charlie came to play a crucial role the day I sought guidance. But there's something else to explain first.

I remember, Brothers, when I was alive and doing normal, everyday things living people take for granted doing—grading papers, answering my phone, washing the car, reading a book, doing my laundry, responding to e-mails "sent" by Brother "Genesius," charting the Provincial's descent into dementia, whatever my fantasy life conjured up—and I would have this thought. It was not a conscious thought, merely an automatic presumption that my life would go on, despite ample evidence daily provided that I was in grievous error, if not deluded. I would be eating an omelet or swatting away a yellow jacket or zipping up my robe before heading down to chapel, and I would take for granted that I would keep doing such manner of things indefinitely. In other words, I would be assuming life goes on. Only a fool assumes as much, and only a masochist makes the opposite assumption.

What if you knew it would not always go on, how would you act differently? If you arrest your attention and realize that it will not go on forever, what difference would it make? The illusion of continuity is powerful, and seductive. Sometimes, however, something happens that ruptures the illusion. I have a great example of the Rupture, not to be confused with rapture, or The Rapture—not at all. Here it comes. It will take a minute to set up.

This is the bargain we make with the primal terror of mortality. We keep the dread in the basement, and promise to tend to it at some undefined tomorrow, and as long as it stays there, lost in the big file box of curling, faded photographs and musty books, we are able to go on living our finite, exhaustible lives.

The story I have been pouring into your reluctant ears, Brothers, is nothing but the transparent chronicle of my loneliness—the account of an ordinary life in our religious order, an existence which provides the ideal occasion for loneliness. Pathetic, I know, pathetic, and I cannot defend myself. But listen. It is also a story about evil. I know. Evil sounds histrionic, even medieval, but I said please listen. The movies don't do justice to the concept. Blood and gore and babies on pitchforks? Sometimes maybe, though not usually. More often, evil has soft hands. Evil smells of talc, evil strums a little guitar, evil looks familiar, an awful lot like you and me.

One day I witnessed the mash-up of loneliness and evil. Who knew they were soul mates? The convergence took place when I was eighteen, in high school the first time, thirty-seven years ago. Brothers of the Definitorium, there is nothing left to be gained by not telling you. I have told you everything else—why not this?

———

It was spring, my memory suggests, because the darkness was nowhere near to descending, the trees were glowing, the birds raucous. I opened the door to Brother Charlie's classroom. It was long after the school day had come to an end, long after baseball practice had finished, and the halls were empty. Charlie was behind his desk at the front of the room, where I could count on finding him.

"Good to see your shining face, Stevie my boy," he said. "Come have a seat." He pointed in the direction of my assigned desk, my home base from which I sprayed the room with ideas like the clean line drives I reliably sprayed to all fields in my dreams, my ideas about God, books, and life as they occurred to my eighteen-year-old self.

"You busy, Brother? We can talk tomorrow." It was such a pleasant prospect, observing Brother Charlie secure behind his desk, surrounded by papers and books, doing his teacher work. What could be more wonderful?

"Never too busy for you. I thought for a second you were the custodian, but he must be gone by now."

"I saw Marco driving off. He needs a new muffler."

"You see anybody wandering the halls?"

"Ghost town."

"Good, we have the whole place to ourselves. I was just thinking about you."

"Really?" I said, though I was only pretending to be surprised. I thought everybody was thinking about me all the time. I was a teenager. I was continually thinking about myself, why wouldn't everybody else enjoy the same ecstatic opportunity?

"You appeared distraught in class."

I was not conscious of being distraught in class. Still, I took a seat, a seat in the back of the room. Why in the back of the room? I have no explanation. I did not want to impose upon him, I suppose, did not want to close the space between him and me, but I did have an important subject to discuss with him. He was my mentor. I was his protégé before I could spell the word with the correct accent marks.

"Brother Charlie, heard a rumor."

"Don't believe everything you hear about me," he laughed.

"You're really going to be principal next year?"

"Loose lips sink ships! Keep it between us, you and me, OK? Besides, that's not half as important as you. Let's talk about Stevie, shall we?"

"There's something on my mind," I began. I could not articulate what I needed to articulate. My silence shouldn't indicate that words were unavailable to me. If anything, I had too many words, and they all fought each other for primacy of position at the tip of my tongue.

"Let me see if I can help, Stevie. You want to talk to me about your relationship with Shannon, your girlfriend." Talk about a leap. No tiny question mark in his voice, either.

"What?" There was a question mark sharp as a scythe in mine.

"It's OK, Stevie, you can talk to Brother Charlie. Is she the first?"

"First *what*?" That was something I thought, but did not say.

I could tell he believed he had figured out what was on my adolescent, hormone-ravaged brain. I tried not to be disturbed by such presumption. Especially because he could be right. Brother Charlie often was, you see. As with any great and beloved teacher, Brother Charlie knew us better than we knew ourselves.

"I get it," he said. "It's normal. Your body is going through changes. That's natural. More than anything, these desires tell us we're alive. It's what you do with your desires that makes the difference."

I had to back him off. "It's not that way with Shannon."

"What way is it with Shannon?" I did not like this question. *Voyeur* had not yet meandered into my SAT-prep vocabulary, otherwise I could have employed it deftly in a sentence. Meanwhile, his eyes drifted up to the corner of the room, and mine followed, wondering what was up there. As far as I could tell, we were both watching nothing.

"What are you talking about, Brother?" Something told me I would be afraid to find out.

"You want to discover the meaning of these turbulent feelings inside, but they are really not so bad. No feeling can ever be truly bad in and of itself, it's how we respond to a feeling that matters, and it doesn't mean that you are a bad boy, or I am a bad man for that matter, only that…"

I blurted out, "I am thinking about becoming a Brother."

"You?" he said.

Could he be that stupid? Why did I come into his room in the first place, why, why, why, why?

"Me, yes, who else are we talking about?"

"Oh," he said, and then Brother Charlie smiled that smile. Even now, years later, remembering that smile gives me the creeps. Even then, I was beginning to have trouble reconciling my mixed feelings about him.

"I've been waiting for this moment since the first time I laid eyes on you, Stevie. You are sure about joining the Brothers?"

"I don't know what a vocation should feel like, so I'm not sure I have one. What about you? Your vocation?"

"Me? I am not always so sure, either."

"Really?" This was baffling.

"Certainly," he said with grave sincerity. "Life is a work in progress, and I wouldn't have it any other way."

Do you see, Brothers? Do you see how Charlie could insinuate himself? Do you see how he could do so because he seemed to have no such intention? No, he wanted me to think he was the vulnerable one, the oldest trick in the teacher's book.

"Life is very mysterious and beautiful, Stephen. You yourself are very beautiful and mysterious, Stephen."

Me? Mysterious? *Me?* I heard those odd words, but would not take in their meaning, because they sounded too strange.

"So you yourself still wonder if you have a calling," I tried. That qualified as a news flash. I was an idiot, supposedly a mysterious one. This didn't qualify as a news flash.

His face flushed red, and his breathing sounded shallow and forced, as he reached behind him and flipped off the light switch on the wall. The classroom turned shadowy. Then he pulled the chair next to his behind his desk, and tapped the seat twice. "You're too far away. Come sit next to me, Stevie."

I will tell you how close he was. If from where I was positioned I laid down a perfect bunt, deadened the ball and directed it to trickle inside the third baseline, it would roll and come to a dead stop directly underneath his chair.

How was I supposed to say no? I loved him, Brothers. We all did. Tell me, how could I say no to him? How? Explain that to me, Brothers of the Definitorium.

I took the seat next to his and I looked into his eyes for just a second. That was all I could manage, all the moment allowed. In his eyes I saw he was registering nothing about me. In his eyes I saw night falling on a prairie. I saw a door swinging closed in a cyclone-ravaged barn. My life was never to be the same.

"You are an incredibly good boy." His voice was breathless, fractured.

Then he reached for me, as naturally as somebody might reach for a book, a cup, a pair of glasses.

—

The whole time, I kept my eyes fixed on the corner of the room. This strategic decision I grasped would not keep me intact, but it would perhaps make the time pass swiftly. I never knew before how the silence could harden inside my chest. It was a mountain of marble, it was a block of ice. My words had fled and flown up to the corner of the room, where they promised to stay still. I followed them, and waited there in the distance, where I would be all right any second.

"Is this OK, Stevie?"

I did not speak.

"Is *this*?"

I was occupied thinking about the kinds of things I would do with my own classroom someday when I was a Brother myself and teaching school. For one thing, I would arrange my desks in a circle, in order to facilitate discussion. The students who didn't speak up in other classes, the shy ones, the insecure ones—they would speak up in mine. I would

put cool posters up on the wall. I would arrange a couple of standing lamps and not use the overhead banks of fluorescent lighting. That
would make the mood conducive to reflection, conversation, the open-
ness that allows somebody to risk articulation. I would pack my bookcases with works I loved, and I would lend them to kids when they were
curious, yearning, ambitious, big with aspiration.

"*Yes, I believe you would really love this,*" I would say.

"*Hey, something you said today made me think you ought to look at
these stories.*"

"*Sure, it's a hard book. But hard books are the kind you want to try
to read.*"

Like that, I would be gentle, encouraging, receptive. Students would
hang around my classroom at lunch and we would discuss the poems
they were writing late into the night. We would talk about colleges,
about courage, about friendship, about God, about love. I would have
profound things to say by then, I felt pretty confident. They would talk
about becoming doctors, scientists, writers, artists, parents. I would
help. They would trust me. They would look at me with admiration
and I would feel blessed and lucky to know them. I would be changing
their lives forever. Years later, at reunions, they would come up to old
Brother Stephen and remind me of something wise and unforgettable
I had said.

"*Remember when you told me I should go with my heart, Brother? I
never forgot. Thanks.*"

It would be different from what was transpiring right now in the vicinity of me, mysterious me. My life was changing forever. I knew this. I
couldn't stop it from happening, but I knew that much. That would not
be the way it would be for them.

———

When it was done, Brother Charlie sighed. "This is our little secret."

I nodded.

"Pull yourself back together now."

Then Brother Charlie added in the soft voice I would one day hear again, during that last session of the Definitorium, when I attended to the crushed red velvet voice of death itself: "Now, where were we, Stevie?" As if we had been interrupted during our conversation about the baseball team, as if the telephone had temporarily called him away, as if somebody in class had asked him a question off-topic.

"*Where were we?*"

Death's oldest question.

"*Where were we?*"

I knew exactly where we had been, and where I had been taken, to the place of evil, but I did not inform Brother Charlie, for I knew it was a place to which, as long as I lived, I would never willingly return. Yes, adverbs are the con men of prose. I used to tell my composition students as much. But I said *willingly*. That adverb tells you nothing that you don't need to know.

"We were talking about Shannon Reed," I said to him with a hush, knowing that was not quite accurate.

"She is such a special girl to you, that Shannon of yours," he whispered. "I have always liked her. But about that vocation of yours, Stevie."

"Yes, Brother?"

"A vocation is a gift."

"A gift," I repeated, taking refuge on the safe ground of repetition, because to venture any more than that would be to acknowledge I had a voice in this non-conversation.

"And you know what we do when we receive a gift? We give thanks."

"Give thanks."

"Yes, we give thanks, sometimes in public, sometimes in private. Some things we keep to ourselves. Some things happen that nobody else can understand. Take you and me, for example. We have a pact. A sacred bond. Nobody else would ever understand if you ever thought to tell them, would they? Of course not, Stephen. Take my word for it, they would not. How could anybody else understand? Because it cannot be explained. Because we don't give back gifts we have been given.

And gifts come in many forms. Take your own life experience. For you, Shannon is a great, great gift."

"Shannon."

"And you, Stevie, you are a gift to her. You are a gift to me, too. Thank you, Stevie. But now I have some work to do, young man. So go on, get out of here!" he said cheerfully. "I have work to do!"

"Out of here."

"To be continued, Stephen, to be continued. Oh, and don't forget. Life is very, very beautiful."

"Yes, Brother."

Never forget for one second, Brothers, that we all loved him.

~

THE GRAND DEPOSITOR

You should have guessed. If you were paying closer attention, I mean. Still, you might have discovered the secret had you been asking the right sort of open-ended questions in your deposition. You are kicking yourself, I can tell. But don't feel so bad, no one has noticed. I have had a long time to perfect my act around Charlie, and besides, it is immaterial now.

What was that you said?

That's OK. Come on, what are you sorry for? The thing is, you don't know any more about me than you knew before. My parents, the same thing. Shannon, ditto. I went back to the practice field, put on my cleats. Nobody was around anymore, but I swung the bat and ran a few laps, and afterward went home. Just like every other day. Talked with Shannon on the phone from nine-thirty to ten-thirty, the way I usually did. Took a book to bed when I was done with homework at eleven, and read for a while, till I fell asleep. At some point my mom came in and turned off the light, but not before giving me a kiss on my forehead. I woke up. "Hi, Mom."

She replied, "Go back to sleep. Sweet dreams, Stephen."

"*You, too, Mom.*"

"*Tomorrow will be a better day.*"

"*Why?*"

"*Oh, honey, it just has to be.*"

"*You just keep telling yourself that, Mom.*"

"*I do, I will, Stephen.*" She softly closed the door to my room and, once I heard her padding down the stairs, I said to her, as I would to anyone else who wanted to know, "*I have decided. I am going to the novitiate. It's the only place now for me to go.*"

But even as she was descending the stairs, she was also back here, in my room, where I needed my mother to understand what I wasn't going to tell her or anybody else. Neat trick, no?

"*I guessed that you were going to make that decision, Stephen.*"

I am one of them now, I did not say to her. It's like what happens in those zombie movies. One of the undead scratches your skin, and eventually you turn, contaminated, and become one of them. You can't help it.

"*I understand, Stephen.*"

She didn't understand. How could she? Brother Charlie claimed me. He scratched me. Made me one with him. Proof? Look what had happened that afternoon in Brother Charlie's classroom after school. That's all the proof anyone could need.

Here is the kicker—or what I thought at the time was the kicker. He wouldn't have claimed me if I hadn't already been one of them. And now I belonged with him and with them, the Brothers. I was one of them. And if I left home and if I left Shannon, I could make my life work. If I was not around home or Shannon, if I could get away from anyone who loved me, I wouldn't have to remember that I really was not whoever it was I once thought I was, before this afternoon. And then Shannon wouldn't be exposed to sick and disgusting Stephen. I wouldn't be able to scratch her, and make her one with my self-hatred.

It's a neat solution, don't you think? And it's much simpler and cleaner than the other, possibly more logical, certainly *messier, solutions: which would be killing myself, or killing him.*

"*What I do,*" *my mom said,* "*what always works for me is, I pretend.*"

"*I noticed that, Mom.*"

"*Yes. When something happens that I wish had never happened, I pretend it never happened.*"

You see, don't you? Nothing had happened. And here's the rock-solid demonstration to the whole wide world that absolutely nothing happened between me and Brother Charlie: I became Brother Stephen. Would I have been willing to become a Brother of the Holy Family if Brother Charlie had done me any harm?

And so, my Grand Depositor, that is the story of how Stevie one day heard his calling and Brother Stephen took this vocation as his own.

TWELVE

Q. 477. Can we resist the grace of God?
A. We can, and unfortunately often do, resist the
    grace of God.
                                —The Baltimore Catechism

I met with The House therapist for my regularly scheduled session. I consulted the notes scribbled in my pad. I was prepared, as ever, and I jumped in with my big swinging crucifix.

"I'm feeling better," I said. "So much better, in fact, time's come for me to leave The House. Can you help?"

"Talk to me about how you are feeling better," said Dr. Samuel Inskeep.

"It's very simple. These feet are made for walkin'."

"You're in a good mood."

"Yes, I am. It's a beautiful day and I don't want to drink anymore. For now."

"*You don't want to drink anymore for now,* you say. You know, Brother, I've never heard it put quite that way before." Dr. Inskeep had bifocals that nestled far down on the bridge of his nose. When he gazed at a patient the way he gazed at me in that moment, he looked how I imagined a Swiss-village clockmaker. He peered over the top of the specs and conveyed benevolent and almost sweet skepticism—shall we call that spekticism? OK, question withdrawn, Brother Provincial. He also conveyed a specialist's determination to dig into the innards of the timepiece. A few seconds twanged off inside my mainspringing soul and it almost seemed as if he could hear that mechanism working within me.

"I am an alcoholic, I get that. But that doesn't mean I will drink again."

"How come *now*, Brother? How come you think you are ready to leave *now*?" Inskeep was the primary treating psychologist employed by the order. According to the invoices I routinely approved in my incapacity as Auxiliary Provincial, he had seen dozens of Brothers over the years, and sometimes he had achieved, word had it, a modicum of success. Then again, to be fair, until recently he had not made the professional acquaintance of Brother Stephen.

"How long have I been at The House? Six months? By my calculations, I've been thinking about leaving for five months and twenty-nine days. I'm not saying I'm cured. I'm *not* cured, but let's be candid, I probably will never be cured if I keep hanging around all these Brothers in The House. Do you have any idea what it is like to deal with Brother Nils, Brother Gene, the rest of them? My life is wasting away. I'm done with Ang/Man and the rest of the program. I need to get back to work. There's so much I need to do. And I don't have much time left."

More silence. Then: "Say more."

He was so irritating that I said, "More."

Inskeep clucked with dismay, shook his head, and said, "That's kind of juvenile, don't you think, Stephen?"

"So's your 'Say more.' If you have a question, take your best shot and fucking ask it." My outburst shocked even me, I have to say, and I considered apologizing, for a second.

"For someone done with Ang/Man you sure are displacing your anger, Stephen. What would you say to Brother Charlie if he were here with us now?"

I groaned. "*This* is the kind of stuff they teach you in Shrink School? Keep Charlie out of this. And don't say *Say more* to me ever again."

In that instant, and fairly accidentally and without provocation or preparation, I was granted a glimmering of self-understanding. What I understood about myself was that I was the kind of man who was ready and willing to say anything to get out of living one day more in The House. And I also came to terms with what I thought about psychotherapy and psychotherapists.

On one level, this psychologist was the garrulous gatekeeper holding the keys to my release. On a deeper level, I had to admit, I thought that he was an arbiter of justice. Therapists existed, I somehow believed, in order to determine who was in the right and who was in the wrong—in addition to saying weaselish things like *Say more*. That *Say more* still pisses me off to this day. Of course, Dr. Inskeep would be horrified to hear of such ignorance and bias, as would any kind and good soul who turns to psychology for a career. But I could not shake the rock-bottom conviction that the institution of psychotherapy was a branch of law enforcement. And what does one do when one has done something wrong, or has been himself wronged, and comes face to face with the forces of authority? Does he seek justification? Does he make an excuse? Who truly knows? What I did was finesse the truth.

"I can control my urge to drink," I continued. "I've located just enough weakness within myself to stop drinking."

"Don't you mean *strength*?"

"No, I mean weakness. I am so wretched, I loathe myself just enough to make a change."

"In my experience that's not the way it usually works, but let's go with this idea for a second. A while ago, you said your life is wasting away."

"All you and I do, session after session after session, is talk, talk, talk, hour after hour after hour. You're a good enough fellow, and a good enough therapist, I suppose, but I got the message, Sam."

"What's the message, Stephen?"

"The message is… the message is… the message is, I gotta get out of The House before I lose my mind. I feel like I'm fighting for my life, fighting to breathe. Plus, I've been praying again, for the first time in, I don't know, years."

"Really?" said Dr. Inskeep. "What's God telling you?"

"You're not going to believe me." I made my face take on the look of injured merit that amounted to Full Pout.

"Try me."

"You're not going to believe me, believe me."

"What's to lose?"

"God was telling me…why not tell you? God was telling me He needs me elsewhere." I mentally crossed my fingers as I said that. I am a good liar when I need to be, Brothers.

Dr. Inskeep said nothing, and I filled in the blanks:

"See? You *don't* believe me."

True, the psychologist could press me, because as I predicted, he did not believe me, though he did not push back. Besides, he probably had an intuition that Brother Paulus had not made him privy to all his deliberations on the Brother Stephen assignment.

"What I believe doesn't ultimately matter, Stephen. Do you wish to talk about what happened to you when you were in high school?" Inskeep was fast on his feet. That was an excellent transition, or would have been if I weren't on the receiving end of that leading question.

"There is nothing to say about what, euphemistically speaking, happened to me in high school."

"Brother Stephen, don't you see? You are exhibiting many of the classic symptoms of a long-term psychological and emotional disability. It's what we call post-traumatic stress disorder. PTSD."

"Mercy, mercy me, but you are going off the shallow end."

"Dissociation, depression, selective amnesia, a tendency toward radical isolation. Inability to trust, sleep disturbance, alcohol abuse, splitting…you have perfected the art of checking out, of just going far, far away. In times of stress, when your job gets to be too much for you, for instance, when it brings up unwanted images, buried memories, you opt for the relief afforded you by dissociation. But you do more than just space out. You go to an altogether alternative world."

"If I were so good at that, what you're calling dissociation, I would be able to go far, far away right now. I'd inhabit an alternative world in which you do not exist."

"That's why I think that your therapy, and why The House, is finally working, Stephen. So when you say there is nothing to talk about relative to what happened to you when you were a teenager, I respectfully disagree."

"I thought shrinks were supposed to listen. I am not a diagnosis, you know. I am not a set of symptoms. And what you're just not getting is, I'm over it. That was a lifetime ago, and I'm an old man. I can't remain stuck in the past."

"No, you can't, you're right. But sometimes we need to go back into the past. For a visit. For a cup of tea."

Cup of strychnine, more like it, but all I said was: "Look. I've forgiven pathetic old Charlie. It is all very ancient news. Check your detailed notes." I pulled out my notepad, for the purposes of a prop, and showed him. "I'll give you mine, if you need them. You'll see that we covered this topic."

"You're being glib."

He was really getting under my skin now. "So are you, Sam. But, well, fact is I have forgiven him."

"Forgiveness does not come that easy."

"Blesséd are the forgivers, for they shall be doormats."

"Maybe you haven't forgiven yourself, Brother."

What crap. "I don't have to forgive myself. What for, and why do you care? And besides, what makes you think I ever will?"

"That's a lot of big questions."

"Say more, Sam." He didn't like that, and I didn't blame him when he stared back at me with his watery-brown doe eyeballs. "Fuck it all, Sam." I tried to make peace. "Did you miss the fact that I joined the Brothers after all, and took a vow of celibacy, which I kept, despite…"

The word broke all the glass in the room. Or should have. *Despite the temptations, Sam, despite all the temptations, and I'm not gay, stop implying I'm gay and that I'm not in touch with my sexuality, that I'm thwarted as a result of this supposed trauma, which you only know about because I told you, because I'm not gay, so I will never be in touch with my sexuality in that way. Or maybe I am, and what difference does that make here and now? Yes, Charlie molested me my senior year, all right, it is true, but he never really touched me, he never touched my soul, because he never could.* I waited the therapist out, and besides, I had nothing I needed to say that he didn't know. I have some advice for you, Brothers, when you are sitting across from Dr. Inskeep, where you will all find yourselves eventually, if I calculate this correctly. Here's the key: shut up and wait.

I shut up and I waited. And waited. And waited.

Sam said at last: "I think we have finally reached a turning point. This is exactly where our conversation should someday begin."

"Well, don't want to disappoint you, Sam, but it doesn't look like today is your lucky day."

"Or yours, Stephen."

Fine, I said to myself. *Or mine.*

———

I left The House. What I mean is, I was sent back to my post of Auxiliary by the Provincial, who shortly after my last session with Sam Inskeep summoned me to his office and gave me my new assignment.

"Stephen," said Brother Paulus, "I see some very nice low-hanging fruit."

I looked around the office, my mind clouded and confused. Nowhere in view was a fruit tree or, for that matter, a fruit bowl.

"It's a B-school term," explained the Provincial, who lamented afresh never having earned that pesky MBA that he wished he had. "Fruit that is low-hanging, see? Easy pickings, get it?"

You know, I did not get it. "Actually, low-hanging fruit is most in need of ripening, so it's just the opposite of what people might…"

"Brother Stephen?"

"Yes, Brother?"

"That's quite enough of that. Why don't you make arrangements to put The House on the market?"

The Provincial's thinking had turned around recently. Selling The House seemed to be the thing to do. The neighbors were getting increasingly restless and vocal about the Brothers' presence, and their complaints were growing more and more strident with each new story in the paper. More to the point, however, the Brothers needed a quick million bucks to settle the most recent sexual abuse claim.

~

THE GRAND DEPOSITOR

Is Brother Stephen a good Catholic? Are you? Name other good Catholics you know.

If I were still a member of the Definitorium and breaking out for discussion the way those guys are doing, I would be thinking a little bit like an English teacher. This is kind of a coming-of-age story, only in reverse, so to speak. That's why this isn't a question. On second thought, do you have any questions? Why not?

You, too, assumed I was gay—admit it. Come on, just say it out loud for once. Look in the mirror and say it, go on. Gay gay gay gay gay gay gay gay gay gay gay gay gay gay gay gay gay gay gay gay gay gay gay gay gay gay gay gay gay gay gay gay gay gay gay gay gay gay gay gay gay gay gay gay gay gay gay gay gay gay gay gay gay gay gay gay gay gay gay gay gay gay gay gay gay gay gay gay gay gay gay gay gay gay gay gay gay gay gay gay gay gay gay.

I wish it were that easy for me. Being gay is difficult enough, I suppose, but for me the problem was I was not able to know myself well enough to say one way or the other.

THIRTEEN

Q. 421. What words should we bear always in mind?
A. "What doth it profit a man if he gain the whole
world and suffer the loss of his own soul, or what
exchange shall a man give for his soul?..."
                                    —*The Baltimore Catechism*

In my afterlife, I was continually on the run from class to class. In this regard, my afterlife was maddeningly identical to my once-upon-a-time life as a high school student, or as a high school teacher, for that matter. Back at Angel of Mercy, I somehow invariably intuited where I was supposed to be, even if I did not understand the whole curriculum, or have in my possession my individual schedule, for that matter.

My next period, for instance, was taught by Brother Charlie. Of course, so far it seemed every single course was taught by him. We all sat at desks exempt from books, so I was assuming there was no assigned text. As I would soon see, in this class, there was no need for external resources.

"OK," he began. "Let's pick up where we left off yesterday. Shannon, would you begin, please?"

"I'm sorry, Brother."

"Excellent! Curt?"

"I am mortified, Brother."

"That's the spirit. Now you, Sally Jean?"

"I can't believe I was so insensitive, please forgive me, Brother."

"You're finally getting the hang of it, Sally Jean. Much better than yesterday, *much better.*"

"Thank you, Brother."

"What was that you said?"

"Oops. I said, thank you, Brother, I'm sorry."

"Not bad," said Brother Charlie. "Pete, you have a question?"

"Yes, I am sorry, Brother, I do have a question. Tell me again where we are going in this class? I know it's a stupid question, so there must be something wrong with me, and I am full of regrets."

"There are no stupid questions asked, Pete, just stupid askers. In our Apology Class we are all working through the essential human opportunity—how to plead for understanding for our shortcomings, how to beg forgiveness for everything we have and have not done."

"I'm sorry I asked, Brother."

"Me, too, but I'm also glad. Remember, saying you're sorry means never having to say *I love you.*"

I couldn't take it anymore. I didn't raise my hand. "Brother Charlie, what happens if I'm not sorry for anything?"

"Besides flunking a required class of your afterlife, you mean? What will happen is that you won't get anywhere."

"Where is there to go?"

"Everybody needs to get to the place of forgiveness. As Jesus teaches us…"

"Some of us need to get to that forgiveness place more than others, right?"

"As Jesus teaches us, we are all sinners."

"I'm sorry, Brother…"

"Good, Stevie, very good, that's what I am talking about."

"I'm sorry, Brother, but you are so wrong."

Charlie looked at the clock on the wall, the one missing time-telling hands, and said, "Where did the period ever go? You have your assignment for tomorrow, right?"

Shannon's hand shot upward and she was promptly called upon. She had the assignment memorized: "Walk up to ten strangers, or at least ten people who aren't friends, and beg them abjectly for their unreserved forgiveness."

That assignment struck me as being insane, and I said, "You can't ask your friends for forgiveness? Makes no sense. That's the only way I can tell they're my friends."

Charlie got the last word: "Class dismissed! Miss Shannon, we'll see you at rehearsal later, don't forget."

~

THE GRAND DEPOSITOR

Do you think you would benefit from taking an Apology Class? Don't you think everybody would? Sorry for asking, but what are some things you might—theoretically, of course, only theoretically—like to apologize for?

I'll be here, waiting for you.

FOURTEEN

Q. 817. If, then, it be a Christian virtue to forgive all
injuries, why do Christians establish courts and
prisons to punish wrongdoers?

A. Christians establish courts and prisons to punish
wrongdoers, because the preservation of lawful
authority, good order in society, the protection of
others, and sometimes even the good of the guilty
one himself, require that crimes be justly punished.
As God Himself punishes crime and as lawful
authority comes from Him, such authority has the
right to punish, though individuals should forgive
the injuries done to themselves personally.

—The Baltimore Catechism

Night fell on my head like a guillotine.

That much darkness descending that fast never helped anybody, least of all me. And naturally, Shannon did not like what I had to tell her. I told her where I was going.

"Stevie, what do you think you are doing, going to the Hanging Gardens?"

I did not see the need to explain why I needed to go there, not that she couldn't figure it out.

"To meet the Longcoats?" she said. "I knew it. Stevie, death has not changed one thing about you. You always could be kind of naïve. You are disturbing me, Stevie."

Her reaction seemed a bit strong, but I really didn't see an alternative to complying with the Longcoats' instructions. I knew I needed to humor them, because I knew I needed something from them, though I did not know what that was.

"Those Longcoats," she smirked. "They are such stupid clichés. Black coats, big boots, tattoos, and all. Clichés."

"You know how to counter a cliché, don't you?"

"Everybody does, Stevie. You reimagine it. But I don't want you going alone to the Hanging Gardens. I'm coming with you."

"You're not scared of them?"

"Don't make me laugh. Besides, you couldn't find the Gardens with a seeing-eye dog and a map."

——

It was dark already and we walked through the woods adjacent to Angel of Mercy, and I reached out for her hand. It is true, Brothers, I admit it. It was cold outside, but her hand was warm. It felt like the most natural thing in the world, strolling hand in hand through the woods, even if to Grandmother's house we were not going. And the winds were unusually fierce tonight, bustling branches and gusts of dirt.

"Don't get freaked out," she advised me, "when you get there. I'll explain everything afterward. You won't understand ahead of time."

We were walking in between the trees, where there was no path to follow, as if we were in a short story by Nathaniel Hawthorne that I used to teach all the time, but she seemed to know exactly where she was going, and who was I to question her? Then we broke into a clearing, and there in the meadow, a medium-deep fly ball away, I could see the Longcoats standing around, smoking cigarettes, muttering to themselves. And beyond them, over their heads, in the next part of the forest, was a spectacle that I could not quite decipher at first, only that I knew it was bizarre. If these were trees, I could not identify them. Not that natural science is my long suit. But off in the distance were big shadowy trunks with enormous, amorphous appendages, the strangest sort of dark fruit.

We approached the Longcoats. I felt disconsolate when she let go of my hand. It was a feeling I was familiar with. Isn't everybody?

One of the Longcoats curtly addressed Shannon. "What are you doing here? Nobody invited you."

"Stevie asked me to come along, right, Stevie?"

I told them she was right.

"That's not cool, Stevie. Not cool at all."

But then they instantly got over their distress at seeing Shannon.

"One day we'll all be one of them," one of them said to me, thumbing over his shoulder, "there in the Hanging Gardens."

I started walking toward the strangely animate trees. Gradually I understood. Hanging from the branches everywhere in the stand of tall trees were bodies, hundreds of kids hanging there, ropes around their necks, twisting slowly and slowly and slowly in the stillness of a moonlit night.

Then off in the distance I saw Charlie. He was entering the clearing. And I hurried to follow him.

"Where do you think you're going, Stevie?" a Longcoat demanded. "Get back here, we're not done yet."

Soon Shannon and I were close enough to Charlie to hear him. He was singing. It was a piece of Gregorian chant, the tune we sang for evening prayers in the Brothers' community. He always did have a sweet tenor voice. Oh, and he was carrying a step ladder and a rope. As we approached, he went up to a tree and positioned the ladder underneath a sturdy-looking branch and climbed up the steps. We were close enough to see his hands trembling, but he either ignored us or seemed not to know we were there. Once at the top, he tied the rope to the tree and formed a noose. Then he slipped the loop around his neck and tightened it. He seemed to hesitate for a moment, as if he were bracing himself, and then he stepped off the ladder and walked onto the air.

His body sounded like a sack of birdseed that hit the floor, and he twisted and twisted around, though his eyes remained open and he never clutched at the rope around his neck, the way you see people do in the movies. I watched and his eyes never closed. He was still singing.

"Let's get out of here, Stevie," Shannon said. "This is no place for you to be anymore."

I stood there, watching, paralyzed.

Charlie smiled, and then, for the first time taking notice of our presence, he waved at us.

"I can't stay here another second," Shannon pleaded with me.

We could not move. I waved back at him.

I also whispered to myself: "Why don't you just please die already?" I was referring to Charlie. I think.

"I have a question, Stephen," Shannon said. "Take this in the right spirit. Are you sure you're still you?"

"Why's everybody's asking that? I am, at least as much as I ever was. And you? Are you still you, Shannon?"

"I don't know why, but I think I may be more me than I ever was."

"That's a good thing." I knew it was.

"But," she added, pointing toward Brother Charlie, twirling in the breeze that was growing calmer by the second, "see him? We're not done with him yet."

"What do we have to do with him?"

"You'll see. We are going to make things right."

"When?"

"When we need to."

Looking at Shannon, seeing her smile flicker, fade, return, and fade again, made me sad, I think, for the whole world I had left behind. It was not right that a world that contained her also contained Charlie.

FIFTEEN

Q. 1397. What does St. Paul say of heaven?
A. St. Paul says of heaven, "That eye hath not seen,
nor ear heard, neither hath it entered into the heart
of man what things God hath prepared for them
that love Him."
           —The Baltimore Catechism

The birch trees surrounding the courtyard sighed and bent in the cool wintry breezes, swaying like tall ashen pompons. There was a huge banner hanging over the makeshift stage, and in dripping blood-red paint it read:

CARNAGE IN THE COURTYARD

Yes, Brothers, Dead Week was upon us then, which was bound to be, under the circumstances, a very special time for me. A crowd was assembled for lunch, and everybody was eating their tuna salad sandwiches and drinking their little mineral waters and waiting this side of patiently for the show to begin. As I gazed out upon the throng, the faces of the audience appeared inky and vague, like blurry fingerprints on rap sheets held at arm's length.

Brother Charlie stepped to the fore: "Welcome, everybody, to DEATHFEST, our Dead Week Performance of Famous Shakespearean Death Scenes, sponsored by the Drama Club, Shannon Reed, President." A few *woo-woo*s rose up among the more hyperactive, un-wonder-drugged students. "We begin our program with the famous death scene from *Romeo and Juliet*, which you know all too well from ninth-grade English—correct? And as interpreted by our own Shannon and Stevie." He shambled off to the side, but not before setting up the dramatic context. He had edited the Shakespeare text a bit, he explained. And we were dressed not in costume, but in everyday school garb. I mean, Shannon was. I could not replace my robe, evidently.

In the hush, Shannon walked onto the makeshift stage in the middle of the courtyard, got down on the ground, and slowly rested her head on a little rectangular buttercup-yellow satin pillow. She nodded slyly to me that she was ready and slowly lowered her eyes as if she had happened upon the ideal venue for taking a little nap. *Sweet dreams, Shannon*, I thought. And I looked up toward the other banner hanging from the classroom windows:

LUNCH OF THE LIVING DEAD

I took a deep breath and walked into the imaginary mausoleum, where Juliet, my life and my love, lay presumably dead, though she was faking it—as every ninth grader understood. Such a dumb plot—lost letters, bonehead maneuvers, attention-deficit-disorder couriers, mothers and fathers all in desperate need of parenting seminars—but there you go. It was not a play understood by yours truly, currently the famous "wherefore art thou Romeo"—now on the verge of speaking wrenching words a little bit too close to his and my heart:

"How oft when men are at the point of death
Have they been merry! Which their keepers call
A lightning before death. O, how may I
Call this a lightning? O, my love, my wife!
Death, that hath sucked the honey of thy breath,
Hath had no power yet upon thy beauty:
Thou are not conquered. Beauty's ensign yet
Is crimson in thy lips and in thy cheeks,
And death's pale flag is not advanced there…"

At which point I paused and studied Shannon's—Juliet's—disordered face. It looked as if she had just been awakened while lost in a bad dream, another way to describe high school, perhaps. Her eyebrows arched. Her mouth quivered. There was a little scar on her lip from the time when—she told me this long ago—she was four and a toy dog snapped at her. This most delicate of all disfigurations was radiant, and it was—though I cannot explain how—extremely erotic. It made me stop breathing. But the show had to go on, so I gathered myself up. All the same, I wished I could take away the pain I had just caused her. I wished I had never walked onto the stage, I wished I could undo and unsay everything that had been done and said.

I should also say that, though up until this very moment I had always hated this play with all my fractured heart, now it was different. I mean that, yes, I still hated it, but in the dramatic moment, I grasped its force. I don't know how it was possible for me to keep my footing. The stage seemed to tilt this way and that, as if this were a ship in a storm and I an unsteady deck hand. Even in my disequilibrium, the scene made sense to me in a way it never had before.

Death, thank you for bringing me here, but spare Shannon, please.

If I had been asked then and there by the Grand Depositor, I would have to testify that I couldn't recall having bothered to memorize these lines, which came to me as naturally as water. Meanwhile, as I paused and took in the scene, Charlie must have thought I had lost my lines, because he called out in a loud whisper, which everybody within a mile could hear, prompting me, "Ah, dear Juliet…"

I looked at Charlie, who had done so much damage to me, to her, to who knows who else?

"Ah, dear Juliet, why art thou yet so fair?" Charlie tried to cue me, who needed no such assistance.

I felt the truth of my lines, and I realized there was no saving her, and no saving me, and living out the play was the only chance for saving us:

"Ah, dear Juliet,

Why art thou yet so fair? Shall I believe
That insubstantial Death is amorous,
And that the lean abhorred monster keeps
Thee here in the dark to be his paramour?
For fear of that I still will stay with thee
And never from this pallet of dim night
Depart again. Here, here will I remain…"

I stopped again, moved by her face, and Charlie tried once again to come to my aid, though I needed none of it: "*With worms that are, Stephen.*" I knew my lines all too well, I knew them better than I'd ever known anything in my whole life.

"With worms that are Stephen," I recited rotely, causing giggles to ripple across the crowd. *No, that's not it.*

"With worms that are thy chambermaids…*Charlie, OK?* O here,
Will I set up my everlasting rest
And shake the yoke of inauspicious stars
From this world-wearied flesh. Eyes, look your last…
Here's to my love!"

At which point I guzzled down my apothecary's fatal potion (cranberry juice, ugh, not my favorite):

"O true apothecary!
Thy drugs are quick. Thus with a kiss I die."

Thus it was that, as I knelt down over her prostrate form, I bent forward and placed my lips on hers. It was a kiss that should have killed me if any part of me still remained that needed to be executed. It would have killed you, too, Brothers, it would have killed anybody. And I watched her eyes open for real and I fell to my side with a thump, acting dead, reprising the last moments in the Definitorium, and wishing it were true, which I didn't need to wish for because it was true. The crowd gasped. Or maybe Charlie did. Or maybe I did. These distinctions mattered less and less all the while.

There Shannon and I both lay for a while, still as, well, corpses, till

Juliet popped up like a Whack-a-Mole and peered into the distance, where the main school building was. She turned back toward my recumbent body.

"What's here?" she said with a hush. "A cup, closed in my true love's hand?

Poison, I see, hath been his timeless end.

O churl! Drunk all, and left no friendly drop

To help me after? I will kiss thy lips,

Haply some poison yet doth hang on them

To make me die with a restorative..." And she kissed me. "Thy lips are warm," she observed, but did not add that they were (key dumb plot point) an ineffective poison delivery system. She resorted to the carefully placed prop of a knife and addressed it passionately:

"O happy dagger! This is thy sheath; there rust, and let me die."

Then she stabbed herself in the heart with the collapsible stage weapon. "No!" I shouted inside my own head as she tumbled elegantly in slow double and triple folds alongside stricken me.

At which point, and after allowing for a pause to become as pregnant as precocious Sissie Stearns had become during our own high school days, Brother Charlie commandeered downstage center to utter Shakespeare's final lines:

"A glooming peace this morning with it brings.

The sun for sorrow will not show his head.

Go hence, to have more talk of these sad things;

Some shall be pardoned, and some punishéd;

For never was a story of more woe

Than this of Juliet and her Romeo."

Applause, polite, rose up among the students, but I suffered an inspiration and popped up to my feet, possessed by an absurd desire that the scene need not end, and furthermore by the requirement that Charlie not get the last word. No, Brothers, listen to me, the scene does not have to end. Charlie would, as it turned out, not be amused. But I had something left to say.

"Not so fast, Charlie impresario.
Life yet goes on for those who may be dead
In words they speak before love's urge has fled.
We say the stars above are out of joint,
And death substantiates words that would be said
It's you must be tasked and punishéd
And not lovely Shannon who has bled."
And then Shannon rose to the occasion—and to her feet, too:
"O Stevie, we each other truly love,
That is an awkward verse, by the moon above.
Your absence is a presence I most crave
Your love for me so many birds on the wing.
I cannot bear to bear your still being gone,
So sing we our love. Come follow along."

Then she took my hand and together we walked offstage, trium-phantly, to the chorus of rapt stillness. Where did her and my words come from? I wish I could say. Though not really, for there was no script in existence for two people such as us.

SIXTEEN

Q. 816. Why are we advised to bear wrongs patiently and to forgive all injuries?

A. We are advised to bear wrongs patiently and to forgive all injuries, because, being Christians, we should imitate the example of Our Divine Lord, who endured wrongs patiently and who not only pardoned but prayed for those who injured Him.

—The Baltimore Catechism

Dead Week, red-blooded baseball fans and anemic Brothers of the Definitorium, did me in.

As a result, I finally did what any red-blooded dead high school boy always secretly desires to do, something I never managed to do in high school the first time through: I tried unsuccessfully to get a little bit drunk (details, details, Bushmills, Bushmills), hopped into the driver's seat of the Prius (which, despite the threats, had not been towed), and, Brothers, I cut school. Sorry, Dr. Samuel Inskeep. I meant what I said to you in therapy, honest, but promises to stop drinking seemed beside the point after my star turn in *Romeo and Juliet*.

I drove the way I normally did, five miles above the posted speed limit, exactly five, windows up, radio off, somebody's sunglasses on. I was the only one traveling on the coast highway. That nobody shared the road with me boded excellently for any deceased traffic safety proponents. Still, Brother Stephen did not require a Breathalyzer to know that he was impaired. Slightly impaired. Not roaring drunk, impaired. Inebriated, technically, though I'm guessing not in a way that quite connects to the Irish whiskey.

~

THE GRAND DEPOSITOR

Brother Stephen was an alcoholic—some would even lie and call him a stinking drunk—at the time he died. Can you explain how you believe his "condition" affects the telling of his story?

How irritated are you now by these leading questions? Do you think Brother Charlie would care about what you have to say?

—

How I had managed in the course of my lifetime never to receive a moving violation, never to have been pulled over, was something I could not account for. In fact, I regarded myself as being an altogether excellent driver. I had not been alone in the estimation of my stature either, for I enjoyed the lowest possible insurance rates due to my spotless record.

I am not proud of my behavior. I am simply telling the truth. Shoot me.

But why bother now?

I was captivated by the call of the open road. This call of the open road was not entirely remarkable to my ear, because to me it sounded indistinguishable from my own all-too-familiar cry of drunken self-loathing. Therefore I responded to this call as so many felons and artists before me had responded: pedal to the metal.

I turned my head and squinted into the distance, toward the horizon, where the blue-gray sky slipped into the blue-gray ocean, where the West at some imperceptible point metamorphosed into the East. Thousands of miles away, I sensed, there was Hawaii, there was China, there was Japan, there was—there was, for lack of a better term, the whole wide world. An unworldly person is someone for whom the "world" exists mainly as an abstraction, someone for whom the word itself designates a vague sense of elsewhere, a sort of placelessness where one makes a stand. And Brother Stephen was not a man anyone would mistake for worldly. Truth is, hardly any of the Brothers would so qualify. Under oath I would stipulate that I knew essentially nothing more about those faraway exotic lands than what would be contained inside the borders of a picture postcard. Had I been curious in my lifetime about the great big world? Yes, but again, abstractly—that is, curious in no way that was desperate for satisfaction. Sometimes I imagined a little life such as mine could almost have been contained inside one of those Christmas-season novelty snow globes.

I had joined the Brothers directly out of high school, several decades ago, as you know, Brothers. As you may not know, however, I did not enter the order after experiencing an epiphany of piety. I never was a pious boy. I felt more at home with the Brothers than I felt anywhere else for reasons I have done what I could to elucidate. Some people would call that a vocation, but *vocation* made me uneasy. How could I claim to possess a vocation? I had a justified reputation for being arrogant and even high-handed when it suited my purposes, Brothers, as it often of necessity did for someone in the position of influence that I wielded as Auxiliary Provincial, but I still would not say I had a vocation to be a Brother. It was a decision I had made, this life, nothing more ethereal than that, a choice made as freely as I could make it.

Everybody makes a big deal out of celibacy, I realize. They think it is a circus act—superhuman and grotesque and unnatural as some bearded lady with a barbell or a set of Siamese Twins playing four-handed piano. To many, celibacy is a denial of fundamental human desire. They blame celibacy for priests' and other religious' turning into pedophiles. Which could not be further from the truth. Choosing a life that disallows the expression of sexuality does not imply a hatred of sexuality and hardly encourages homosexuality. If anything, quite the opposite. And being celibate doesn't amount to a free pass to molest children, give me a break. Plenty of molesters have spouses and families and are the picture of social conventionality. Don't you read the newspapers? Every single time one of them is arrested there appears the obligatory set piece: "He was the nicest dispatcher/electrician/landscaper/coach/neighbor in the whole world. I would have trusted my own children with him. I had no idea." And celibates aren't all prune-faced Puritans—excluding members of the Definitorium, of course.

You see, you only renounce that which you love. Otherwise, you wouldn't have to renounce it. You would just ignore it. Renunciation, then, you might say, is an affirmation. It is not about loss. Renunciation is a romance. It is even, in a way, sexy. For all these reasons, I say it is a beautiful thing, celibacy.

Ever since I saw Shannon Reed again, celibacy was a beautiful thing that was giving me fits.

Brothers, don't go there, you sicko voyeurs. It wasn't that seeing her caused me to reevaluate my sexual wants. I always sensed those needs. I was continually reevaluating them even as I was renouncing them for thirty-seven long, cold, solitary years. And don't get this wrong. After Joel or Charlie molested any one of his students (and if you think Shannon and I were the only ones, you don't know how to make change for the bus), he was still celibate, because he was not having a sexual relationship, not at all. He was denying everything that sexuality means by exploiting these students.

I must also admit, though, that death plays some funny tricks on the sex life of a celibate like me. As you will see.

∽

THE GRAND DEPOSITOR

And now, in response to your crude, insistent, unvoiced inquiries, let's have a brief consideration of celibacy.

Let us stipulate the following, my Depositor: we are men and we have dicks.

If there is any disagreement on this score, please discuss... with somebody else.

(Except for Brother Harold, I should say. He is a true dickless, gutless, witless, senseless, clueless, hopeless, ageless wonder. Eunuchs have more testosterone than he has. And except for Brother Paulus, who is totally a dick.)

And we Brothers—we band of brothers, we precious few who have freely taken vows of celibacy, poverty and obedience, but most memorably, on the toughest days and nights, celibacy—we think with our dicks just like sports stars and construction workers, but with a difference. We practice three key strategies of compensation: Two, Four, Six, Eight... Repress, Stifle, Sublimate.

Repress: "Dick? What dick? I don't see a dick."

Stifle: "Please be a nice dick, please. Sit down. You cannot stand up. I will not take you anywhere if you insist on acting like that. I'm warning you. I'm counting to three. One. Two. Th... OK, that's it. If you can't be a nice dick, you will just have to go to your room and stay there till you calm down."

Sublimate: "This afternoon, I am going to build a suspension bridge over the Seine right after completing the Tour de France and before settling down for the evening translating the entire corpus of Proust."

Which compensatory strategy knocks your athletic socks off?

What was that you were saying? No, no, no, but nice try. You cannot retire to another room and sit in a circle to discuss.

———

As for the elephant stomping around in the middle of the room, swinging his phallic trunk, shaking the coconuts down from the trees:

Brothers, why after Charlie—why would I want to become one of you? Why didn't I run away as fast as I could from Brother Charlie and all that he represented? Is it possible I felt I deserved what happened to me? Or did I feel guilty afterwards? Did I think I had somehow brought on his behavior—that I myself was responsible? And afterwards, did I simply deny it ever took place? Denial is a powerful force. It is one of those famous stages of grief. Without denial, it would be difficult to imagine how any of us go on in life, day after day. Or was I your most pathetically typical victim, blaming myself and unconsciously defending Charlie because it was too terrible to admit that Charlie was the guilty one and that Charlie was simply who he was?

These are good questions crying out for good answers, though I am not sure I am the best candidate to provide them. Then again, I may be the only one who much cares anymore—because as you may have heard, I am still dead.

Here's the core of my answer: despite how it must appear, the truth is that I did not become one of *you*. I did not become one of *them*. Perhaps it was trickier. Maybe I became a Brother because I would vow to be the sort of Brother who would do no such thing to a child, thereby demonstrating, psychologically if not logically, that no sort of Brother would do such a thing as happened to me and that therefore it never happened, or that if it did, it was not really an act committed by a Brother, not a real Brother of the Holy Family, not a Brother like the Brother I was or the Brother I would be. But then, why would that matter to me? Was I trying to clean up the order, you think? Riding into town on the white horse to introduce law and order? Pretty grandiose, Brothers, don't you think?

I do not know, but maybe I was trying to salvage the past—to recreate my past—by joining the Brothers. Gearing up, heading willfully into the belly of the beast, you might say, or into the lion's den, or into the dragon's cave. Pick your poison. Maybe those experiences with Charlie taught me what suffering is all about. That's a good thing, right?

You know, maybe I was even trying to save Charlie. Maybe I cared for him nonetheless. Crazy, I know that's how it sounds to you, totally nuts. But I am a little bit crazy, and so is love. Then again, Brothers, maybe I was simply trying to save all the rest of you from Charlie and his kind. You know what makes a savior a savior, don't you? A savior is somebody who, trying to save others, is ultimately trying to save himself.

We shall see about that, won't we?

I'm glad I got that out of my system. Perhaps I *have* gone to a better place.

—

But no, I guess not. I don't feel any better. I cannot get it out of my system and I am not glad.

It now felt to me like a cool, lovely late afternoon at the end of March, the time of year with which I am so familiar, the time of year when the brutal winter rains let up. And it felt like a Thursday. I could not say why, but if the afterlife felt like any particular day, it would have to be a Thursday. Certainly not a Monday or a Friday, or a Sunday. Thursday was a day of summing up, of looking forward and of looking back. A day of letting down your guard. A day to let go of your guilt over what hasn't been accomplished this week, and a get-out-of-jail-free card to roll your dice into the waiting arms of Friday and the weekend.

I drove and counseled myself to take in everything and mentally record it, for later indigestion. You never know, I figured. Some people obsessively collect matchbooks, paper clips, rubber bands. Some have garages stuffed with newspapers and magazines. I collected my thoughts and stored them in mental boxes lining cerebral shelves in the internal storehouse of my mind.

The highway passed marshlands. There the white egrets were high-stepping in the shallows and hundreds of sandpipers were flashing and several hawks were suspended high above, wings extended, riding the wind currents, surveying everything, looking for lunch. In that instant a seagull dive-bombed at a ninety-degree angle into the shallows, came up with a fat fish and flew off.

I passed by another one of those Luna Park billboards, which were beginning to grate on me, and almost certainly on you.

Luna Park, It's Luna Park!
Was life worth living?
Did you make your mark?

I had promised to take Shannon to Luna Park, and I would keep that promise. But I wasn't looking forward to the place. I was tired of being pestered and harassed by Luna Park's existential claims and queries. Maybe I would burn the damn place down when and if I ever got there.

Sobriety was another word I hated. I preferred (and at one point in my life hoped to achieve) *not-being-currently-smashed*, which despite being a mouthful, was for me precisely on the money. As for money and its powers, my testimony should be regarded as suspect. That is what comes of taking a vow of poverty, which was, like celibacy, another one of my sacred sworn promises when I embraced being a Brother. Consequently, I lacked for nothing to satisfy my material needs.

Now the sun was turning orange and beginning its slow, nostalgic descent, and I glanced pointlessly at my wristwatch again, which remained blank. Having eaten nothing since I couldn't remember when, I let myself feel the pangs of hunger, though, as I often said to myself, I could afford to skip a few meals, especially now. But what was with the hunger? How many other disappointments would death eventually deal me?

~

THE GRAND DEPOSITOR

How many little disappointments do you expect your death will deal you? Explain—go ahead, try to explain that one.

—

When I still held my Auxiliary position, I had the energy to put in twelve-hour workdays at the office and then continue to work some more into the early morning hours in my bedroom in the Brothers' quarters. This wasn't how I expected to feel after receiving the terminal diagnosis.

We are all dying, I had always acknowledged matter-of-factly to myself, and each of us has to die of something eventually. No wisdom to be gleaned inside the cracked kernel of that commonplace. In my case, I happened to be diagnosed with—

It doesn't really matter at this point, does it? And it had not required much contemplation on my part before I rejected my physician's facile recommendation as to the indicated medical regimen (amounting to the massive introduction of toxins), which was readily conceded to be a long shot anyway. I informed no one of my condition, not even you, Brother Provincial, and had no intentions of informing anyone. Was it anybody else's business that I was dying? I was going to live until I died. Simple as that. Not that I was ever regarded as being a simple man. Unworldly men rarely are. But the revised outlines of my life were simple. I was dying. No news there for anybody other than myself—and now, for you, of course.

Today, however, I simply wanted to drive my Prius. It was so much fun to drive and I needed a little time to think. It had been a very trying time of late before I had died. And a very difficult year. But then, had it ever been any different, really?

I had progressively less and less time in the afterlife to ponder those rhetorical questions.

My eyesight 20-20 even in my current state, I saw in the near distance, off to the side at the approaching intersection, the black-and-white Prius of a police car, practically camouflaged by the canopying Monterrey pine trees, pointlessly lying in wait for speeders on this two-lane country road. The logic of the existence of law enforcement in the afterlife (as well as the rationale for my trepidation) was not in the instant, to me, airtight. Nonetheless, reflex caused me to lift my foot lightly off the gas pedal, and experience cautioned me not to hit the brakes, a fatal giveaway. Besides, if the car I was driving was on the radar gun, and if the highway patrol officer was a pathetic observer of the letter of the law, I was dead meat anyway, as it were. Nonetheless, I held my breath. I wondered if I could do that for hours now if I so elected.

First chance I got, I would go to the notepad and inscribe: *Breathe. Hold breath. Experiment.*

I was relieved as I drove past, keeping my eyes straight ahead, when I wasn't pursued and pulled over, though why I was relieved I would be hard-pressed to explain. How much more trouble could I be in? What difference could it make if the insurance companies raised my rates ten-fold or if I was stuck in the slammer?

As I went around the bend, and exhaled, I reached over for the fifth of Irish whiskey lying on the empty passenger seat. I put it between my legs and unscrewed the top. I lifted the bottle, tipped my chin back, and took a drink. Then I lifted the bottle level with my eyes and gauged that I had about half the bottle remaining, which meant I was hypothetically prepared for wherever the road would hypothetically take me. Actually, despite sipping from it, the bottle had never been any more or any less than half full. I can remember when this miraculous development would have cheered me up beyond words. But now? I took it for granted, or deemed it to be yet another instance of my afterlife's black sense of humor.

In a few minutes I needlessly flashed my turn signal for the nonexistent benefit of nobody who was following me and deliberately pulled off, slowly entering the familiar clear-out. This clear-out led to a path, which in turn led down to the beach. This is precisely the sort of place where I always liked to pull off. I stopped the car and stepped out. Mine was the only vehicle present. And about that cute little snub-nosed creature: You might have thought, considering that this was *my* afterlife, I would have had the bright idea to come up with some flashier wheels. A Ferrari, perhaps. No such luck, however.

Meanwhile, the scent of the pine trees filled my lungs. And the temperature was dropping, so I was glad that over my robe I was wearing my old letterman's jacket (AMHS BASEBALL). What was also useful about the old jacket was that it featured capacious pockets, with one big enough for me to carry the bottle of Irish. Like old Auxiliary Provincials, old habits die hard.

I closed the car door, leaving it unlocked, and walked the path down to the sea. I heard a distant, muffled, mysteriously disembodied voice cry out, echoing as if it were inside my own head: *Why are you stopping? What are you doing now? It's not too late. Get a grip on yourself before you've gone too far.*

———

Along the path to the sea, the birds dazzled me as ever: the industrious terns, the delicate scampering quail, the predatory crows. At the same time, I attended passively to the myriad of irrelevant to me official signs and warnings: *Dogs Must Be Leashed... Shark Alert: Low... Fire Level Today: Medium... No Littering... No BBQ... No Sleeping on Beach... Severe Undertow! ... Do Not Swim or Surf Alone... Be a Buddy, Save a Life ...* All bases indeed seemed covered, didn't they?

The sand seeped into my tennis shoes as I made my way onto the beach, which appeared to be deserted. It always took an effort of the will to trudge through the sand down to the surf, but the inviting roar of the sea spurred me forward, nostalgically propelling me toward the setting sun. I stepped over the strands of seaweed and the driftwood and the crab carcasses that had been picked clean. I snapped up my jacket buttons to the neck and, with the big wind picking up, I tugged down on my baseball cap before sticking my hands into my pockets.

I realized what it was that I wanted and from whom. It was what I always wanted when I took myself down to the lonely seashore. I wanted something from God, assuming it was not too much to ask, and assuming God had a horse in the sweepstakes of my life. Big assumptions to be sure, but I was badly in need of some wisdom, if any were available to somebody like me, or, failing that, at least some provisional sign that my life had not once been the total travesty I feared I had allowed it to become.

My stomach empty, I bent over at the waist and thought for a second that I would become sick, but it was a false alarm. My head was spinning, the sun was kaleidoscopically wheeling, silvering the surf with oscillating spots like quaking aspen leaves. I might have had too much to drink. Or too little.

I stretched out my arms as if I were able to collect the winds.

Brothers, I collected the winds.

———

"Charlie," I recalled saying not so long ago to my old friend, when I called him into my office about the problem that had been dumped on me, as Auxiliary, to solve on behalf of the order. "Charlie, what do you need to tell me about Shannon Reed?" We had yet to receive the lawsuit at that time, but we knew what was coming.

"Shannon Reed! My, my, my. Now, there's a name I haven't heard in a long time."

"Well, you will be seeing her name in the papers a lot in the next few weeks. And yours, too. You'll be reading all about her and about you and about when…"

"You're enjoying this, aren't you, Stephen? Ah, sweet role reversal."

"Try to take this seriously, because I'm going to ask you one more time what this complaint is all about."

"OK, Stephen, we'll play it that way if you insist. I have no idea. I'm innocent."

When I took vows and donned the robe, Brother Charlie was assigned to be my mentor, or what the order called my Angel.

"Do I need a lawyer, Stephen?" asked my Angel.

"You may need a confessor more, and maybe a shrink, but that's your decision, not ours."

"And what I say is confidential?"

"Come on, Charlie. You of all people know the limits of confidentiality, you were a school counselor, for crying out loud."

"You're really dying to know, aren't you, Stephen? For old time's sake, what the heck, I'll just tell you. It's too late for me anyway."

So Brother Charlie told me.

"Shannon Reed was a precocious young woman. Seventeen or eighteen, and going on thirty-five. And she had a very active imagination.

Are you upset, Stephen?"

"Just go on, Charlie."

"I am sorry to speak of your old friend this way, but you have given me no alternative. And she *was* curious, you know what I mean? Always asking coy, leading questions. Personal questions. It was obvious what was on her mind. Totally obvious. What am I? A robot? I have feelings, too. One day, things happened. It was springtime. Her shirt was seductively unbuttoned. Never mind, it doesn't matter, and you don't believe me anyway. I'm not proud of myself, but it takes two, Stephen. It takes two."

"You are a very sick man." I didn't believe a word he said, but I believed everything he did not say.

"Stephen, you're taking this very personally. You know what they say about upper management—in order to manage people effectively, never take anything personally. I love it when you manage me effectively."

When Charlie stopped talking, and despite alternating between feeling faintly nauseated and understanding he was totally out of his mind, I had one further question.

"What is it that you are leaving out, Charlie?"

"What do you mean?"

"What is it that you are leaving out?"

And he provided one additional detail. He was lying about his story of Shannon's coming on to him in his office. "You were an idiot to take that bait, Stephen." At which point he issued a veiled threat.

"Remember your first year teaching? Who can forget the first year? Remember that tenth-grade boy you once upon a time found yourself caring for so much? You were new to the classroom. Remember how compelled you felt? *Compelled*: I remember that was the word you used."

A long time ago I had made the terrible mistake of trusting Charlie with my innermost thoughts on a certain subject—the subject tantamount to the love that dare not speak its name.

"Who *was* that boy again?" Charlie said. "I think it was—"

Charlie's subject was different from mine. His was the love that dare not shut the fuck up.

"Charlie, you are a slime ball. Nothing happened and you know it."

"Billy, right? That was his name, yes, of course. It's all coming back to me now. Now, I assume nothing happened between you and Billy, Stephen, because that is what you told me. Probably nothing happened, Stephen. You wouldn't let anything happen. Would you, Stephen? That's what you confided to me. But teaching is a romance, Stephen. Our students fall in love with us, and we have a sacred obligation to love them tenderly in return. *Tenderly.* They are so sweet, so trusting, so needy. You know as well as I do, we can do nothing wrong when we love them. Did you forget that?"

The son of a bitch, he was speaking about a student of mine named Billy, Billy with the sleepy green eyes and the hair flipped behind his ears, the boy who wore a green army fatigues jacket zipped up to the neck in any weather. Billy who had the voice of an angel. Billy who sat in the back of the room and stared off into space during class, but not in my office, with me. Billy who appeared in my dreams. Billy whom I never—since you are wondering out loud, Brothers of the Definitorium—someone whom I never touched. Whom I never really seriously contemplated touching. Billy, for whom I felt something that wasn't quite love, but was a feeling related to love, I admit.

In my afterlife, while I apparently have the opportunity to reflect continually on such matters, I begin to see that very few feelings I ever had in my lifetime were completely unrelated to love.

"Stephen, you're not going to believe this, but I'm sorry for what happened," Charlie said. We both knew what he was talking about. "I'm not a bad man. And you're not a bad man, either. We're both good enough men. I'm capable of doing some good, you know. Much like you. We're not that different, you and I, not that different at all. I just wish I could go back in time and make everything right."

"I wish you could, too." Not that I was aware of this development, but that was perhaps the precise moment when a plan to deal with Charlie and with Shannon's case began to form in my unconscious. I jotted down a few notes, after Charlie departed, including this one, which amounted to an injunction that the Definitorium could never enforce: *Put a stop to Charlie once and for all.*

—

I continued to walk along the windy beach, allowing myself to absorb everything, including the fine dust of sand that tickled my face. Then, out of nowhere it seemed, a dog appeared.

It was a white greyhound, with a green tennis ball lodged in his mouth, ready to frolic, with no other human being in the vicinity. I was more than willing. More than that, I was helplessly happy for an instant. Stupidly, mindlessly, goofily glad. I had always had dogs at home when I was young. There was a basset hound named Elvis, a Jack Russell named Cleo, a whippet named Eddie, who was the dog I loved with all my heart. Somehow, I figured, the aristocratic beast's arrival was a pretty good omen.

The greyhound wagged his tail and taunted me with the precious green tennis ball, and he dared me to catch him. Brothers, I chased him. Such a powerful, beautiful dog, loping along with a sleek coat glistening in the fading sunlight. Then the dog ran back to me, stopped and dropped the ball, and cued me as to what I was supposed to do.

So I picked up the spittle-sopped ball and threw it far as I could down the beach. The dog raced off to get it. It was a gorgeous thing to see, a silky white and sinewy dog running for pure joy along the surf. I turned away for a second, trying to get my bearings, trying to catch my breath. And when I looked back in the direction of the dog, he was no longer in view.

But then, in a heartbeat, he was back. In fact, he was speaking to me.

"Brother Stephen, how are you feeling?"

I regarded this little development as a personal affront. "Dogs cannot talk." Death was toying with me again.

"That is true, most dogs cannot talk. But that's not because they don't have things to say. Now, you have to admit, I just asked you a question."

"How am I supposed to feel?"

"Reason I ask is, maybe I can be of service."

"I don't know where I am and I don't know where I am going."

"Excellent."

"*Excellent?*"

"You have your work cut out, even though it isn't exactly work, and when you need to know where you are and where you are going, you will."

"That explains everything, doesn't it?"

"Think of me as the narrator of your life."

"I always wanted one of those. Somebody to make sense of the turbulence of the heap of days."

If the dog had the facial structure to convey a wince, he would have. Which was something I detected to my post-mortal mortification. Here I was, put down by a superior greyhound. Death was never going to be easy to endure.

"That did sound pretentious," I conceded to the dog, "you're right. How about a voiceover, though, like in a movie? Funny how I didn't see the credits and THE END roll up before I keeled over so ignominiously. It would have been a nice touch on the part of a master director."

"Does the movie have a happy ending?" wondered the greyhound. "Maybe we'll find out eventually when you watch the director's cut."

"I used to like dogs—they're man's best friend—but you're becoming irritating."

"Thought you said dogs can't talk."

"You have a name?"

"Mort."

"Don't mess with a dead man, Mort. A dead man's got nothing to lose."

"OK, I see my work is done." He began to lope away.

"Wait a second. Your work hasn't even begun. Come back!"

I watched the dog run down the beach and out of my afterlife.

So much for solitude and self-reflection on the windswept shore. I retraced my steps, headed back to the car hundreds of yards away. Once I arrived there, I removed the whiskey bottle from my pocket and contemplated what course of action to take. I decided what to do. I tossed it into the garbage can.

Dusk was approaching. The *gloaming*: that was the word for dusk in the old poems. The *gloaming*. A marvelous, mouth-filling word. I would change my life from that moment forward, coming out of the gloaming for good. I had received the sign I was looking for, even if I could not explain what it was.

The sea wind pounded my ears, the salty air infiltrated my nose. I unlocked and lifted up the trunk.

"How are you feeling, Charlie?" If a dog saw fit to ask me a question like that, why couldn't I ask Charlie the same thing?

Lying on his back, Brother Charlie nodded, said nothing, communicating to the effect that he was all right, all things considered, and that Stephen was a son of a bitch. His reddened eyes gleamed with anger and defiance.

"Remember, Charlie, what your old school pal Marcus Aurelius once said? 'Pretend that you died and imagine that you have received a gift of a new life.' And then he said, 'Now live your life full of gratitude.' Remember? Remember you quoted him to us in Latin IV?" It was dirty pool, quoting the stoic emperor to the old anything-but-stoic Classics teacher.

Charlie smiled. "In all the excitement of being kidnapped and transported to the underworld, I seem to have lost track. When is cocktail hour, Stephen?"

"As Marcus Aurelius says, we only live in the present anyway."

"How about letting me have some of your Irish, Brother Septimus. I know you have a bottle wherever you are."

That was rich, calling me *Brother Septimus*, a veteran move by Brother Charlie. It had been a long, long, long time since anybody had called Brother Stephen *Septimus*. Since cars were all made in Detroit and had fins, since grown women were not offended by being called girls, since atomic bombs were tested in the Mojave, since presidents were assassinated by lone or lonely gunmen. Unlike a nostalgic vision of a cherry-red Chevy Impala or a mushroom cloud, the old name did not induce in me even the flimsiest frisson of nostalgia, however. After all, I had been Brother Stephen for years, since just about everybody in the order reclaimed their family names in the burst of enthusiasm that followed Vatican II in the '60s and '70s. Septimus was, however, the name for the young man Charlie had once upon a time had a part in creating. Septimus was therefore decidedly somebody else, somebody who was no longer Stephen.

Septimus means "Seventh" in Latin, but don't ask me to explain how I came up with the name. I was probably nineteen, maybe twenty, when the thought occurred to name myself that. Whatever the inspiration or reasoning may have been at the time is something I could not reliably recreate. I would feel fairly confident in testifying that I did not have, though, a mystical connection to any lucky number. The explanation is more mundane. As you appreciate, back then all Brothers took exotic-sounding, Latinate and Greekish names like that: Eugenius, Demophile, Giles, Marcus, Genesius, Roggan, Paulus, and so on. Peer pressure of a rarefied sort. It was a very different world.

This is another curiosity. I just realized my old friend Brother Charlie was an exception in this respect, as he was in so many others. My once best friend and teacher and ally was always Charlie, Charlie from the first. And Charlie's calling me Septimus was a brutal reminder of the past, tantamount to calling me a betrayer.

"Good guess on the Bushmills, Charlie. Just your bad luck I threw it away a second ago."

"I was always skeptical about your choice of libations, Stephen. Jameson's is the Catholic Irish whiskey. Not Bushmills—that's the Protestant. Bushmills comes from goddamn Londonderry, for Christ sake."

"Can't disagree, Charlie, but deciding between Catholic and Protestant whiskeys here and now seems about as pressing as choosing between swallowing a bottle's worth of Valium and taking a razor blade into my warm bath."

"I was prepared to go along with you for a while, till you had your little laugh and made your pathetic anarchic point. But now you have to let me go. I won't tell anybody, I'll make a deal with you. You won't have to answer for this craziness, Stephen, I promise. It's just between us. And we know how to keep our secrets, don't we, Stephen?"

I nodded, because Brother Charlie was correct. "But you see, Charlie, I really don't care what happens to me anymore. Especially now. But I do care what happens to you, and I want to be certain it happens in just the right way."

"I get it. You're the avenging angel. I get it perfectly now. You do realize, however, what happens to avenging angels, don't you? Those arrogant bastards are themselves all revenged upon. What else do you think you are doing here?"

"Charlie, this may be the best thing I've ever done, maybe the only honest, pure thing."

"That's the Protestant Bushmills talking, not the Brother Septimus I used to know."

"The Roman Catholic Brother Septimus you used to know is no more, *Brother* Charlie."

"You're going to be sorry, Stephen, you ever met me."

He was half right. I was already sorry. "One last thing, Charlie. Maybe you can shed some light."

"We have to think outside the box now, Stephen. Though I'd also like to think outside of the trunk."

I flipped through my notepad pages. "Right," I said. "My question is this, Charlie: does it ever end?"

"Sure, it does. Wait. What? What are you talking about?"

"Does the suffering ever end, does the pain, does the love and the responsibility, does it ever just come to a halt?"

"Close the trunk and leave me the hell alone."

That was his final word, for now anyway. I let down the trunk.

I drove back the same route by which I had come.

As I headed past the intersection where the patrol car had been positioned, I noticed it was not there anymore. I felt saved. I felt vindicated. I had made a good decision, throwing away the whiskey. Being dead, I would be a better man, a better Brother, a better Auxiliary, a better friend to Shannon Reed, who now needed me to do my job and do it better than I had ever done it before. Maybe that was my purpose in the afterlife.

That was the moment when I witnessed, in my rearview mirror, the police car boring down fast upon me, red and blue lights flashing. Then the car's siren went off for a second, *whoop whoop whoop*. Obediently, fatalistically, I pulled to the side of the road into a gravel patch and waited for justice to be delivered. I was honestly curious.

On this occasion, justice took a surprising turn, however. The police car zoomed past and disappeared around the bend ahead.

"My lucky day," I said.

From the trunk, Charlie cried out: "You wish!"

◆

THE GRAND DEPOSITOR

Do you believe death was Brother Stephen's wake-up call?

SEVENTEEN

Q. 792. What should we do if we cannot remember the
number of our sins?

A. If we cannot remember the number of our sins, we
should tell the number as nearly as possible, and
say how often we may have sinned in a day, a week,
or a month, and how long the habit or practice has
lasted.
                              —*The Baltimore Catechism*

The winds were still for a change, and I walked out onto the wooden
dock—

Go with it, would you, please? It was a dock. Which was there.
Which I was walking on. Where I was alone—though, guess what? Not
really. I'm never alone for long. You're getting on my nerves, Brothers,
always hanging around, wanting to know more, lifting your eyebrows,
casting petty doubts around, raising trivial questions of logic and pro-
gression.

To return to the place I was before I lost it with you: I walked out
onto the wooden dock that oonched into the crystalline lake, and the
water softly lapped up against the sunken piers. Before my eyes there
was a lovely little body of water, about the size and shape of a baseball
field, surrounded by tall evergreen trees. I had this incredible and irra-
tional need to fish—a desire I had heretofore never experienced. And
maybe since this was my afterlife, well, presto: dock and lake—a lake

containing, with any luck, a cooperative fish or two.

It appeared as if the sun had just begun to come up, and that the air was still bitter cold from the night before. I reached into my robe pocket and came up with a handful of worms (yummy) for the fishing pole and line that were in my grasp. I baited my hook (conveniently lodged onto the front of my robe) and gave thanks for my robe's unanticipated grubby largesse. I dropped the line into the water that was still and deep blue and wanted to settle in for a nice, slow, quiet morning of fishing.

But complicating matters was this: Charlie was there, somehow out of the damn trunk again, though he wasn't joining in the fishing expedition. He was standing where the dock began at the shore, and he was—surprise!—complaining. "I don't like this," he whined. "Why are we here?"

"Got me."

"I really don't like this."

"Don't like fish, or don't like to eat fish, or don't like to fish?"

"All of the above, wise guy. But I have a question for you: where is time?"

"You mean, *what* is time?"

"No, I know what time is, but I don't know *where* it is. Is time in us, or are we in time?"

"Charlie, you are annoying. Time is the place where you are in the moment, which is all we can ever know of time."

"OK, Stephen, I like that. We live in the moment. And that's all there is. The moment."

"Yes, living in the moment is all there is, but you need to pick the right moment. You don't want to elect being in a really bad moment. Like, for instance, you want to be careful and not be like me, choosing this moment, talking with somebody like you on this lake. Say, Charlie, how'd you get out of the trunk again?"

"I can't follow you, Stephen, so why don't you tell me: how was your time on earth?"

"Who wants to know?"

"*You* do, Stephen, don't fool yourself."

"I'm trying to fish, Charlie."

"Maybe it would be easier if you thought your old friend and mentor, Charlie, wanted to know. So tell me, how was your time spent on earth?"

"Come on, Charlie, you're killing me. I'm not sure I know why but I'm trying to fish here in peace and quiet."

"Just answer the question, it'll do you good. How was your time spent on earth?"

"OK, I'll answer and then you will shut up? My time went by very fast. You know, I always heard people say don't wish away your life. But looking back, I think I probably did just that."

"You're not answering the question honestly, and you know it. You can't help yourself from blaming me, can you?"

"All I can say is, I miss my life, I do. There, I said it. And it happens to be true. How about you, Charlie?"

"This is *your* afterlife we're in, Stephen, not mine. What would you do differently, if you had it to do all over?"

"If I had to do it all over again? Let's see. I feel pretty certain I would decide not to do it all over again. I think it's clear by now that that's not how the world is set up. That is one truth that comes through in *The Baltimore Catechism*, something I agree with. Beyond that, life is something we spend because we have to spend it. It is there to be spent. I wouldn't take up some new hobby or career, I'll say that. I do wish I had learned to play the piano, but I really don't think that would have made a great difference, ultimately. And I also wish I had arranged to have you put out to pasture a long time ago, to get you far away from kids like me, whom you damaged in ways you don't care to know. You see, I think you are a pathetic, terrible man."

"Good one. That's something else we have in common. I also think I am a pathetic, terrible man."

"Like I care."

"I always knew you did."

"But these big questions of yours—about how I spent my time on Earth—they really are not helpful. They really do not further the cause. You see, right now, fishing on this dock, it's amazing how few regrets— aside from my failure to deal with you—I feel. Not that I was perfect, far from it. But mistakes and missed opportunities are the essence of life, or so I now think from my currently distant vantage point. Now can I fish?"

"You're making a big mistake, Stephen."

"Why? It looks like a nice lake to fish in."

"It's a mistake the way you are treating me—in your report to the Definitorium."

"What do you think my mistake is, Charlie?"

"You see, your story is simply not believable. Brother Paulus and Tom Newgarten and the rest of the Definitorium are not going to buy it. And I'll tell you why. You hate me too much, is why. You're really nothing but a victim? That's your big point? Well, that is something you cannot finally sell. And I am a monster? Really? I never did anything good for you? Never? Give me a break. You need to present me in a more complex way, otherwise your audience is going to discount everything you have to say. Throw me a bone, Stephen. Come on. Even a movie villain would, in real life, help a blind lady cross the street."

"I never saw you anywhere near a blind lady. Well, did you?"

"Did I what?"

"Did you ever help a blind lady cross the street?"

"No, I didn't, but you're missing the point. And not for the first time. Didn't I ever do right by you, maybe once or twice?"

That was a fascinating question, I had to admit. "You know, Charlie, I have to say that you did, once or twice, do something right. When I came down with the flu, early on as a Brother, you brought me a bowl of chicken broth. That was very kind of you. Thank you. And when I was a student in high school, you taught a particularly great class one day, on a poem by Keats, 'Ode to a Nightingale.' That was amazing. *Was it a vision, or a waking dream? Fled is that music:—Do I wake or sleep?*"

"And don't forget: *Now more than ever seems it rich to die, To cease upon the midnight with no pain.*"

"I learned something about love, Charlie, about how it never dies once it finds its way into a poem."

"You're welcome, Stephen. I appreciate that. Let me ask you again, then: was your life worth living, Stephen?"

"They say the unexamined life is not worth living."

"Same goes for the unexamined death?"

"Still don't understand the question."

"Sure you do, Stephen. Was it an experience that you value now?"

"You're kind of slow on the uptake, you know that? Everything you seem to want to know is kind of academic."

A flock of geese flew overhead, blowing their horns like five o'clock commuters.

"For instance," he asked, "looking back, are you glad you became a Brother?"

"Glad? No. It's harder than that to explain. How much do we choose in life and how much chooses us, after all? Being a Brother was good for me in a way that, say, being a bus driver, a doctor, a carpenter, whatever, wouldn't have been, not that there is anything wrong with being anything else. No, being a Brother meant living in a community that enabled me to be more perfectly alone. It was disappointing, the life of a Brother, which makes it an excellent introduction to mortality. And in this regard, Charlie, you were a big help. That unease with my life felt comfortable to me. And now, since you won't let me fish in peace, let me ask you something, Charlie. You keep asking me about the past, so tell me something. What is the purpose of memory?"

"I have no idea."

"Come on, Charlie. Play along. What is the purpose of memory?"

"Why, to remember."

"Sounds right, but you know what I think? I think the purpose of memory is to forget."

"I knew you were going to say that. It's so you, Stephen. But forgetting is not the purpose of memory, that's its consolation."

"I have a question, Charlie."

"What's new?"

"What is the purpose of memory, Charlie?"

"I will tell you what the purpose of your memory is now. To forget me once and for all, to forget what I did. This is your chance to take back your life."

"That's funny."

"It's not funny, what I said."

"No, I mean, look at this."

I felt this tug on my line. And I reeled in a silvery trout, which hardly put up a fight. There it was then, flailing and flopping on the dock, at the end of my line. Somehow I managed to pick up the fish, though it was so cold and slippery, and I stared into its opaque unblinking black eyes. Life was a choice, I realized, and Brother Charlie was right. I slipped the hook out of the fish's mouth and tossed it back into the lake and it made a splash, and swam away.

"Thank you, Charlie," I said. "That was one more good thing you did."

"Now where do we go?"

A cold gust pierced my robe like a thousand hooks. The trees shuddered.

"Are you still you, Charlie?"

"Again? Well, I'm not you, Stephen, if that's what you want to know."

The winds picked up high in the trees. I didn't know how much I would miss the winds till they were gone.

EIGHTEEN

Q. 778. Is it ever allowed to write our sins and read
them to the priest in the confessional or give them
to him to read?
A. It is allowed, when necessary, to write our sins and
read them to the priest, as persons do who have
almost entirely lost their memory. It is also allowed
to give the paper to the priest, as persons do who
have lost the use of their speech. In such cases
the paper must, after the confession, be carefully
destroyed either by the priest or the penitent.
                                    —The Baltimore Catechism

ADRIAN F.

Between the ages of fifteen and eighteen, diminutive Adrian was sexually molested, by his and his lawyer's count, on forty-three occasions by Brother Jonas. What an astonishing, what an incomprehensible number. Remember that case, Brothers? And how disturbing it was that Adrian was able to reconstruct a chronology, and that it seemed totally credible. Times, dates, details of the deeds, right there in black and white. Wasn't there anybody in the Brothers' community who ever once noticed what Brother Jonas was doing, or asked where Brother Jonas was going with little Adrian? Nobody detected anything even a little bit bizarre on one of these forty-three separate occasions? How could that be? Nobody observed all the times Adrian, the smallest boy in school with sunken black eyes and pale pockmarked skin, was by himself in the company of Brother Jonas? Inside a classroom, during lunchtime in the band room, in the Jacuzzi in the gym, even in chapel. Brother Jonas's preferred activity, however, involved driving Adrian to the hamburger joint, getting takeout, and parking at the back of the lot. Brother Jonas had to sign out for a community car. How come nobody stopped to wonder what he was doing with a car during some of those forty-three times? Adrian said he would eat his hamburger while Brother Jonas busied himself. Eating slowly, hoping for the moments to pass, that was all Adrian could do. By the time he ate the last bite of his chili cheeseburger Brother Jonas was done. The lawsuit was filed seven years ago. The Brothers authorized a settlement, and I signed the check, and the lawsuit was dropped. I drank a whole bottle of Bushmills that day, not that it helped, and not that I expected it would. Adrian said that he was self-destructive throughout his twenties, but saved himself by becoming a marriage and family counselor. I acknowledge that I have some simplistic if not naïve questions, but I have to ask myself: why didn't Adrian ever make a single attempt on Brother Jonas's life? Forty-three occasions. At least twenty hamburgers, I estimate. Not once did Adrian shove his chili cheeseburger into Brother's ravenous, greedy maw. At the same time, I know why. It would have been impossible for Adrian to resist, impossible. Then I think about Brother Jonas. I would also like to know how come not once did Brother Jonas stand in front of the car and beg Adrian to please please please just run him down and put him out of his misery. I concluded then, and accurately, that I would never understand. This was the first negotiation I conducted in my capacity as Auxiliary. As for Brother Jonas, he left the order fifteen years before and was long dead by the time the Holy Family Brothers settled the claim. $725,000.

CONNIE S.

Brother Michele-Paul, Connie's college counselor and her confidant, one day when no one else was in the school building, politely asked her please to unbutton her pale blue school uniform blouse. She was so stunned to be asked by the Brother she trusted, and since he asked so sweetly, she said, she complied. She further testified, after she came forward six years ago, that he buried his bald head in between her budding breasts and brought himself to climax beneath his robe. Not long afterwards, she dropped out of school and became a hairdresser in Hollywood, where she was the highest-paid hairdresser to the stars. She claimed that she forgot about what had happened until the moment she received the school alumni magazine featuring a photo of Brother Michele-Paul, who was receiving some important award for distinguished service to children and education. She said she felt a duty to set the record straight about his so-called distinguished service. We wrote her a check for $25,000. She didn't need more money, she said. She needed an acknowledgement of culpability, which the check provided. Brother Michele-Paul denied the allegation at first, but we counseled him out of the order. Last anyone heard he was working as an instructor at a community college in the California desert.

Mark H.

One afternoon, Brother Benjamin fellated Mark inside the tool shed when he was the fifteen-year-old president of the Chess Club, of which Brother Benjamin was the moderator. Mark dutifully told his parents, which was brave on his part, but they did not believe a Brother would do such a disgusting thing, and when had he ever learned about such disgusting acts? They went to their grave not believing him. $75,000. Brother Benjamin left the order and moved to Paris, where he was the executive director of a small museum in the Marais district until he died, rumor had it, of AIDS.

Hillary F.

$1,000,000. Brother Francis impregnated her during her senior year. Her child was born with Down's syndrome. When she graduated from Yale Law School, she caused a lawsuit to be filed. I had never met anyone as calm and dignified as Hillary F. In a strange twist, Brother Francis offered to marry her and be a father to the child. She took a pass. We counseled him out of the order, too, and according to Hillary, he recently hired his own attorney in order to establish paternity. He works in the technology field and was, until the bubble, a dot.com gazillionaire who contributed lots of money to causes such as the local teen runaway center. She is to this date using every legal means at her disposal to shield the child from his father.

PETE T.

$1,333,333. Brother T. Thomas was the principal of Pete's school, Saint Rose's Academy, and he vowed to tamper with the official transcript and lower Pete's grades—he was a straight-A student—if Pete told anybody about their mutual masturbation fests in his paneled principal's office. Brother Thomas is now in the Brothers' Senior Community at the monastery up in the mountains, and he is never permitted to have any dealings with children. He is eighty-nine years old but showing no signs of imminent physical or mental deterioration. Initially, Pete asked for $3,333,333 for some reason I could never fully understand, except to this extent: he wanted an odd number and a big number. He has been married five times and has nine children, none of whom he has seen in years. He took the money and established a trust fund for his children.

BILLY O.

Here comes the tough part: my relationship with a student of mine who was named Billy. *Relationship* is one of the ugliest words in the language. *I'm having trouble with my relationship. How is our relationship going? We are having issues in our relationship.* We only use the word when we are at a loss, when we are disappointed, frustrated, confused. Like *issues,* now that I think about it. But no matter. The time is long past due for me to unburden myself about this relationship. If this is another way to say, Brothers, that it's your problem now, so be it.

Poor, sweet boy with the slow-lidded eyes—Billy, you loved me. It's true. I know this. I need to tell the truth all over again. I did not mean for us to become intimate, or I should say as intimate as we became. You know this. You trusted me. Sometimes I would have to walk away from you when our paths would cross at school, and you always looked disappointed, hurt. But you see, I was your teacher and I truly loved you more than I loved myself. Where have you gone now?

Some nights are destined to be long ones. Life teaches us one thing over and over again, and that's it. Some days are full of tears, I understand. All this I know. But there are things I do not know still. Why were you, such a beautiful boy, so lonely? Why were you so sad? I would have taken away your pain if I could have, as you would have taken away mine, had I invited you in.

What brought you to that terrible night? And when you held up the convenience store, what were you thinking? What did you need the money for? And when the police surrounded you, why didn't you drop to the ground, as they shouted at you to do? Why did you raise your gun and point it in their direction? That toy gun. What ravenous joy suffused your face in that instant as you smiled and refused to put the gun down?

I keep looking for you in the afterlife, because I must, and thus far you are nowhere within reach. Tell me why it must be this way. That is me calling out to you all the time, begging you to answer, wanting you to understand you will always be loved and be safe with me forevermore.

Speak to me in your silence if that is what you prefer. I can hear you perfectly that way. Your presence is rough and overwhelming as the cresting sea in a hurricane, the purest song pouring out from your bullet-riddled heart.

———

Just then, a sign appeared on the side of the road:

CLOSURE, POP. 000

NINETEEN

Q. 275. What do you mean by the remains of sin?
A. By the remains of sin I mean the inclination to evil
and the weakness of the will which are the result of
our sins, and which remain after our sins have been
forgiven.
                                      —*The Baltimore Catechism*

Every self-respecting town, I suppose, even one situated in my afterlife, needs a dining establishment. A place where you can hang out, see friends of yours who may be or will soon be dead, spread rumors, hold hands with your spouse, lover, or date, and complain about the food quality and the service. Evidently this densely unpopulated locale, the gravely unincorporated ville called Closure, required at least one restaurant to cater to its nonexistent residents.

The malfunctioning flashing red neon sign indicated that the establishment I had come upon was the Crestfallen Café and that it was O-P-E-.

Ope is always the last thing to die.

Charlie cried out from within the trunk's confines: "Who writes your material, Stephen?"

"Ope springs infernal."

"Get me a rewrite."

Where was a nice big pothole when I needed one?

I parked the car in the deserted lot. It seemed to be the thing to do. Night had fallen, and apparently the dinner crowd, if it were to materialize, would be one of those late-arriving ones. Therefore I determined that I stood a pretty good chance of getting a table without a long wait. I used to hate waiting in a restaurant. I don't need to tell you that I likely would never embrace a Zen, detached approach to human experience, or at least my human experience, certainly not at this current rate of non-progress. Meanwhile, the transfixing neon sign kept blinking at a constant, panicked rate, as if it were suffering a seizure. If I continued staring maybe I would suffer a seizure myself.

I got out of the car and for a fleeting second considered liberating Charlie and taking him inside, but I wasn't ready for his company. I didn't know if I ever would be again. I assumed, without any justification, I had plenty of whatever was the local equivalent of time available.

I advanced toward the entrance. The gravel sounded beneath my soles like the noise made by chewing what was formerly my daily dose of Grape Nuts. My golden fifties had brought about many such mundane adjustments to my diet, not all of them savory ones. Legumes, anyone? At least now I would never again be forced to hear my internist advising me to consume my nine servings of fruits and vegetables every day. I glanced at the posted menu of the Crestfallen Café for a second. My mouth did not salivate for the stir-frys and omelets and hoagies.

The lights inside the restaurant burned brightly, but indifferently and uninvitingly, much like the eyes of you, Brother Paulus, Provincial. The black canvas awning over the front door was rent and flapping in the breeze, tattered as a singed sail on a burning sea vessel after marauding pirates depart with their spoils.

Aaargh, me bucko and me beauty, what be havin' eight arms and eight legs?

Eight pirates, you lily-livered scurvy dog!

Splice the mainbrace—mighty Crestfallen Café, prepare to be boarded!

I heard Charlie cry out, at the top of his lungs, "You need psychological help!"

"Go to Davey Jones's locker, landlubber!"

—

As for spoilage, once I was inside I could see that every table was crowded with dirty plates and glasses and shredded paper napkins. Where did all the customers go? Had they suffered a siege of second thoughts or ptomaine poisoning? Had the café been evacuated by emergency edict of the pointless-at-this-point Health Department?

My tennis shoes on the gummy white-and-black linoleum flooring made flesh-crawling sounds, octopus make-out kiss-kiss sounds: squish, squish, squish. Tiny bandage de-application noise-rips. I stopped and soaked in the establishment's ambience, using the term loosely, very loosely. I reconsidered ordering those crepes I had briefly cast my eye on from the menu outside, or anything else available from the hidden back kitchen. I normally didn't care for so-called background so-called music, but I would have preferred anything to the silence that gathered like an unlanced boil in the middle of the room.

Besides, I was almost happy that my appetite seemed to have vanished.

Meanwhile, the solitary employee—a squinty-eyed, crystal-meth-skinny, bare-armed, sullen, and t-shirted young woman—leaned her back against the cluttered counter, one hand cupping an elbow, the other holding aloft a smoldering cigarette at a thoroughly hostile angle. She listlessly blew a single smoke ring up to the paint-chipped ceiling. "Practice Safe Sex" proclaimed the bunched-up words that constituted the printed legend gracing the front of her shirt. Her hair was tussled, as if a minute earlier she had been disturbed while living up to her motto. Then she turned around to extinguish her cigarette in a half-filled coffee cup, making a sizzle, and the legend imprinted on her back was revealed: "Practice Makes Perfect."

"Hello, how are you?" I risked saying anyway to the back of her head. She turned to face me. "Uh-huh. What you want?"

"Compassion. Justice. Wisdom. Understanding. Also a hot shower."

"That's too bad, because we're not serving up any of that here at the Crestfallen. I *can* give you some more grief, which is our house specialty."

"I kind of sensed that."

Resigned to the limited options before me, I ordered a cup of coffee. I had counted on that being a relatively safe choice, even if I had witnessed how she had disposed of her cigarette. Still, I analyzed, when in Rome or the Afterlife…and so on. And besides, what difference would a little case of salmonella or botulism make to me under these circumstances?

"You want some cream and sugar with your coffee, don't you?"

"Sounds good."

"I know it does. Only guess what?"

"Don't tell me. Let me guess. You're fresh out."

"You're a whole lot smarter than you look."

"Thank you."

"Don't mention it."

I miserably carried my miserable self and my miserable black tepid coffee to the table farthest in the back, facing the entrance, near the hallway that seemed to lead either to restrooms or to eternal fires. Is a terrible wreckage of a restaurant the most depressing place imaginable or not? I cleared away the dishes and cups to the next table and wiped the surface down with a less-soiled napkin, and then sat down to contemplate exactly what I was supposed to do now.

I was not going to be sitting alone for long. Brothers, if I had learned anything so far, I should have learned that my afterlife, much like the previous stage when I was living with you in community, was destined not to be an opportunity for solitude.

———

"Stephen, may I join you?" That was Shannon Reed (who else?), and she was standing tableside and addressing me softly, looking the way I would have expected her to look. Oh, and by the way, she looked older, no longer like the high school girl I remembered.

"Shannon?" I said like an idiot, though I had no doubt and it was therefore not a question. She always could mash my brain cells simply by paying attention to me and I was, therefore, often an idiot around her. Death changes a lot of things, but not that.

"Who else could you be expecting at the Crestfallen?"

I regarded her question as strange and decided to reply with silence.

Shannon smiled. "*Beatrice*, Stephen? You're expecting *her*? You read too many books. Well, news flash, she's been Dante's date for centuries, not yours. You have to settle for me."

I had to admit that in fact a second ago I *was* thinking Dante. I wondered if everybody was going to be able to read my mind from now on. Not that it mattered much, really, when you factored in what else had already trans—

"I wouldn't put it that way," she derailed my train of uncoupled thought. "It's just that the dead cannot lie even if they try. No false moves anymore. You are *who* and *where* you are now, period. No pretending, no fooling around."

"Death makes lying irrelevant? That's a relief, plus it frees up a lot of time and brain space."

"Think about it. Deception serves no purpose now. Why bother faking anything anymore?"

"But how come I can't read *your* mind? Maybe there's a chance I'm not really dead after all?"

"You're not really dead? That's funny. Maybe it just takes getting used to, being dead and not lying. My hunch is you'll come around. You will get the hang of it. Trust yourself. You always had that ability when you were alive, you just forgot most of the time. Don't be hard on yourself."

"And what's the point of talking to you, Shannon, if you know what I'm thinking before I say it? Not to mention the problem that I don't even know what I think until I say it, and even then…"

"Maybe we're just playing along with you. You're the maestro. It is *your* afterlife, after all. But actually, to tell the truth, I'm still puzzled myself. Nobody ever thought for a second I had all the answers."

"You know what they say. Where there's death, there's hope."

Shannon contemplated that statement seriously, as if I had handed her the map to buried treasure. Clearly, she needed to take this conversation in another direction, fast. "Hug, you silly goose, *hug*. Though I guess I should say *Brother* Silly Goose."

I slowly rose to my feet and reached out to grasp her hands in mine. Then I leaned over and kissed her cheek. She smelled of apples in autumn, tasted like fresh butter.

"Add flour, Brother Stephen, and you got yourself an apple crisp."

I can't believe I set her up like that. Even in death, a straight man. So to speak.

For the first time I could ever recall, it almost felt liberating to be so transparent.

"My just dessert," I remarked. "But you knew that, didn't you?"

Then the two of us hugged each other, an affectionate hug, a sweet hug. Her head landed in the middle of my chest, where, when the two of us were teenagers, she had sometimes rested it after she almost made out with me on a few occasions. Standing across from me at a slight distance, she had appeared larger. Once I collapsed the space intervening between us, and once she was encompassed by my arms, though, she felt smaller. Not to say manageable. She never was.

Then, before I was conscious of doing so, in unison we sat down, facing each other across the table. That was better. That was also the happiest I had been since—since I had arrived wherever it was that I had arrived.

"You look just like you did in high school," she said. "Every bit as handsome. I always loved the way you looked. Your brown eyes, especially. You always had that sad, kind look that used to knock me out. But now I like all the salt and pepper in your hair, which I find very distinguished."

"I thought you said nobody could lie anymore."

"Exactly."

"Maybe death has been kind to me. And look at you." She appeared radiant.

"My skin color comes from my Italian mom," she said. "The blue eyes, from my Irish dad. But you know this. You remember my folks."

I did, and I really did know all that.

"I have a question, Brother Stephen. When are you going to stop drinking?" she asked, almost innocently.

"What did you say?"

"I recognize the signs. I'm an expert, recognizing the signs."

"Fair enough. OK, maybe I will stop now. It does seem beside the point."

"I'm happy to see you, Brother."

"Shannon, you have to stop calling me Brother soon, or I'm going to cry."

Shannon looked over behind the counter. She addressed the girl as she lit up another cigarette: "Those things'll kill you, Molly."

The girl passive-aggressively tugged on her blue-jay-plume-colored bangs.

"She's my daughter," Shannon advised me, though I had gathered as much. Shannon had always been the ultimate monitor. In a span of seconds, she had given both me and her daughter instruction. On the other hand, we both could probably use some instruction. By way of reply, Molly saluted us both with her middle finger.

"Lovely child," I said.

"You bet. You should have met her father. He was a piece of work. He was a DEA agent. The things I could tell you, Stephen."

She gave me an inspiration, and a plan. "Tell me everything, Shannon. Pretend I never knew you before. The things you could tell me: just tell me."

"For real?"

"What do we have to hide? Besides, isn't the air we breathe piped-in sodium pentothal?"

"Death is a truth serum more powerful than sodium pentothal."

—

"It's weird. I like your idea. OK, here goes. My name is Shannon Reed. Is this mic on? Good. I am fifty-four years old. I am five-foot-six. I weigh one-hundred-nineteen-and-a-half pounds. Which is what I weighed in high school when I was totally in love with you. And when you were semi-totally in kind of love with your idea of me. Come on, admit it. My hair, I cut most of it off a while ago and what's left is mostly a nice sweet friendly platinum burr that feels like the pelt of an animal when I rub my hand across. I have a little scar on my upper lip, which you're close enough to see, see?

"I will get to the subject of my husband eventually. Give me a second, I need to work up to it. There is a little tattoo on my left hip. It is a red rose. These things happen. After tequila shooters especially, not that I remember the occasion very clearly. My daughter Molly is nineteen. She is a very beautiful girl but I don't think she likes the way she looks. God, I used to be that way. I don't enjoy remembering that time. Molly was supposed to be doing homeschooling. I was supposed to be her primary homeschool teacher. Which is not quite the joke it probably sounds like to you, being already pretty skeptical.

"I actually did very well academically in college. I can show you my transcripts. No, really, I can. Anyway, Molly and I, well, we were not enjoying excellent results in the academic arena. Molly was not valuing her education. Molly was not taking advantage of the opportunities presented her. Molly did not have good career prospects in her future. I worry for Molly more than I let on to her. To this day she refuses to have dinner with me. Actually, she can barely sit across from me for a minute. I tell her to stop smoking cigarettes. She lights up another one.

"I drive an old Toyota pick-up truck that I think was probably once red. I own one dress, blue gingham, naturally. Hey, we live in the country, in this place called Dogtown. I am usually wearing blue jeans at home and I am sitting before the potbelly stove, upon which I have placed an iron water pot, filled to the brim, to keep the air from getting too dry inside my cabin. I am a vegetarian. I am a fundamentalist Christian. My parents have passed away. They kind of liked you, you know. I have few fond memories of them myself, and even fewer snapshots.

"My ex-husband is a DEA agent, or maybe was. I just said that. I met him when they raided all the farms nearby and found a few tons of marijuana, none of it mine. I cannot smoke anything, much less weed. It was love at first sight. For him, I mean. He had names for his two service weapons: Junior and Senior. He had similar names too for the other important appendage in his life. If you know what I mean. He called me *Shanns*. He called Molly *Moll*. I guess you could say he was a man of few syllables, one at a time.

"Our marriage was all right for a second. He traveled a lot, as you can imagine. I never had a thing for law enforcement officers, by the way. Don't think I'm that type woman. When he asked me out the first time, I asked him shouldn't he be reading me my rights first? He laughed. I remember the times he laughed. All three of them. I am a Cancer, Aries rising. I used to do astrological charts for free when people asked me nicely. I could tell them what the stars said awaited them in their lifetime. I can provide no similar service for myself.

"This is what Del used to say—the ex-husband. I say ex-husband, but I cannot be sure of that. If there were court proceedings to dissolve our union, I missed this development. Whole years I missed, to be honest. I have not seen him for seven years. One day he said he was going on a bust of a crystal-meth lab in Mendocino County. He himself liked to do plenty of crystal meth. He wanted me to try, but I never did. I do not need drugs to be high. I told him this about myself, I did not keep secrets from him. I am naturally high. That became Del's joke about me, that I was naturally high.

"I wouldn't be surprised if Del remarried. He was an attractive man, in a DEA-ish kind of way. He would have hated Molly's boyfriend. They're too much alike is why. His name is Les. I tell Molly that *Les* is the totally perfect name for her boyfriend, because he has less to offer

than anybody I have ever met. Stop it, she tells me. He's growing marijuana, Les, I am pretty sure. He rides a big black Harley. She sits on the
back. Sometimes, I think he is a Hells Angel. There are a lot of them
around here, you know. Have you seen them riding along together?
Hard to miss.

"Along about now I should probably mention that Jesus is my lord
and savior. I cannot tell you how happy I am that I have accepted Jesus as my lord and savior. Molly has not accepted this or anything else
about Jesus. I went to Catholic schools when I was growing up. Which
obviously you know. I enjoyed school all right at first. Jesus would not
be a Catholic, that's what Pastor Robideaux said to me. I was a little bit
in love once with Pastor Robideaux. More like a crush, I suppose. It is
not easy to admit this. He had a wife and seven children and he drove a
Mercedes when he visited me here in Dogtown. He was misunderstood
by his family. The congregation loved him, but they may not understand him either. Del would really have hated Pastor Robideaux. Pastor
Robideaux said I owe it to myself to get my thoughts down on paper. He
was a very wise man. Who am I to disagree? He said I have a sacred duty
to be kinder to myself. Jesus would say exactly that to me.

"Once I put my thoughts down on paper, thoughts about Brother
Joel and Brother Charlie especially, Pastor Robideaux had somebody
call me. A lawyer he knew. He was a smart man, this lawyer, and I went
along and signed the papers he wanted me to sign. Next thing I knew I
heard from the Brothers. I met with one of them, the big cheese, at some
restaurant. We had green tea, which I love. It has antioxidant proper-
ties—the tea, I mean, but maybe the love, too. The Brother wanted to
know if I was OK. He had received the lawsuit, he said. He was worried
about the state of my soul. He apologized for what may have happened
when I was in high school. That's how he put it. *What may have happened when you were in high school*—as if I had a screw loose, which
may have been true at one point but not then. I told him thanks and
asked him if he wanted another cup of tea. I thought for a second he
was going to try to talk me out of the lawsuit. I wish he had tried. I

might have dropped the whole thing.

"High school was hard on everybody. Take Molly. She hated high school. I had no choice but to remove her. The boys never left her alone. She never studied. She never brought books home. She changed the color of her hair every month or so. I hope she doesn't stay with Les. He is not a good boy. He is not very nice. A good mother has a sixth sense about such things. Even I do. Les carries a gun. I saw it. I told Molly, and she goes, So? He needs a gun, she said. For what? I said. To deal with all the stupid people, she said.

"I'm scared, honey, I told her. You're scared of your own shadow, she said. Please, listen to me, I said. I'm going out now, she said. I'll be back Wednesday, she said. Where you going? I'm going with Les. Don't go. I'm an adult, she said. No, you're not. All you think about is being molested in high school by some priest a hundred years ago, she said. Not a priest, a Brother, I corrected her, for the thousandth time. Well, maybe you were molested, big deal, get over it. It was a long time ago, it doesn't mean anything anymore. You are letting that one thing define your whole shit-storm of a life, get over it! Sometimes I think she may have a point. Maybe Molly will come home tonight, maybe she won't. People have a habit of leaving me. When I least expect them to leave me, usually. Now *you*."

"I'm not planning on leaving you, Shannon," I said. "Where am I supposed to go now?" The words had tumbled out of my mouth before I realized exactly what a big thing I was saying.

"No, I mean now *you*."

"Now me, *what*?"

"Now you tell me your story, Stephen."

"Oh," I got it now. "My pretend-you-never-knew-me story?"

"You have something better to do?"

So I agreed, and I began to tell Shannon my story. It seemed to be the thing to do. It would feel like hours passed before my story came to an end. I did not realize there was so much that I needed to say. I also didn't know that she had to be the one to hear it.

—

I finished speaking—a few minutes, a few years later, who can tell? Not me, Brothers, and not you, either.

"Thank you, Stephen. I had a hunch back then."

"It's an old story, though, isn't it? We thought we knew everything about each other. How wrong we were. Maybe we were always more alike than we realized."

"You know, I'm making your favorite dish for dinner. Want to come home with me?"

"What is that?"

"Home is where, when you have to go there, they have to—"

"You know, I never believed in that Robert Frost poem. What I meant, though, was what is my favorite dish?"

"The *late* Brother Stephen," she said, laughing a little. "You know what your favorite dish is."

"Can we really do that, Shannon, just go home like that?"

"Stephen, open your eyes, look around. We can do anything you want."

"You're inviting me home?"

"I'm trying hard to."

I was never going to get used to Shannon's surprises.

"Sure, you will," she said, reading my mind again. "But hey, look at this, here is something you should have expected." She pointed toward the entrance of the Crestfallen Café.

"Someday, sure, Shannon, someday we can go home."

That is when a highway patrol officer came through the front door. He had a bad limp. He dragged his leg like somebody resisting arrest. He approached our table. Blood was seeping into his shirt from the vicinity of what appeared to be a gaping wound in his left shoulder. I had the intuition it was the same officer who had been lying in wait before and who had later passed me, siren blaring, on the road. My intuition, I would slowly realize, might or might not be incorrect.

"You're making things too complicated, Stevie, just pay attention," said Shannon.

"That your Prius out front?" Highway Patrolman Brother Charlie addressed Shannon, somehow managing a glare through his sunglasses.

She shook her head no. "That's a pretty impressive sight, that wound," she said. "Where did you get it?"

He spoke to her and pointed at me. "Ask your friend. He knows where I got it."

I denied knowing anything about it, and added that he was crazy to think I did.

Shannon said to him, "You should have somebody look at that."

Charlie addressed me instead: "About that car out front."

"There a problem?" I guess I was supposed to play along.

"I got a piece of advice for you, mister."

"Call me Stephen, Charlie." I waited for the advice, knowing I couldn't use some.

"If I had any advice for you, my advice would be, don't order the tuna salad, mister."

"Thank you, Charlie."

The highway patrolman took my measure.

"Can I help you, Charlie?" It was an honest question on my part.

"I kind of doubt it."

I had a question: "You see a greyhound on the loose anywhere?"

Brother Charlie in his Highway Patrol uniform smiled his odious smile. "You kids have a nice night." And on that sarcastic note, he departed, leaving a trail of blood in his wake.

THE GRAND DEPOSITOR

You're used to leaving a trail of blood and tears in your wake, too, aren't you? Did you really think you could get away with everything forever? And now I know for sure what I always guessed: We are Brothers, joined forever, Brothers.

———

Shannon told me she was ready to go.

"Is it weird," I asked, "to keep seeing Brother Charlie over and over again in the afterlife?"

"Not really. It's where he finds himself, and it is certainly where he belongs. Besides, he pops up in my dreams all the time."

"I wish he would just stay in the damn trunk. *That's* where he belongs."

Shannon said, "I don't think that's going to happen. He's on the loose. You could not keep him contained forever."

"I think I should track him down and put a stop to this."

"Maybe. Your decision. I will be here, waiting, and I will be *there*, waiting. You can always count on me. And you'll know where to find me. It's a small town, Dogtown. And you'll have plenty of opportunity to decide."

"Are we really dead, Shannon?"

"Indications from the Stevie Afterlife seem to point in that direction. Seems hard to believe, though, doesn't it?"

But now I discovered that I could also read her mind.

"Yes," I answered her next unasked question. "You know I do."

"Good," she said. "Even though I knew from the first I ever met you—that we wouldn't—that we couldn't—that you were—"

I reached across the table and put my finger up to her lips. I would not let her finish. "No, I'm not."

"Stephen, it's OK. You are who you are, aren't you?"

"But I'm not." That sounded like the right answer to the wrong question, or maybe that was the wrong answer to the right one.

"It's OK, it's really OK."

"When did you reach that conclusion?"

And I.

And she.

And he.

And they.

And we.

As we all did once upon a time, and as we would once again, perhaps, from now on.

"Remember, Stephen, what you told me, the night before you took off for the novitiate and joined the Brothers? You were packing up your boxes in your room, pulling stuff down from the walls, picking out the books and the sweatshirts you were going to take, and I was crying my eyes out, remember?"

"Remind me." I knew she had all the facts wrong about being in my room, but I wanted to hear her say it out loud.

"You said, 'I will always be your soul mate.'"

I did say that to myself all the time, because it was true then. Was it still true?

Shannon replied: "Yes, it is still true. And do you remember what I said back to you? I said, 'Maybe in the next life, Stevie, maybe in the next life—that's the time when we can finally be together.'"

I did remember it all, as if it happened a minute ago.

"Well, Stephen, take a good look around. Guess where we are."

Shannon, where did our lives go? I must have known when I was in high school that I was not able to make my life work as long as I was alive. Maybe being dead was my golden opportunity.

But all I said was: "And do you remember the other thing I told you?"

"Of course, I do, Stephen. Now you know I meant what I told you when I was eighteen. What you have discovered—maybe what we have discovered—is that I would die for you, too. But there is one thing I'm kind of upset about."

"Just one?"

"You know what tonight is, don't you? The prom."

Now I knew what was producing that sinking feeling inside. "Why does everything keep sneaking up on me?"

"Well, are you going to ask me, or not, Stevie?"

I was obedient to my heart's demands—hers, too. "Do you have a date for the prom, Shannon?"

"Now I do, bozo."

"That's Brother Bozo to you."

TWENTY

Q. 479. Does God give His grace to everyone?
A. God gives to everyone He creates sufficient grace to
save his soul; and if persons do not save their souls,
it is because they have not used the grace given.
                        —The Baltimore Catechism

The theme for the Angel of Mercy Prom was "Island Paradise." Can you detect the ukulele strumming in the hot Polynesian breeze? It is pretty faint, I agree. We must try harder to capture that music, because that is the mood effect I am striving to reproduce for you. Oceans slipping and sloshing while the golden sun is setting. A warm breeze rustling the hibiscus, the lilacs. Night-blooming jasmine adrift in the warm air.

The gym was tricked out exactly as you might have expected. Swaying fronds on phony miniature palm trees. Painted sea and shoreline backdrop. Big puppet macaws strung along invisible wires overhead, along with fluffy white cloud cardboard cutouts. The tables were laden with coconuts and pineapples and mangoes. Where the tropical produce was coming from in my afterlife, I have no idea, Brothers, so don't ask.

The only thing missing from the scene, as far as I could determine, was the grass skirts. Shannon, for her part, was regal in a long creamy satin sleeveless gown, which matched perfectly my blindingly white dinner jacket, donned rakishly over the black robe, of course. I took a pass on the bow tie, as you might imagine, not only because, possessed of ten thumbs as I am, I could never have tied it, but also because it would have conflicted with my clerical collar. Shannon looked delectable. Her hair was done up in a bouffant, straight out of the '60s, and her wrist was graced with a little corsage constructed around a white orchid.

Full disclosure: tonight was my first prom. I mean, I chaperoned lots of proms as a high school faculty member, but I never went to my own prom. You are not surprised, Brothers, I can tell. Shannon and I took a pass back when we were in high school, figuring it was too ridiculous for people like us. Fair enough, but now I was going to make up for lost time. I was going to have a great time if it killed me.

You know what I mean.

We danced every dance, Shannon and I. I use the word "dance" loosely, but God knows what word I really should use. Stomp? Thud? Creak? Lurch?

After many dances, to quench our intense thirst we retreated to the refreshments table and lifted fake coconut cups of cloyingly sweet so-called tropical punch to each other's lips. Then we encouraged the sweaty-pawed portly photographer to take pictures of us against the plastic palm tree backdrop. I can wait to see the results till the next time I die, though I do have every reason to suspect I was probably smiling like old, flatulent Brother Genesius, which is to say pretty much like an idiot.

It was all perfectly and ridiculously idyllic, this island paradise prom. Complete with the requisite presence of a snake: by which I mean our very own Brother Charlie, who was hanging around the punch bowl, ladling out his own pink brew of a concoction for the benefit of unsuspecting adolescents.

———

The music came to a brutal stop when the three Longcoats rushed into the middle of the gym floor. They took command of center court, and stood on the painted image of our Fighting Irish mascot (a pixilated little Elvis-sideburned gent in a green hat, serpent under his boot heel). Flared open were their bigger-than-ever coats, which were so enormous that they could have been piped with helium or stuffed with rocket-propelled grenade launchers. The situation looked dire, and all the prom-goers cowered at the edge of the floor.

"We have something special for you," one of them shouted. "Listen up, all you losers!"

"Something you all deserve," said another.

"You all can thank Stevie for what's coming down on your heads," added the third. "Pay attention—we want your last prom to be unforgettable."

Panic ensued. Everybody hit the deck or scrambled up the bleachers, like Shannon and me, or headed for the exits.

That was when, on cue, after waiting to let the tension build a bit longer, the Longcoats opened wide their arms. They simultaneously released what seemed to be hundreds upon hundreds of white doves. The birds exploded up to the rafters, whistling as they streamed to the top. It was a stunning, blinding, thunderous storm of white wings. We all watched with a sense of rapture and of wonder. Once the birds settled, we all applauded. There was nothing else conceivable to do.

Brother Charlie got onstage, grabbed the mike, and said:

"Ladies and gentlemen, the Longcoats. Let's hear it for the Longcoats!"

We all took our cues and responded with loud huzzahs.

Charlie continued: "The only question I have, all you crazy Longcoats you, is: who's going to clean up after these doves?"

Not the Longcoats, because they marched like royalty or rock stars through the gym doors into the night, waving to their adoring, clamorous fans.

Please come back, I said to their retreating forms. *Please stay away*, I added.

"See?" Shannon said to me. "See what you have done?"

"I haven't done a thing."

"What are you talking about? You saved us all."

I wondered if that could be true.

"Wonder no more. You're cleaning up what you left behind in your life."

Now, I wanted to leave the prom. To go where, you are asking? I had no idea. At the same time, I was more than idly curious about something. "Shannon, in my afterlife, do we ever at any point, you know, make out a little bit? You and me? I'm just curious, I can take my answer off the air."

"Come on, Stevie, be serious, would you?"

I deserved that.

"Of course," she said, "of course, we deserve it. Eventually."

The festivities were not quite over.

———

We heard the dull, muffled, distant roar of a fleet of motorcycle engines. Then the side of the gym collapsed and what seemed like a hundred Hells Angels rolled onto the floor. One of the bikes drove right up to Shannon and me and skidded to a stop, inches away from us. A young woman had her arms wrapped around the waist of her charioteer.

"Molly," said Shannon. "What have I told you about crashing parties?"

"Mom, don't cop such a rude attitude. It doesn't go with your sweet little slip of a white dress."

"Stephen, remember Molly?"

"How could I forget?"

"And this is Les."

"I've heard about you, Les."

"Like I care," he said to me, and to Molly: "Your mom is weird, Moll. Let's trash this dump, I hated high school."

"How about," said I, "you don't?"

"Really?"

"You made your point, more or less, Les."

Les glowered. He had a goatee that seemed to have been composed of pencil shavings and eyes that had been polished with a sander. He spoke to Molly.

"This is your dad, huh? Not much of a manly specimen."

"I'm not her dad, Les," I offered in the interests of clarification.

"Actually, Stevie," Shannon began. "Actually…"

———

The two of us walked outside, where the full moon was up to its usual tricks.

"I figured out something just now, Shannon. I believe I understand why I am with you in the afterlife."

"Really, Stevie? Why are we together here?"

"I've been sent here to save you."

"You think?" Her face turned elastic as a clown's. Her forehead ratcheted up and her lips curled down. She was so adorable. "You really *think?*"

"Doesn't it make sense, Shannon?"

"I do see the logic, I'll give you that. So, are you going to ferry me back across the River of Time—or whatever?"

"Would you like to go back?"

"It's a possibility, I suppose, but before I decide, I think I should tell you that I might see the whole thing differently. What about this? Maybe I've been put here in your afterlife, Stevie, in order to save *you.* And I'd been meaning to speak to you about Molly."

"I'm not her father," I protested. If you think about the logistics…"

"Why start now, thinking about logistics?"

That was a development. "It's got plot-twist potential, Ms. Alfred Hitchcock."

"Come on, you'd have to be a fool not to see that unresolved paternity question coming a mile away."

"Exactly, Shannon, exactly."

"Why not first let's go to Luna Park, Stephen?"

Why not, indeed. Why not? When in doubt in the afterlife, all you have to do is change the subject.

"When shall we go and how do we get there?"

"We're already halfway there, Stevie. Just open your eyes."

I could do that, I could.

TWENTY-ONE

Q. 461. What is sanctifying grace?
A. Sanctifying grace is that grace which makes the
soul holy and pleasing to God.
—The Baltimore Catechism

Luna Park, It's Luna Park!
The shadows are bright!
Cold hearts need a spark!

Shannon and I passed through the redwood-high, ornately baroque steel gates. Little baby gargoyles were perched here and there on the fencing, stonily protecting and warning at the same time, the way you count on gargoyles doing. YOU ARE HERE NOW explained the looming sign under which we entered, words of wisdom obviously drafted by a philosophy graduate student forced to take a marketing job in the private sector. I presumed there had to be a slack academic afterlife for the Humanities.

Inside, the place was packed with visitors eating cotton candy and hotdogs and candied apples. In many ways, the expected prevailed for an amusement park—though *amusement* did not stand out as the correct term. Boys showing off for girls, girls showing off for girls, at the heavy ball toss and the hammer gong and the weight guess. Anachronistic ladies under twirling parasols, anachronistic men in Panama hats.

Organ music played in the background and the smell of barbecue and popcorn filled the air. In other respects, however, this amusement park was not as you might have expected, Brothers, as you will soon find out.

"Let's start here," Shannon decided. She was referring to the exhibit that promised, bafflingly I thought at first, "Rain."

We walked through the entrance and into the clearing, which is where we waited, though not for long. You could hear the wind picking up and almost feel the air molecules expand, ripening with our expectation.

There was a clap in the stratosphere and the rain, as if on instruction, poured down upon us. We stood underneath the cloudburst with our faces turned up and let the rain fall for a while. We opened our mouths, thirsty as parched plants. Here is a mystery that lingers from my past life: Why do umbrellas exist? Why must we keep the rain away? The rain feels so cool and so clean.

"Rain," I observed, while the water was streaming off my head. "It is just like the rain."

"Can't slip anything past you, Stephen."

We walked back outside, where there were clear skies overhead. I should probably add that we were dry as if we had walked out of a desert.

Shannon had her dance card filled out, and she was anxious to move on. "And now that," she said, pointing toward the little cathedral.

"You are in charge, Shannon."

The little cathedral toward which she pointed was—a little cathedral, which we soon entered. Rose windows. Stained-glass haloed saints. Glass-walled crypts jam-packed with bony relics reclining on red velvet. Marble statuary. Flying buttresses in the twilight. The air was drafty and cool, the way I like my cathedrals. The stones were enormous, and seemed to be breathing. The candles flickered, the unicorn tapestries billowed.

A column of black-cowled and black-cloaked women was moving on their knees slowly up the center aisle, heading in the direction of the altar. Their heads bowed to the floor, their countenances concealed from view, together they collectively resembled a gigantic centipede. Off to the side, a troupe of mumbling monks flagellated their backs as if they were coming down the stretch to the winner's circle, and a smaller group of sad mendicants shuffled along, aimless and begging for alms, the skin sliding off their leprous faces, tiny shadowy caves where noses used to be.

After we departed the Middle Ages, and not a moment too soon, we proceeded to other tourist attractions. We visited "The Library," "The Board Meeting," "The English Class," "The Operating Room," "The Forest," "The Black Hole," and one or two others that slipped my increasingly porous mind. In "The Library," the books were checking out the people. In "The Operating Room," the physicians were applying their scalpels to themselves. And so on and so on. As for the "Old Bushmills"—now, that was one exhibit we decided to take a pass on. I knew in advance that all that attraction could possibly promise was at best unreliable.

"The Black Hole" was particularly fascinating. Instantly, once you were sucked inside, you could hear nothing and see nothing. I felt like I was moving—if I was moving—through some milkshake-cold, gelatinous, viscous element. For some reason, which I might identify as blind panic, because that is closest to expressing what I felt, I started running and kept running and running till I was out of breath. At one point, I recall attempting to scream out Shannon's name, though that must have been an illusion because I could not hear myself. And she did not hear me, either, or so she told me after, because she was screaming out my name, too.

Once outside—and how and when and where we exited via the wormhole, you think I can figure out, Brothers? Once outside, I asked her what she thought.

"Nothing is so exhilarating," she replied.

"I'm sensing a theme, Shannon. The theme is that there is no theme in Luna Park."

"As the sign said, YOU ARE HERE NOW."

"And we are where we are?"

"You're getting smarter the longer you are dead."

"Thank you."

"Where to, Stephen? 'Lovers' Lane'?"

Why not, my coy little darling? That was to be our next-to-last attraction. We hopped into a little car on the track, broke through a curtain of glass, and headed into a gauzy space. Rose petals were falling everywhere. Breezes scented vanilla. The call of birds, like waves breaking on a distant shore. We held hands. We never would leave this place, I resolved.

We left Lovers' Lane still holding hands.

———

It had to be here, Brothers. There had to be an attraction called "Charlie's Greatest Show on Earth!"

Charlie was taking tickets at the turnstile outside, and when we presented ours to him and he handed back the torn stubs, he smiled and roguishly said, "Glad to see you kids."

We walked through the door and looked down toward the spectacle of the three-ring circus below.

"You sure about this, Stephen?" Shannon asked, clearly uncertain.

"Not really."

"We don't have to do this, we can turn away and leave him behind us."

"I don't know how to do that yet."

"OK then, here we go, it's your funeral."

Shannon and I walked into the big top tent for our final Luna Park experience, and in no time Charlie took over the center ring as ringmaster, illuminated by the burning golden footlights. He was a vision mostly of the scarlet type. Scarlet cutaway-tailed sequined coat, scarlet cummerbund, scarlet bowtie. His black satin jodhpurs billowed about his calves and waist, the bottoms stuffed into the tops of tall, black, shiny riding boots. The black top hat, one size too small, looked to be perched precariously on top of his head. In his left hand he held a whip, and in the right, a handgun that looked to be fashioned of chrome.

Shannon and I were the only ones in attendance, and we had taken our seats midway down.

"Ladies and gentlemen!" he thundered. "WELCOME... come ... come... come... come," sounded the echo. His tremendous baritone voice lifted and trembled and trilled all the way to the top of the tent as if on the wings of a dove.

"Charlie," I replied. "Charlie?"

"Yes, STEPHEN... even... even... even?" he boomed like some latter-day William Jennings Bryan.

"Charlie, it's just Shannon and me here, you KNOW...know... know...know."

"Ladies and gentlemen!" he thundered once again, discounting the accuracy of my crowd count. "We have sights that will amaze, that will amuse, that will stun! Please remain calm throughout the program! Please stay in your seats once the action begins! We cannot be responsible if you do not cooperate! You will laugh, you will cry, you will go dizzy with glee! The white horses will fly, the tumblers will tumble, the trapeze artists will swing through the air with the greatest of ease!"

Shannon tugged on my sleeve, twice I think, because I couldn't take my eyes off of Charlie. "I want to go, Stephen."

"Really?"

"This is going to end badly, can't you see that gun?"

I didn't know this for sure, but then again, I had not always been thinking so clearly since I died. So when she grabbed my hand and stood up, I stood up, too. We made our way to the aisle.

Charlie's voice dropped to a whisper. "Please don't go, Stephen. Just give me a second, Shannon, it'll be worth it to you."

Shannon was perturbed. "Spit it out, Brother Charlie. I don't have any more time to waste on you."

"Ah, this is the way you treat the Drama Club moderator now? Well, you are giving me no choice." He put the gun to his temple. "Leave and

I shoot the pedophile in the head."

Shannon was blasé. "Let's go," she repeated to me. "Blow your brains out, Brother Charlie. Like we care."

"Soft, you!" he said. "A word or two before you go. I have done the state some service, and they know it, no more of that. When in your letters, these unlucky deeds relate, speak of me as I am, nothing extenuate."

Shannon agreed to that: "Fine, we will nothing exterminate. You are a bad man, Brother Charlie. You deserve whatever befalls you."

"I wasn't always a bad man."

"So you keep saying," I said. "When was that, exactly, when you were not always a bad man?"

"I don't blame you for being angry. I'm angry over what I did."

Shannon addressed me: "He's pleading for sympathy, do you hear that?"

I knew that, but all I could say to her was, "Who doesn't need understanding? Aren't we all guilty?"

"Stephen and Shannon, I have done you grievous harm, the both of you, and I beg your forgiveness."

"I'm not forgiving you for what you did to Stephen," she said. And I couldn't forgive him for what he did to Shannon.

"Tell him, Shannon," he said. "Tell him that you made all of that up. You trumped up these charges about Joel, and when I called you on it, you never forgave me."

I did not see that one coming. "That true, Shannon?"

"Let's go. Let him kill himself, it's only right. He'll feel better after. He can't feel worse, you know, because he probably can't feel anything. He's a monster."

She took my hand and pulled me out of the stands. As we approached the exit, our backs to the three-ring, a shot rang out. I froze and held my ground, horrified, sickened, wanting to turn back.

After an agonizingly long moment, the next sound we heard was Charlie's voice. "You see, Stephen? You can't leave, can you? You do have a conscience. You do."

I turned back and shouted at him, I was so furious. "No, you're wrong, Charlie. I don't care, not at all." When would the mind games end?

Perhaps the mind games would end soon, or so I hoped when I heard the next shot ring out, and the lights blinked out inside the big top and a thudding noise was made when something, or someone, fell to the packed-down dirt on the ground. We broke through the tent and raced into the sunlight, where Charlie did not greet us.

I asked her, "You have something you want to tell me, Shannon?"

"Luna Park, Luna Park," she said. "Where night is bright."

"Where day," I added, "is dark."

TWENTY-TWO

Q. 413. What is Hell?
A. Hell is a state to which the wicked are condemned,
and in which they are deprived of the sight of God
for all eternity, and are in dreadful torments.
—The Baltimore Catechism

It was nighttime and I was sitting in my cell, soaking my weary, aching feet in scalding water and Epsom salts. I heard the knock on the unlocked door. I quickly hid the bottle of Old Bushmills beneath my chair, behind the hem of my robes, and I called out, "Come in."

Enter, though not pursued by a bear, Brother Charlie.

You are very sharp tonight, Brothers, paying unusually close attention. I took us back almost thirty years, to the time when Charlie and I were working at Angel of Mercy and living in community together.

"Septimus, mind a visitor?" He took a seat on my narrow unmade bed.

"Why don't you make yourself at home, Charlie."

He chuckled. "How'd classes go today?"

Charlie was an eminence and a legendary teacher at the school for many years before I was assigned. He had been unceremoniously relieved of his principalship, but he was still revered. It was easy to see why. He had a way of talking to kids that I wanted to emulate, a precious way of saying to each of them: you matter simply because you do, I want to hear every single thing you want to tell me. He inspired such confidence—no, he inspired such passion. Other teachers envied and despised him. His freckled, flushed face and his bright eyes threatened no teenager—or so I believed they believed. He had no interest in being popular, I'll say that, and that solidified his hold on the kids. He curried no favor. A's were hard to come by in his classes. There did not seem to be the slightest trace of disingenuousness about him. His laugh was light and musical, like a flute in a Debussy symphony. His gaze, direct as a sunbeam. A sunbeam bounced off a magnifying glass into your eyeball.

Nobody was using the word "gay" back then, as I said, and nobody was willing to speak openly about his or anybody's homosexuality, but that didn't curtail everyone's glib assumptions about Charlie's orientation, which was another word nobody used yet.

To return to his innocent-sounding question as to how my day had gone, I was a young teacher and didn't know any better. One day I thought everything was going swimmingly. Next day, I was scrambling for the Titanic lifeboat. I was teaching a curriculum handed down to me by the dean and every day building up my limited enthusiasm for books I would never have personally selected. Not that it mattered much. It was a strange era. Anybody who survived the '60s deserves a medal.

That was when Charlie noticed I was soaking my feet.

"That looks inviting."

I told him it felt pretty good, that it was something I did every single night.

Charlie made small talk, and I followed along: the new cook, the old cook arrested for shoplifting, the show now in rehearsal, the planning that was going into some assembly, the letters of college recommendation. But Charlie had something else on his mind. His voice barely above a whisper, he spoke hesitantly: "Been meaning to ask. How's Billy?"

I instantly regretted telling him about Billy that time he asked me about my students.

"Oh, he's fine. Excellent student. I don't understand why he gets mostly D's in his other classes. He just turned in— " I pointed to the stack of papers, "—a brilliant little paper on *Tale of Two Cities*."

"Best of crimes, worst of crimes, right, Septimus?"

"Is there something particular you want to say to me?"

"Septimus, I'm still freaked out."

"Billy will be all right if we take good care of him. He's a sensitive plant."

"No, I'm freaked about what you told me during community walk. Are you seriously thinking about leaving the order?"

"I'm not thinking about it tonight, Charlie," I said. "For one thing, I've got too many papers left to correct." True, my tone was a little dismissive, and a bit insincere. I had been vaguely contemplating such a course of action, but lately I just couldn't think of a good reason to leave. At the same time, I couldn't think of a good reason to stay. I had a retreat arranged for spring break, at which time I was going to give myself the chance to think through my options. Before, when I had vouchsafed this confidence to Charlie, I had done so with the idea of gaining his advice. But tonight, my feet aching, I almost wished I had never tipped my hand.

"This have anything to do with Billy?"

I pretended that I did not get the connection. "What are you talking about? He's just a sweet kid, a student who needs extra attention."

"Sure, he is. A sweet kid. Don't take my question in the wrong way, Septimus."

"Have you been talking with Billy, Charlie?"

"He's trying out for the play. I think I see a role for him one day, who knows? I'll keep my eye on him, just for you, Septimus."

I wanted to be alone again, in my cell, if it wasn't too much to ask.

"I hope you'll talk to me before you leave."

I promised him I would. I wouldn't think of doing anything like that without him, I might have said.

"And for the record, I hope you don't ever leave."

I was unaware of anyone's keeping a record, so it was easy to say

"Why not?" This sounds like a semi-sarcastic comeback, I understand. Not that I am above such pettiness, but in this case, I was curious. I wanted to know why he didn't want me to leave.

"Why not?" he parroted. "*Why not*, he wants to know. Well, because I'd miss you, Septimus, *that's* why not."

I was touched, and, besides that, I deserved his mock scorn. "Not to worry, Charlie. I'm a long way away from a decision, honest."

We pledged to resume the conversation at another time.

"Want to go to dinner Friday night?" he asked. "Just us, we can catch up."

"Sure, Charlie." Anything to get him out of my cell.

"Good, I'd like that," he said and stood up, gathering himself for a second, standing close to me. He touched my arm and wheeled around to go, adding over his shoulder, "Hope your tootsies feel better."

"Thanks, Charlie."

"And another thing. I maybe shouldn't say anything... so take this in the right way..." He pointed toward the leg of my chair. "Septimus, there's no answer to be found in that bottle."

"You're right. But it does contain all the questions."

I shouldn't have said that. It was true, but I shouldn't have said it. I hurt his feelings, and he left my cell.

When he was gone, I said to myself, "Me, too, Charlie, love you, too."

TWENTY-THREE

Q. 327. Which are the sins against hope?
A. The sins against hope are presumption and despair.
                                    —*The Baltimore Catechism*

O nce again, I found myself behind the wheel of my reliable Prius, tooling silently down the open road. *Damn. Damn. Damn.* That's my father's prized phraseology blazing into my brain: "tooling down the open road." Another example of his pet phrases was his response to less than optimal planning or execution on my part, when he would accuse me of running a so-called loose operation. Such "loose operations" were, to him, a by-product of "pipe-dreams," my insidious, debilitating fantasies unrooted in practicality. These he picked off like snipe, one by one, from the blind that was his conception of being my loving dad.

Sometimes, I confess, as my Prius and I tool along in my loose operation of an afterlife under the influence of my pipe dream, I wonder if I will ever again run into him, so to speak. The old man and I, we were the perfect pairing—matches and lighter fluid.

That is when I saw looming in the rapidly closing distance a forlorn hitchhiker. Even in the afterlife of somebody like me it might not be a very advisable proposition, hitchhiking. But as I approached the out-stretched thumb and the expectant face of the hitchhiker, things grew weirder still.

I slowed down when I saw who it was standing by the side of the road, dressed in green army fatigues jacket and hiking boots and blue jeans. Will wonders ever cease, goes the old chestnut. Nope, evidently they will not. I stopped. He opened the car door and hopped in.

"Hi, Brother Septimus," said Billy, who didn't look a day older than when he slumped and gazed dreamily out the window of my classroom thirty years ago. "Thanks for stopping."

"Billy, my God, it's you."

"In the flesh. Or— " He looked around as if the test answers were hanging in midair like figs on a tree. "Whatever."

"But it's Brother *Stephen* now, Billy." Like this made a difference, Brothers.

"Really, Brother Septimus? OK. Hi, Brother *Stephen*. How are you?"

"Hi, Billy. I'm—" What was I supposed to say? *Fine? Dead?*

He graciously filled in the gap of my awkwardness and surprise: "Going my way, Brother?"

"Seems like it. Where is that?"

"Good question," said Billy, but something told me he had a better chance of knowing than I did.

I hit the gas pedal and the two of us were on our way, together again.

———

"Nice car, Brother. I been looking for some transportation, where'd you get your wheels?"

"I have no idea."

"OK, if that's the way you want to be. Kind of a weird-looking car, I like it."

I made a half-hearted effort to defend my default afterlife selection of an automobile.

"So what's new, Brother? Where you been keeping yourself?"

Where to begin? My heart grew faint, so instead I asked Billy if he wanted me to put on the radio, and he ignored the question. I was glad, in case there was a repeat of the radio interview, or maybe an interview with that ambitious charlatan, Dr. Inskeep.

"I didn't intend to get shot, you know," Billy volunteered, reading my mind, I have to say. "That was not part of the plan. Not that I had one. A plan, I mean. When I started out, I mean."

I said I was devastated when I heard.

"Yeah. I know. Me, too. I'm sorry."

"So you weren't trying to get yourself killed?" I kept my eyes on the road, not that it mattered much, of course.

"Not really. Though I was a pretty miserable teenager, I'm probably not the best source of information. Which you know."

A billboard popped up. Take a guess. Second thought, don't bother.

Luna Park, It's Luna Park!
Chapter 10, verse 31,
Gospel According to Mark!

Billy noticed and he sounded disappointed: "Damn, I need to go there sometime. I heard about Luna Park, that it was pretty cool. I wish I had gone there when I had the chance. You been there, Brother?"

"You've already been there, Billy. Like most places, we missed it the first time."

"That bad, huh?"

I had another subject on my mind. "Billy, you know when people we care about die, we wonder how we might have let them down."

"Get over it, Brother. People make choices. Though to tell the truth, when I was bleeding out in the 7-Eleven parking lot, funny the things I was thinking about. Like about you. About how you were going to feel bad I had done something so dumb as to get myself all shot and killed. It wasn't the cops' fault, either. I would have shot me, too."

"I wish it were that easy to forgive myself, but I can't."

"That's just how you are, Brother. You miss me?"

"All the time."

"Well, we have the opportunity to get reacquainted now." If only the wisdom of staying in the moment had occurred to him three decades ago. "What is chapter something, verse whatever, Gospel of Mark?"

"This is weird, but I actually recall that we talked about that passage at length in class, remember?"

"Sure I do," he said, before admitting: "Well, not really."

"*The last shall be first and the first shall be last.* That's what Jesus said, and who knows better?"

"I never understood that part."

But I knew he really did. He would put it all in place. Of the four evangelists, Mark was the perfect reporter. Luke's Jesus was all sweetness and light, lambs and friendship and family. Matthew's was infused with politics and religion. John's was the poet's Jesus, perhaps the greatest gospel of them all. But Mark's was different—his was the emotional Jesus, the man with feelings bigger than the universe, Jesus with an attitude, spoiling for a fight, with a "Get a load of this" implicit in everything he said and did. But such discussion and such catching up for us were destined to be, at the very least, forestalled. Because when I went around the bend, there was a roadblock.

"What are you going to do, Brother? This looks serious. Hey, wait a second. Is that Brother Charlie there? It *is* Brother Charlie. Now there's one serious nutcase of a Brother."

Billy was right, it was Charlie, and as it turned out he was present alongside every single one of you, Brothers: Brother Paulus, Brother Harold, Brother Ignatius, Brother Gregory Called G, and old Tom Newgarten—the entire Definitorium.

"Brother Charlie told me I could have a part in the school play. *West Side Story.* I was going to be a Jet. When you're a Jet, you're a Jet all the way, from your first cigarette to your last dying day, you know."

"So I heard."

"He said I had the electric stage presence of a leopard."

I winced and flinched. So downtown Charlie. I said, "That was probably intended to be a compliment."

"But I said no, thanks, if I wasn't Maria, I wasn't interested."

I fell silent.

"*Brother?* That's a joke, Brother."

I hit the brakes. I needed to know something. I needed to know for myself what happened with Billy. And to do that I had to put myself back there, into Billy's climactic scene. What's being dead good for if you can't resolve a mystery or two?

———

So there we were, transported (just go with it, Brothers), deposited in the parking lot of the 7-Eleven. It was a cold and gorgeous night and Billy had run out from the store, with me in close pursuit, two steps behind.

"Stop," I cried. "Billy, just stop, this is crazy."

Then, miraculously, Billy did stop, if only to utter the following: "Too late, Brother Septimus. I told you, there's no turning back now. Nobody asked you to come back into my life. And nobody asked you to bring me back into mine." He was agitated. "You can be such a pill sometimes, Brother, you know that? Not everything gets to be made clear to you. You think it's always about you, don't you, Brother Septimus?"

That was fair enough, if harsh, and his anger might have been richly merited by me, so all I could say was: "It's not too late for a different outcome."

He stopped and faced me. He decided, fine, let's all play along. "Look, see? I told you." He waved the paper bag in front of me, the bag filled with the money he had made the clerk pull from the cash register drawer. "What kind of outcome did you have in mind?"

The police officers were positioned behind their cruiser, pointing guns at us.

I stepped in between Billy and the cops, to shield him. "Officers, wait, slow down, everybody just be calm. This is not what it appears. This is a confused young boy. He is going to cooperate. Give me a second, please, to talk some sense into him."

"Brother," said Billy. "You realize it's not going to end well, right?"

"You know, Shannon said something similar a minute ago."

"Who's Shannon? Never mind, but no matter what you do, it'll end just like last time for me, just so you know, OK?"

"You can step back from the brink, all you have to do is want to."

"That is the catch, you're right."

The cops screamed at us to hit the ground.

"Billy," I said, "just think for a second. You made a stupid mistake, that's all. We all make mistakes."

"Not like I do. Let's review facts. I'm a robber. I have a gun. We're in the crosshairs of these cops and they're going to shoot me dead. They don't have a choice."

"But you do, Billy."

"Now you're telling yourself a story, Brother."

"You didn't kill anybody."

"God, you are slow. I have a fucking gun, Brother, excuse the language—the fucking part. You should get out of the way now, because things are going to get messy."

The cops screamed again. The red and blue lights were flashing on top of their car.

"Put the gun down!" one of them said.

"Hit the deck!" said the other. "Now!"

"We can work this out later, Billy. I'll get you a lawyer. You haven't killed anybody."

"No, it's too late, Brother. Don't you know anything? It was too late for me from the first minute I walked into your class."

I faced the cops and pleaded, "Give us a second. He's just a mixed-up boy. Don't shoot. Don't shoot."

"Tell him to put down the gun, Brother Septimus."

Shocked, I looked toward the speaker, whose face was impossible to decipher in the glare of searchlights.

The cop spoke again. "It's me, Brother."

How the hell was I supposed to know who "me" was?

"Kenny?" he said. "Kenny Cochran?"

"Kenny?" This was a former student of mine. Like so many of my former students, he had been drawn to the ever-expanding professional opportunities available for a career in law enforcement. Maybe I could make that career choice work to our advantage. "Listen to me, Kenny. Listen carefully. Billy is just a crazy kid."

"Remember me, Brother?"

Not really. I remembered the so-called sentences and the alleged paragraphs he submitted but not quite his face.

"You gave me a C, Brother Septimus."

"*What?* What are you talking about?"

"You gave me a C when I was a senior."

Was he bargaining? "I'll change your grade, Kenny, I promise, just be patient."

"No way, I earned that C fair and square. That was the highest damn grade I ever got in English."

"OK, then. You're a cop, you went to Catholic school, you of all people understand how people sometimes aren't completely conscious of their motivations."

"Which is what we have to figure out, as readers. Just like you taught us, Brother."

"Exactly. Exactly right, Kenny. Here's your chance to read some pretty complex motivation. This kid is not thinking clearly."

The light must have gone on in Kenny Cochran's brain. I could practically see the night go soft with illumination around his haloed head.

"Hey," he said, musingly, "didn't you used to talk about something called a 'unreliable aviator'?"

"Yes, Kenny, yes. An unreliable narrator."

"Well, this boy here is pretty unreliable, as are most people who got a gun in their hand after committing a arm robbery. Which he's got a gun, Brother. That's pretty clear. Can't overinterpet a gun."

"Of course you can, you can overinterpret anything, Kenny, which is something I learned too late in…life. I wish everybody would just slow down."

"A gun's a gun and a robber's a robber, Brother."

Billy agreed, nodding and saying, "He's got a good point, Brother. Hard to argue with facts."

"There are no facts, Billy!" What a move on my part. Here I was picking an argument with a young robber who had a gun. How was this the appropriate occasion for a discussion of epistemology? "OK, maybe there are *some* facts. Maybe just a few."

"Time's running out," said Billy. "Don't worry, Brother. I made a pact with God. If he gets me out of this one, I promise I will be good forever. I'm putting God to the test, you see? It's going to be all right, trust in Him."

"Are you nuts? God tests us! We don't test God!"

"Don't be such a virgin, Brother. And don't tell me you of all people haven't been testing God your whole life."

Kenny called out: "Brother, we gotta come to a resolution here pretty soon. There's a guy with a gun we gotta disarm."

"Kenny," I said. "Give us a little more time, please."

"Brother, wish I could. If he was to up and shoot you, that would be on my head."

Life is all about timing, and, as I recalled, Kenny (who never turned in work when it was due) was the sort of guy who couldn't time an egg.

"Kenny, he's not going to shoot me. Tell him, Billy."

Billy started to think. I could tell. I didn't like that development.

If we had had the time, Billy might have wanted to put his hand on my arm. I could tell he needed to touch and be touched. Life could be pretty simple, when you boiled it down to the elements, assuming there were elements that could be reduced and you had the opportunity.

"It's going to be OK, Brother Septimus," said Billy, "don't worry." He gave me a look that communicated *What difference does it make now?* It also said *I'm really sorry* with a little bit of *Things are going to get pretty interesting pretty quick and if I were you I would get the hell out of the way.*

That's when I remembered: *Oh, yes, of course, certainly. Only the old are afraid of dying.*

And I remembered that all over again for the following reason: I was old, and I was afraid of dying, even here and now.

But Billy was not afraid, which I think will be clear to you in the next instant because he took that gun, that realistic-looking fake gun, and aimed it at my chest.

"Don't do that, kid," Kenny cried out.

"Sorry, Brother, goodbye," said Billy.

Billy head-faked left and went right, as if this were a pick-up basketball game, and I went with the fake, so he was in the clear, nothing between him and the drawn policemen's service revolvers, which instantly rang out, *pop pop pop pop pop pop pop pop pop pop pop pop pop pop pop*. The bills were sent flying, released from the bag like confetti from a magician, and Billy dropped to the asphalt parking lot, where he would soon be bleeding out from his chest wounds, dazzling red flowerings, and in a moment, maybe two, he would be totally dead to me once more and to everyone else in his or anybody else's world.

The ground is where he stayed, until he was hitchhiking on the road to wherever it was we were now going. On my tongue I tasted salty tears.

———

A herd of cars was positioned in the middle of the road, and a large war party had assembled, everything and everyone illuminated by flashing lights. I recognized the sedans from your carpool, Brothers, all those anonymous four-door black Fords we checked out when we needed to go off campus. Charlie held a bullhorn up to his mouth. "Stop!"

I stopped.

"Stephen, you and Billy get out and put your hands on top of the car! Move very slowly! And keep your hands visible."

Everybody was giving me orders. I guess I looked as if I had turned into somebody who needed them.

I called out, "Why?"

"We have a few questions to ask you, Stephen."

So Charlie was there with all the rest of you members of the Definitorium. Talk about strange bedfellows. And stranger bedfellows were in attendance, too, for the Longcoats were present, too.

"Stevie," one of those jackbooted nutcases yelled out, "we have Shannon, she's cooperating and she's looking forward to seeing you, so come on in, big fella."

Something told me that the Shannon reference meant they were overplaying their hand, so I didn't believe it, though don't ask me why. Besides, I was tired of being told what to do. I leaned out the window and shouted, "You're not taking me alive, Copper!"

Charlie shrugged his shoulders. "Yeah, sure, of course we're not taking you alive, and your point is?"

Billy weighed in: "I think we can get through this, Brother."

I turned toward Billy. "You are not going to do anything crazy, Billy—not this time, please."

"Crazy didn't never stop me, Brother."

Charlie spoke again into his bullhorn, clearly enjoying the stage. "Stephen, looks like the shoe's on the other foot."

That's when I realized I was lost in a moment of truth.

Billy sensed it, too. "Go for it, Brother. Just drive."

"Think so, Billy?"

"It's what I would do. And you know how successful I was. Call me crazy, but something tells me we can literally drive right through this problem."

"You think, Billy? Right through it?"

"Yes, that's what the gas pedal is there for, you know. To fucking floor it."

"Last shall be first, Billy!"

So they would, so they would. Jesus said so, didn't He?

"Mark 10:31!" Billy shouted. "Mark 10:31!"

I hit the gas pedal, prepping myself for the inevitable impact. What difference would it make now? I was living a charmed death so far, wasn't I? I kept accelerating, pedal to the floor, beyond the point of impact, and Billy screamed *Yes!* the instant before I was about to make contact, and to tell the truth, I kept accelerating beyond that point, and Billy screamed *Fuck yes!*, and we broke through to the other side of the roadblock, which is where, go figure, the last would be first once again.

———

If there were dust to clear, the dust must have cleared, or perhaps I missed it, and in a heartbeat or two the Prius was now zooming down the road, taking us away from your clutches, Brothers. Don't forget to call when you get a chance.

When I glanced back to see what I could see in my rearview mirror, which is really the preferred point of view for a Brother, as you know, or any human being for that matter, there was nothing left to see. They were all gone, Charlie and Company.

And when I looked over to high-five Billy with gratitude overflowing in my frazzled, drained, and distorted heart, he was gone. He was missing all over again, gone to wherever the likes of my Billy must go. I missed him. I would always miss him, wouldn't I? Heartbreak and death are versions of the same thing.

Off to the side—what else would you expect? There was another billboard, my last billboard of the afterlife, as it would turn out, this one conveying news that was very much like most of the news available about the goings-on in the world I had left behind but could not help recalling, a sad and unsurprising double-message:

COME TO LUNA PARK!
Luna Park, It's Luna Park!
Closed for Repairs, Stage is Dark!

TWENTY-FOUR

Q. 273. Should we wait until we are in extreme
danger before we receive Extreme Unction?
A. We should not wait until we are in extreme danger
before we receive Extreme Unction, but if possible
we should receive it whilst we have the use of our
senses.

—The Baltimore Catechism

I was bone-tired and battered, and even my ears throbbed, and the cartilage in my knees had gone to lead, and my arms felt heavy and slippery as two sea lions scooped up from the sea. Maybe I did have a car accident. If so, I was evidently going to be the last to know. The next thing I was aware, I found myself in a strange bed in an unfamiliar room.

If these wicked turns in my report to the Definitorium have been giving you Brothers a case of whiplash, imagine how much pleasure such transitions are providing for my cervical vertebrae.

I wonder what old Saint Thomas More would have to say about this particular Catholic operating horizontally under the current set of circumstances. It was he, as you recall, who once upon a time had a lot to say about Catholics' feeling pretty good about their ever-after prospects after having taken refuge in their Catholic deathbeds. I wasn't regretting being in this bed, that was for sure, and I certainly could not fathom the prospect of leaving it any time soon without benefit of a Fire Department stretcher. And I guess it would have to be considered my de facto deathbed, as any bed I was in would necessarily have to be so considered, and I suppose I was as good a Catholic as I was ever going to be. Score one for foresight on the part of the eminent Man for All Seasons.

As for me, I was a Man for One Season, and a strange season at that, waking up in that strange bed. Not that I can verify anything from personal experience, but I recall having acquired the information at some point in my existence that this was not an uncommon occurrence, waking up in a strange bed. Unless I was wrong, it happened all the time to mortal beings, apparently after Saturday nights on the town spent in the world I had recently departed.

The prom, Luna Park, Billy, and the blockade: all that seemed so long ago. Yet I kept thinking about what these experiences meant for me now and also what Shannon would say once we reconnected. Where she was now, I was about to find out.

It was a four-poster bed with a billowy lime-green canopy high over my head. The mattress was unbelievably, I might even say obscenely, comfortable: soft and firm at the same time, nothing like Brother-issued and -authorized sleeping supplies. The white down comforter was somehow cool and toasty at the same time, and it seemed to float an inch above my outstretched body. Eucalyptus scents threaded the air, tinged with undertones of something savory, rosemary perhaps. Shadows swathed the prominent bookcases lined along the wall, as well as the dresser where there gathered elegant little bottles (perfumes? essential oils? nitroglycerin? how would I know?). Shadows also touched the red Chinese armoire, the ship's lithograph on the wall, and a gilt-framed picture of a smiling mother holding an infant with a man (the father?) standing behind them, proprietarily. A pretty blue French baroque chair suitable for the toilette of a tiny baroness was positioned next to a petite table holding a flickering votive candle. There was one elaborate, frilly, gossamer-curtained window, a large one, and one door (to a hallway?), which was closed. The whole room was luxuriously sepia-toned, like a daguerreotype from another century.

Then I had a grim, grim thought. Did my afterlife traffic in those bed-and-breakfast joints? So be it, I supposed, as long as I didn't have to make small talk with elderly, noisy strangers on the landing about their choice antiques and their fascinating medical conditions.

I was never much of a sleeper, as I think I may have mentioned one or two hundred times, and on this occasion I do not recall feeling rejuvenated. So I do not remember sleeping, much less sleeping in this bed, only the moment of evidently waking up in it. If you have been following along, Brothers, you would know that I had not dozed since before that last unforgettable session of mine in the Definitorium. On the admittedly limited basis of my own personal research, I can report to you that sleeping, which barely makes logical sense in our mortal lifetimes, and appears to have no physiological justification for its utility, makes less sense at the next stage.

Even so, I was wearing a nightshirt, though a nightshirt that was based on the design of my Brother's robes: black and long, made of coarse fiber. As for my robe, it was draped over a piece of modular furniture that resembled a kneeling bench, a prie-dieu, which is a word, though not as much fun to say as *revenant*, nonetheless lovely to roll around in one's mouth. Abandoned across the room, my garment was made to look bleak and sad and disembodied, and I was almost lonely for it. Clothes apparently do make the (dead) man.

I took another glance at that picture, the one that featured the something-told-me not-quite-deliriously-happy family unit. The very pretty bespectacled mom had the wan half-smile that comes with being resigned to a marriage and a love that had gone a little bit sour over time; the handsome dad with the big cliff of a forehead, the bleak gaze of a man who had grown professionally accustomed to disappointing friends as well as colleagues, subordinates as well as superiors. And I gradually realized, the longer I studied it, that though I had never seen this particular photo before, it was a picture of my parents taken when they were quite young, and which indicated that the infant had to be, well, me. Or *I*, if you must insist, Brothers, who are busy poring over your *Elements of Guile.*

OK, then. Where was I? Had I managed to work my way into my own childhood home, you think? Wrong, Brothers, very wrong.

There were pointillist streams of sunlight flowing in through the gauzy curtains. Beyond the window covering I could make out the shadowy outlines of tall, slender trees that seemed to be bending slowly left, then right, like the necks of graceful foraging giraffes. There were no clocks that I could find in the room, but nonetheless I was slowly coming to the awareness that perhaps it was not morning after all, but the equivalent of a late afternoon.

The other realization gradually dawning was that I was not alone under this comforter in this strange bed.

When I turned my attention to the side, I learned that I was indeed lying next to somebody, in this case somebody named Shannon Reed, whose head and hair and bare arms were visible. She appeared to be, as far as I could tell, sound asleep. And preliminary reconnaissance indicated that she did not seem to be wearing that pretty prom dress I so vividly recalled. Though naturally curious, I was not quite prepared to do much more in the way of research as to her current habiliments, such as they may or may not have been.

Maybe this is Too Much Information, and maybe the truth is obvious or possibly irrelevant, but I had never before found myself in bed with a woman. Based upon my fresh experience, however, I could appreciate the appeal, certainly, of waking up next to one. Yes, that is an understatement.

Shannon was turned away from me, but I could hear her breathing softly, deeply, sweetly, her respiration calming me, calming the whole world, to tell the truth, the way the sea does when you sit in a cabin near the shore and read a book before a flickering fireplace, sipping a cup of tea, or something more potent.

The body of a woman recumbent beneath a down comforter is a sight to see, Brothers, not to flaunt my experience. And the bed's resultant topography? It is exhilarating.

To cut to the voyeuristic chase: Did I break my vows at some point in the recent past? Oh, like, say, last night? Wouldn't you like to know, Brothers? That would have been something we would have had in common. I would like to know, too. For I am not prepared to say yes, I will admit that. Though let me also add that I am not prepared to reveal anything, keeping intact my personal record of always being the last to be informed.

From far away I heard a voice that seemed to be part of the room, full of sepiated shadows and of radiating warmth. "You awake, Stephen?" Shannon's husky, sleep-seeped voice rocked me.

I murmured yes, that I was awake.

Slowly, slowly, slowly she moved toward me. Inhale, Brother Stephen, exhale. My eyes turned away, looking up in the direction of the green canopy, where they would remain fixed for the time being while her body-shifting-under-the-comforter sounded like the incoming surf and I was on the shore waiting for the veritable message in a bottle.

"You OK?" she said after the sea sucked back out, and the silence died again.

"I don't know. I think so. How about you?"

"I am happy."

I quickly turned my head toward her. She was still there. "You are *happy*, you said?" I thought I had better double-check, having never heard anybody use the word in such close proximity to me.

"How can you not know this, Stephen?"

Now, that was a concept: *happy.*

Perhaps it was high time for me to embrace it.

And her.

And she, in the same instant, me.

Or what was left of me.

And both of us.

—

"Your flesh, *my* flesh."
"My flesh, *your* flesh."

~

THE GRAND DEPOSITOR

I have been ignoring you for a long time now, sir, for reasons that are so obvious they must be personal. I have to grant that I have greatly enjoyed the sweet little respite from your increasingly annoying pestering. You see, I have concluded that you and I no longer have anything worth talking about. There remains an excellent chance, to be sure, that we never did. But I see from the way you are wildly gesticulating off to the side that this bedroom development has caught your attention, and because I find myself in a generous, expansive mood, I don't see any immediate downside to acknowledging your wretched, piteous, voyeuristic existence. I do so even though I do not think you will ever understand what took place between Shannon and me, because, to tell the truth, it is even somewhat vague for me. What brings together two people, do you suppose? You may be thinking that I am speaking in genteel euphemisms. But I am not. The longer I am dead, the less I can explain myself. Love, our highest and purest state, is inevitably combined with elements that are not so rarefied, and so what? If death has taught me anything, it is that the hierarchies of body and soul were never absolute in our lifetimes, and they are not so later on. We are capable of love only because we have bodies, because we are bodies, because we are or were mortal. Philosophy 101, right? Go on, make fun of me, I don't care. Perhaps that we were born into our physical bodies in the first place is the reason love must exist, if it ever does. And love is pretty rare, when you get down to it. It might qualify as a miracle. And if someday I am ever about to be canonized, let some Devil's Advocate weigh in, let him try to tarnish my reputation by suggesting that love is no miracle, because I hope somebody will step up and, in a rush of sanity, tell the ridiculous watchdog that he is simply in mortal error. I wish I had known all this before, when I was alive and could have done something about it. But then again, maybe I have finally done something about it. Who knows? Any second now, imagine it, I may just burst into bloom. As Salome says, "The mystery of love is greater than the mystery of death." And I don't know about you, but I would avoid antagonizing somebody like her, somebody with a sword and a waiting silver platter in her hands. So, please, go, please, and leave Shannon and me to ourselves. There is nothing here for the likes of you.

—

"Remember what you said to me, when you decided to join the Brothers?" I thought we had covered this ground before, and besides, I was finding it tough aligning my speech faculties with what was left of my increasingly limited cognitive function. "You said, *Maybe in the next life we can be together.* Do you remember saying that?"

"I do remember, and I did mean it, Shannon."

"In case this matters, when you said that you broke my heart."

"I was eighteen and I'd made up my mind to go to the novitiate, what else was I supposed to say?"

"You said it wasn't personal, joining the Brothers. If I could have, I would have let myself hate you."

"I was an idiot. Everything is always personal."

"And everything is serious and everyone plays for keeps every single minute. Or they should."

"I know that now, Shannon."

"You knew that then."

"Well, maybe in the next life we *can* be together."

I looked around. I felt increasingly at home here, here in the room Shannon would obviously call her own. Almost as if I had been here before, but then again, that couldn't be true. But what difference does such a fine distinction make anymore? The family photo was confusing. Maybe dreams in the afterlife were like the other kind.

"I'm going to whip up some dinner, stay here and rest." She swooped out of the room, not wearing her white prom gown but still trailing clouds of glory. I always wanted to use that phrase, *trailing clouds of glory*, not that I knew what it meant any more than I would bet Mr. William Wordsworth did when he wrote that poem.

Death is the mother of invention. And, I think I can faithfully say now, of plagiarism. And of desire. And perhaps of Whoever God Himself may Be.

———

I have been telling you the story of a love that never managed to happen, oldest story in the books. But Brothers, this was one time it finally did manage to happen, in ways that were as sweet as they were inconceivable, which describes the ways of the world and my world pretty well. How could I have missed, in the course of my first fifty-five years, understanding something so fundamentally self-evident? I loved her, Brothers. When people love each other, they show each other how much they care. They can't help it. You are not going to understand what happened in that bed, in that room, but it isn't what you think, that I can guarantee. It wasn't like that. The images in your head will not correspond to the actuality. It was different. It was everything. It was. We were Shannon and Stephen, together all over again as never before.

TWENTY-FIVE

Q. 813. Which are the chief spiritual works of mercy?
A. To admonish the sinner, to instruct the ignorant, to
counsel the doubtful, to comfort the sorrowful, to
bear wrongs patiently, to forgive all injuries, and to
pray for the living and the dead.
                                        —*The Baltimore Catechism*

"Put your feet up, Stephen," Shannon called out from the kitchen. I was in that part of her cabin I might call a living room. I die and I find myself spending quality time in a *living* room. What can I say? It's too late to try.

I have come to appreciate those peoples who buried their warrior kings in big vaults with their loyal dogs, their sacred texts, their slick longboats, and their trusty bows and arrows. You never know. Such things might come in handy for the dead. No point in taking chances. It is the same principle I would have applied to my former lifetime. In a perfect world, I would have packed *everything*. The desk, the microwave, the Oxford English Dictionary, the croquet mallet, the TV, the basketball, the stemware, the wisteria in spring bloom, everything. With all that baggage, it would take me a year to get through airport security. So what? You never know, I say. Now that those deceased warrior kings and I have one experience in common, I can testify with more energy than a sweaty lumberjack that you just never know. I am glad that at least I took the notepad in my robe.

I listened to Shannon at work on dinner. I could hear the chopping on the counter block, the clinking of glass, the refrigerator door opening and closing, the clang of a pot and a pan and a spoon, the cabinets snapping closed. It sounded so pleasantly normal, so human, so different from the level of noise that emanated from the Brothers' refectory kitchen when the employed prep cooks were making meals.

"I'd like to offer you some wine," she said, "but since I don't have any, I won't."

That was all right by me. "Work your magic, Julia Child," I said. *I should probably offer my help in the kitchen*, I thought. That was what modern men were supposed to do. But I had taken my place in the easy chair, near the crackling fireplace, settled down with my enlightened reflections when the phone rang. It better not be Charlie.

"Stephen," Shannon called out after the third ring. "My hands are full, get that, would you?"

I picked up the phone, and before I could get out a cheery hello—

"Brother Stephen? Tom Newgarten here."

"Tom!" Why wouldn't I be surprised?

"Tell me something, Brother."

"You got it."

"What the hell do you think you are doing?"

"Tom, nice to hear your voice, too. It's not what it seems, though."

"It better not be. As you are well aware, we're not supposed to have ex parte communications with Shannon Reed, not under any circumstances. We have a legal process underway, you know, and you could royally fuck things up if you're not careful."

"That's not my intention, Tom, to royally fuck things up. But since when did my intention matter? Tell me that, would you?"

"The fiscal viability of the order hangs in the balance of negotiations like this. This is business we're talking about."

"You have a point, I suppose, but that's not really my problem anymore, and besides, I gotta go, Tom."

"Where do you have to go?"

I looked outside the window to the tree stump. Nearby, an ax leaned up against a cord of unsplit firewood, inviting this squire to activity, industry, purpose, not to mention the avoidance of Tom Newgarten, Esquire. "The fire is going out. I need to go cut up some kindling."

"We're not done talking."

"We are, Tom, we are truly done. I'm having dinner."

"With Shannon Reed? I knew it. I have to advise you that you cannot have dinner alone with Shannon Reed."

"Have it your way. Join us."

"Stephen, listen to me. You don't know what you're doing."

I didn't bother to respond, because I would have said that, for a change, I knew exactly what I was doing—or that, if I didn't know now, I soon enough would.

I hung up the phone. Shannon called out: "Who was it, Stephen?"

"A voice from my past," I said, without pedantically adding that all the voices I was hearing emanated from that place.

Shannon hurried out into the living room, a stricken look on her face, her hands worrying the *Luna Park!* logo imprinted on her apron. "What is it that you told your voice from the past?"

"I forgot we got you that apron. Quite a place, Luna Park, and I was just…"

"Stephen."

"Shannon. OK, I told him I was not available anymore."

"Good."

"Good, you say?"

"Yes, good."

"You know, Shannon, it is good. Just like you."

She pointed out the window. "We need kindling. Get to work, Paul Bunyan."

———

After I chopped the wood, I was tired all over again. After not sleeping for what felt like my whole life, I seemed to be cultivating a nice new habit. I closed my eyes and for a few minutes I must have dozed off. When I woke up, the house felt different, as in spectacularly warm and cozy. In addition, night, or its equivalent, had fallen. The lamps in the room were all burning brightly, even ferociously. They were gorgeous retro standing lamps, with beautiful gold glass kitschy globes that I had not noticed before. And there was piano music coming from somewhere. I'm guessing it was Satie, it was so plaintive and inviting and deviously simple, like some people I could name, or be.

"Daddy?" said the little girl from across the room. She was sitting cross-legged upon what appeared to be an ancient Persian rug. She held a book that was almost as big as she was. Her yellow hair fell in ringlets. She was wearing a red velvet dress, complete with a little black bow beneath her dollhouse teacup of a chin. She looked to be five, maybe six. "The fire looks nice. It's toasty in here. You did a good job, Daddy."

I nodded, buying time, inviting understanding to pay a visit.

"Daddy?" she said again. She was speaking to me.

Tell me, Brothers, how was I supposed to answer a question like that?

"Should I have Mommy make you a martini, Daddy?"

Precocious little child of my imaginings, don't you think, Brothers? Still, I didn't believe that a martini was such a good idea under the circumstances. I said nothing because I had been fresh out of good ideas since the time before I first left her mother after high school, before the girl had ever existed.

Shannon came out of the kitchen into the living room.

"Is dinner almost ready, Mommy? I'm kinda hungry."

"Yes, precious, any minute." Then Shannon addressed me: "Why don't you read Molly a story, Stephen? You know how Molly loves to hear you read to her."

"I do?"

She tilted her head side to side and mouthed, "Follow the bouncing ball, Stephen."

"Molly?" I whispered, seeking clarification.

Shannon's eyes opened wide, which was on her somehow a delightful mannerism.

"That's quite a little bouncing ball," I said to Shannon, and then I said to Molly, "Why don't you come here with your book, sweetie, and we can read it before dinner."

Molly yipped with glee as she scrambled up onto my lap with her book, which I could see was titled *Delia, A Duck*. I opened the cover and read to her. What else was there for me to do?

—

Delia was a duck, and who doesn't love a duck?

Now, you should also know that Delia was a very beautiful duck. If you saw her swimming in her lake, or bobbing her head above the water, or walking along the shore, you would smile, because she would make you so happy.

As you would imagine, all her lovely little ducklings adored her, just as you would if you were a duckling. They never had to say to her, "Mom, slow down, you're going too fast!" She knew exactly how slow to go and what her little ones liked to eat. And boy, did they like to eat. They were hungry because they were so busy growing—just like you!

One day, the clouds turned black overhead. Surely, a terrible storm was coming. That was the day all the ducklings would find out how brave Delia the Duck was and how much she loved and cared for them. It was the scariest and the best day of the ducklings' lives. And soon you will hear why, for this is the story the ducklings would tell over and over again for the rest of their lives—to their own ducklings, when the time came. This was the story I heard when I was a child, which I am now telling you.

"Mom," said one of the ducklings, who was named Danny. "I'm scared of the rain."

"Nonsense, honey," Delia said. "It's just water."

"But water in the wrong place," cried out another duckling, Debbie. Debbie sometimes liked to spark with Delia.

"And the wind," wailed a third duckling, Donny. "I'm scared of the wind. It just might carry me away, into the trees."

"Oh, Donny," said Debbie with her superior airs. "You are such a silly duck."

But that hurt Donny's feelings. "I am not a silly duck. Tell her so, Mom."

And Delia did. Then she gathered all her ducklings around her, including the ones who had not worried about the rain: Denny and Delilah and Dominick and Dunstan and Darlene and Dmitri.

"Darlings," she said. "This is your first rainstorm. Such things happen in life, you will see. If we stay together, though, everything will be fine."

Even Delia was a little bit concerned after a while when she felt the rain coming down so hard. So she huddled everybody up beside a big oak tree, which provided a little bit of shelter. But hours later, it was still raining hard and the ducklings were growing more and more distressed.

"We're so far from the lake!" cried one. "How did we get so far away?"

"The wind is scary!" said another.

And Delia noticed the water coming down the hillside in bigger and bigger rivulets, and she had an idea.

"Follow me, my little ducklings." She stepped into

one of those little currents, and the ducklings followed bravely, good little ducklings that they were.

Soon the current was carrying them downhill, and so fast!

"Whee!" cried Danny, and so did Donny and Denny. "Whee!"

In only a minute or two they were approaching the lake, which was their home.

"Hang on, my little ducklings, this is where we get off!"

And one by one they splashed into the little lake.

"We're home," said Delilah.

"Where we belong," said Darlene.

"Stay together," Delia encouraged them. "That's what we have learned today. If we stay together, whatever happens, we can always find our way home."

———

That was the story of Delia, who was a duck, a story I read to Molly, who said she loved that story best of all and who was still seated on my lap long after the ducks found their way home. Brothers, are you following the bouncing ball? If you are, you can see I had had my glimpse into a life that once upon a time might have been mine.

———

After dinner, my first and only meal of my afterlife, Shannon and I sat at opposite ends of the table, which was lit up by a dozen candles. By now golden Molly had retreated to her room, into that infinitesimally small window before emerging a homeschooled teenager employed at the Crestfallen Café with a biker boyfriend by the name of Les.

"How did you know that was my favorite dish?"

"Are you going to stop asking questions like that, Stephen?"

"OK, right." I changed the subject, which is something I do when at a loss, which is something I usually am. "I'm sorry the lawyer tracked me down," I said.

"No big deal. Besides, it's sort of beside the point now."

"Are we ever going to talk about it?"

"It" did not refer to the phone call, of course. "Do *you* want to talk about it?"

"I think we probably should. Better late than never." I couldn't corral the sigh before it seeped out of my chest.

"There's nothing much to say. Still, one thing I'll never get is that you never got what Brother Joel was up to. How could you have missed it?"

"You never told me, for starters."

"It was obvious."

"I'm sorry, I was a teenager. I didn't know such things happened."

"You sure about that?"

"I could never let myself think that way, I know that much."

"Let's stop. This is not a good idea."

"No, tell me what he did. Just tell me the truth."

"You can't do anything about it. Even the Brothers know that, which is why they're offering me all that money. I don't need money."

"But you were the one who sued the order. You were the one who called the question."

"What option did I have?"

"Let's go."

"Where, Stephen?"

"There is another option."

I didn't know why and I didn't know how, and I didn't know what I was going to do when I got there, but I knew where to find Charlie.

———

Dinner must have gone on longer than I supposed, because the sun was coming up as we drove along the coast highway. We both were so silent, we might have been traveling on a magic carpet. I guess we felt the grim weight of impending resolution that we could only find at one place, the Hanging Gardens.

Meanwhile, winds violently whipped the trees, and I worried they might snap. Branches were bending severely, here and there almost scraping the ground. Strangely, our car was unaffected. We turned off the gusty road and drove along the gravel path up a hill until we came to the awful place Shannon had taken me before.

"Now what?" she wanted to know.

"Now what? Now we make this up as we go along."

We hurried up the sharp incline, face first into the stiffening wind. I don't know why we hurried. I know I dreaded what awaited us.

After a steep trek, we reached the clearing, the dreary spot where Shannon and I had gone once before. We were not the only ones present. The winds had calmed for a bit. The Longcoats were there, as before, only this time in the company of Molly. Not little Molly who loved *Delia, A Duck,* but the post-adolescent Molly who was sitting on the back of a Harley with legs wrapped around *Les, A Loser.* There were dozens of school desks in place, all occupied but two. Also in attendance were a few classmates with whom I had long ago gone to Angel of Mercy High School, as well as many students Charlie and I both taught a long time ago, including—you guessed it—Billy. At first I was delighted to see Billy—delighted until, that is, the larger purpose of this strange convocation dawned.

I may not be telling you something you do not know, for all of you Brothers of the Definitorium were there, too, along with Tom Newgarten. Brother Provincial Paulus, you looked uncharacteristically distraught that for a fleeting moment I grasped the possibility that you did possess a soul after all. Were you sent back here to this assigned desk in search of that long-lost soul? Maybe that's why we return over and over again to our memories of high school. As everybody knows, that's when we first become conscious we have a soul.

Oh, and look who else was there. The legendary Brother Joel.

Yes, here we all were, the lost tribe, the remnants of Charlie's handiwork, apparently summoned together for a reckoning.

There was Charlie himself, standing tall in his black robes before us, black scarf tied around his neck. It seemed as if he were preparing to hold forth, like some evangelist under a revivalist's tent. He appeared the way he always did when he assumed his position of preeminence in front of a class, absolutely sure of himself, captivated by the prospect of entertaining all who had gathered.

In a flash, I recalled the counsel he gave me about the art of teaching. "Teach to please yourself, Septimus. Do that and your students will follow you anywhere. Anywhere you want to take them." He was right, I realized all over again, and his counsel cut at least two ways, as did just about everything he ever said. I wanted, all over again, to hate him. "We do not truly know," he once said, "what effect we have on our kids' lives, but every now and then we get a glimmering—some sense we have made a difference." Yes, indeed, Charlie, such a big difference you made.

The pink sun was rising up through the evergreens, spilling light on the shadowy faces of all those Charlie had damaged in the long, long course of his miserable career.

"Charlie," I called.

"Stephen, nice to see you."

"You sure?"

"Stevie, take your seat. You and Shannon both. There are your desks, go on. And if you have something further to say, you will have to raise your hand."

"Charlie, I have a question."

"You always have a question, don't you, Stephen? Take your seat, would you?"

"One question on the table is, what did you do to Billy? That boy did not deserve what you did to him. Nobody did. But here's my point: I trusted you with what he told me. I trusted you with my feelings about him."

"Quite a little reunion here in your afterlife, Stephen," he said, changing the subject, arching his eyebrows, grinning as if recollecting a sweet little thought. "Excellent organization on your part, Brother

Auxiliary Provincial, bringing us all together for the roundup. Stephen, you're lucky, you're here in time to hear the testimonial letter Brother Paulus penned on the occasion of my twenty-five-year jubilee. I happen to have a copy handy for the inevitable deposition. Would you like to hear it? Good. It goes something like this."

Brother Charlie has enjoyed a marvelous, fruitful teaching career in the Brothers of the Holy Family. For generations he has sustained his students with his special brand of intellectual fervor and passion, loving each of them according to their needs, serving the entire community of Brothers and believers according to its desires. Along the way he has made an unforgettable contribution to the life of countless grateful young people, who are the hope for the future, and we stand forever in his debt.

Congratulations to our much-admired Brother Charlie on his magnificent career, and long may he flourish!

In Jesus' name,
Brother Paulus
Provincial, Western Province

Paulus, you poor man, you cringed to hear your words parroted. It looked like you wanted to slip down under your desk. I almost felt sympathetic. I told Charlie that I didn't care what the letter said, that maybe he had succeeded in fooling us before, but that now he must make things right with everybody, that this was his chance.

"None of you are going to forgive me, least of all you, Stevie. Not that I have justification to ask, and not that I have given you cause, but why would you consider being kinder to me than I ever was to any of you?"

Why not take the high road? That was my bolt of insight. Forgive me, Brothers, but I tried. "You can do it, Charlie. For old times' sake. Last chance."

That was when I assumed my seat in the last available school desk, alongside Shannon's.

I watched Charlie metamorphose before my eyes. His chest seemed to expand and he threw back his shoulders. He was now in absolute command. Maybe reading the testimonial had lit a fuse, for his eyes brightened and something powerful and enchanted came over him as he went into his great teacher mode:

"Are there any questions? Come on, don't be shy."

Billy raised his hand and Charlie called on him. "Yes, my Billy boy, what's on your mind?"

"I've got a question, Brother Charlie. Can you tell me *why*?"

"Why? Not a very precise question, but then, ah, Billy, why not? Why should I spare you? And why bother now? I could tell you why, though I regret to inform you that you don't have the capacity to understand."

Billy would not let him get away with that. "Reason I ask is, from where I sit, you are just a monster. Help me understand, help me hope to forgive you."

"The evidence seems to point in the monster direction, doesn't it, Billy boy?"

"Did you ever care about anybody beside yourself?"

"You've gone and done it now, Billy. Where is your evidence that I cared for myself? Think about it. I destroyed myself, too, which is why we are all here now in Stephen's teeming, stinking, overcrowded, stupid, clownish mess of an afterlife, where I guess we belong as well as anywhere. Besides, unfortunately, your question is a *bad* question, Billy. All yes/no questions are simplistic and flawed."

"No, it isn't a bad question. It's my only question."

"I can't help you, Billy. Let me point out, however, that whatever transpired between us, I have also given you something very special."

"A complete set of nightmares? Terror of the unknown? A desire to get myself killed? Is that why my eyes jump around in the sunlight, and I can't look at anything steady and whole?"

"Listen to me. I have given you, Billy, one thing everyone desperately seeks. I have given you a reason you were ever alive. Is there a higher calling for a teacher? I don't think so. You and everybody around this improvised classroom, you are now in possession of a most excellent reason. You have endured suffering necessary to remind you of who you are—and of why you were ever born. We are none of us spared the suffering of once having been alive. I have granted you nothing less than a purpose, an organizing principle, which is your memory of me. What is purer, more sublime, more bracing than hatred? It's the next best thing to love, isn't it? It might even be the flipside of love. Which I also showed you, yes, love. What's more, ever since we knew each other, since circumstance drew us together, ever so briefly, from that point forward you were able to justify all your future failures, all your ambitionless, empty, futile little designs that added up to nothing, and you could dump all your misery onto me, and why? On second thought, maybe I will tell you why. Here's why. Because I shared with you intimacy and affection—"

"You know you are a sick man," I interrupted him. "You know that, don't you?"

He glared at me. "Yes, affection. Yes, intimacy. Love scars people, Stephen—grow up, would you?"

I stood up. "This is your idea of apologizing to everybody you betrayed? Your show's over, Charlie."

"Sit down, Stevie!"

"Answer Billy's goddamn question, Charlie. Why? All of us need to know."

And Charlie lashed out. "You always tried to protect Billy, didn't you? But not me, you didn't try to protect me, not once, not ever. Sit down, Stevie, and curb your inappropriate language, or I am going to have to ask you to leave and go to the principal's office."

Charlie stood ramrod straight and clenched his teeth, as if he were facing his executioners with the last shred of his dignity intact. All he was missing was cigarette and blindfold. "You want me to pay for my sins? Fine. It's a human urge you are obeying, so fine. We shall do it your way, since you insist. Be advised, though, that it won't help you or anybody else, not a whit. Knowledge is overrated. Knowledge never saved anyone. I refer to the Garden of Eden. And so on."

Charlie's face turned red and he pointed at Shannon with a trembling index finger. "Let's get the record straight, shall we? Never, not once, did Joel touch Shannon. I will prove it. When you study her charges, when you closely examine the lawsuit, it becomes clear. The details do not hold up. For instance, she swears she was molested by Joel the night of the cast party after the spring show, on campus, in my office, far away from the cafeteria where everybody was gathered."

I was not going to let him talk his way out of this. But my voice was not the only one rising up.

That's when Joel said, "You know what I was doing at eleven o'clock, Stephen?"

How the hell would I know what he was doing?

Joel said it was the spring show, the cast party, and the school building was deserted, the parking lot was jammed, the scratchy phonograph music coming from the cafeteria, the dancing, the yearbooks being signed, the kisses and hugs exchanged. I was not there at the party, either, though I wish I had been. But I could see it all taking place at the party, because I visualized it a million times, what took place without me that night. Joel said he was with Charlie that night in his office.

"So what?" I said. "This night, that night, big fucking deal."

That is when Shannon piped up. "Enough, Stevie. Enough already. He's right, Stevie. Brother Joel never did molest me that night—or any other time. I was willing. He was in the wrong, but what difference does that make? I'm sorry. I should have told you."

"You lied, Shannon?"

She shook her head. "I told the whole truth, Stevie, only not the whole truth about me, but the whole truth about *you* and the whole truth *for* you. You couldn't say the truth, I had to do it."

"I never told you, I never acknowledged it myself."

"You didn't have to. You changed. You were not Stevie anymore. When you joined the Brothers it was all totally wrong, I could tell. I couldn't let Charlie get away with it—he needed to suffer for what he put you through. Suffer for what he put *us* through. I knew Charlie had been molesting you."

"Plot twist," said Charlie, "that's what I call a plot twist. Nevertheless, children, when Shannon filed suit, I knew my performance was over. And Stephen, I knew you would eventually track down the facts about Joel and me, because that is the way you are. The exposure, the embarrassment, was going to be more than I could tolerate. I have my pride, you know. Pride may be all that remains for me. A little decorum, please. True, it's a false poise, but a man needs self-respect any way he can get it. I decided to do something. Because the one person who would be hurt the most by this revelation was not me, Stevie, but you. It was the least I could do for you. And that's when I strung myself up here, in the trees your afterlife calls the Hanging Gardens. It is a good enough place for me to slip away and be done once and for all with my sins. I won't ask the girl to apologize for lying. Shannon did what she did for love. Just like I did. Just like I did. For love. And if you don't think I loved you and Billy and everybody else here, even Joel a little bit, I deserve my fate. Which I do." Casually he removed the black scarf wrapped around his neck and revealed the burn tracks made by his rope.

"Charlie, please tell us why you selected us."

"Oh, Stevie, Stevie. Selected? *Selected?* Isn't it obvious? You were special. You were noticed by me, that's all."

"But I'm talking about you, how'd *you* do it? How could you do it?"

"That's simple. Simple and banal. One day you begin to believe you are above every petty consideration, you believe that somehow no threatened sanction applies. You fold yourself up in a cocoon of your own devising. Once I was a good man, you know. Don't look like that. Don't mock me, it's true. Then it occurred to me that I could do what I desired because I desired to, and nobody else needed to know. Everything is permitted, Stevie. Haven't you learned that yet? Every. Thing. Is. Permitted."

"Permitted? *Permitted?*"

"Just listen to yourself, Stephen."

"Permitted by whom!"

"Have you missed everything? Have you been asleep for fifty years? Time to wake up."

He walked over and leaned over me in my desk. I tried to will my arm to rise up and stop him, but I failed, I failed. I could not push back. At the same time, and this is as strange as anything else I have told you, I also wanted to embrace him, also wanted to take him and me back to a time before it all happened, to the time before I ever entered his classroom that spring afternoon to ask for advice on my vocation. But I did not budge and Charlie placed his parched lips on my forehead once, and softly. Then he whispered a single word into my ear. In the rush of revulsion, it sounded as if he said "sorry," though perhaps it was "hurry," or maybe even "horror."

Not that words mattered much, except of course words are all we have, and they will have to do until somebody conceives a better alternative. Any of those words would fit perfectly the circumstances: *sorry* and *hurry* and *horror*. Preach the gospel, said Saint Francis of Assisi, and if necessary use words. Speak to me from your heart, Charlie, and if necessary use words.

He turned on his heels and walked toward the far stand of trees, where a rope hung down within easy reach of a ladder.

I tried to stand, I tried to run over and stop him. I could not move.

He stopped and called back to all of us who had made him what he had become, all of us who wanted to remake what was left of ourselves. "Children? Children, I'm done with all of you. For your own sake, I hope you will one day be done with me. Of course, you can look at it another way. Think of it as just one more unforgettable scene for Dead Week."

"Don't, Charlie." Those were the words screamed inside my head, words I tried to force out of my mouth.

"Listen to me, little ones," Charlie said. "I have done the state some service and they know it. No more of that. When you shall in your letters these unlucky deeds relate, speak of me as I am, nothing extenuate."

Shannon stole his thunder. "Spare us the Shakespeare, Brother Charlie. You loved neither wisely nor too well. You're sick. You're evil."

"Sick, maybe. But I am not evil, Shannon," he said plaintively, as if he almost cared to change her mind. "If I have learned anything, it's that there is no such thing as evil. Evil's not a thing outside yourself. But if there is anything that is evil, evil is what you do when you think somebody like me is evil. *That's* evil. You know that better than anyone. I was good to you in the only way I knew how to be. Who besides me helped you find your voice? Keep hating me, Shannon, and you won't be able to go on."

"A little late," she said. "But you know, you could be right about one thing. Maybe you do not descend to the level of evil. You are sad, you are feeble. What you did never finally mattered. You're done."

But to me, it did matter. To me, Charlie mattered. I wanted to forgive him. And at the same time, I could not forgive him.

"Ah, you're reading my mind," Charlie said to me over his shoulder, resuming his passage toward the fateful tree. "I feel the same. You see, Stevie, I was always your mentor, always what we brothers called your Angel. Goodbye, children, goodbye. Class dismissed."

No one made a move to stop him and soon, too soon, not soon enough, Charlie was swallowed up by the Hanging Gardens

Molly and Les zoomed off in a cloud of dust, and then The Definitorium slowly processed, along with Billy and everybody else, in the opposite direction down the hill, where I lost sight of them.

Shannon and I were left by ourselves.

THE GRAND DEPOSITOR

You get it now, don't you? Tell me finally that you see. We never get it right about those we once loved, neither those who harmed us as a result, nor those who loved us in return. We think we

understand their pain, but we barely have a clue as to our own. It is a frayed, bloodied patchwork, our understanding. A quilt of flesh and tears we wear like shrouds to our own last reckonings. Your work is complete now, my Grand Depositor, at last. Thank you for your questions, after all. I believe you and I both possess the only answer that matters now. That there is, finally, no answer available to us in our lifetimes.

———

Shannon and I made our way back to her cabin. We had become different people in the interim. Sadder people, wiser people? I only know this was not the rime of another ancient mariner.

After Charlie left us to our own devices we took our places in the Adirondack chairs on her deck and watched the sun play on the branches. There could have been food on the table, perhaps some fruit, perhaps freshly baked bread, but I cannot recall, because my recollections from here on out begin to grow progressively dimmer, vaguer, my convictions more attenuated.

Too much had happened before and after, far too much.

"I'll miss you, too," she said, using an odd verb tense, turning away, shielding her face from me.

I didn't get what she was talking about, and I didn't get the verb tense, either. We had each other to ourselves at last, didn't we?

She turned back to me. "It's over. It's done."

How could that be?

"You don't get to stay here, Stevie. None of us do. You know that, don't you, honey?"

I looked down at my hands, which I had folded and placed in my lap like a good schoolboy. A gorgeous orange glow was gathering in the near distance.

"Do you see that?" I pointed toward the emerging butterflies, whose wings were tinting all the branches.

"That's why I planted the milkweed, to attract those Monarchs you love so much."

I looked at her and said: "So beautiful."

"Unbelievably beautiful, aren't they?"

"You are more beautiful. I realize my whole life, and even after, you have been there."

I got up to go. She was right. It seemed, despite everything, to be the thing to do. Not that I wanted to, but I felt myself being lifted and pulled slowly and gently but inescapably away.

"Stevie, wherever you are going is going to be fine."

I wanted to take a closer look at that butterfly. I had the sense I was supposed to follow wherever it was to take me, but all I could say was, "Are we sure, Shannon?"

"I can't keep you company, Stevie. That's the way it works. Though to tell the truth, I'm only guessing."

"Will you be here when I return?"

She smiled. "Sure. Sure, I'll be here, when you come back."

"This is the only place I ever felt at home, alongside you."

"We found it out in the nick of time." Her voice was growing softer and softer, more and more remote, and I was straining to hear every syllable. I was desperately reminding myself *remember this, remember this, remember this, remember this.*

The winds were growing calmer and calmer, too, and we both seemed to take notice in the same instant. I was trying to understand what the winds had been telling me ever since I had come here.

"Now we both know about the winds. You have been carrying inside you a world of sighs," she said, her voice barely above a whisper, "and that's been the truth about your life in your world—till now."

Remember this.

She seemed to be receding slowly from my gaze, or I was moving away from her, or both.

"Now your sighing can finally stop," she seemed to say.

Nothing was left to sigh about anymore.

A butterfly had lighted on a branch within my reach and fluttered its big bright wings and I was moving away. "But I bet I'll probably return before you even realize I was ever gone. I've got to go back. There are matters only I can set straight." But I didn't want to believe a word of that. "It's time for me to go," I said.

"It's a beautiful day, Stevie. The Monarchs will keep you company. You can return right now to your life."

"For a second I was sure my life was right here."

"That's what I have been told."

"You've been told?"

"All for now, Stevie, all for now."

"I don't want to leave you."

"It's not my decision. You know, it's probably your decision. But don't worry. I'm right here, Stevie. Close as can be. All you need to do is look."

"Where?"

"In the same place I've always been, Stevie. Inside yourself."

I knew that now. Still, that is the most optimistic thing anybody ever said to me, and, Brothers of the Definitorium, it's the last thing I would hear uttered by Shannon Reed, whom I had loved for what felt like my entire life, and whom I knew I would love forever. That is the truth I would take away with me from wherever I had been. I had learned all over again what she had taught me when I was too foolish to believe. The next world would be the only one possible for Shannon and for me. If you take away anything from this report, Brothers, know that there is always a next world.

But that was all for now.

Soon I was passing swiftly over a carpet of golden leaves, as if I had become one with the diminishing winds. The sky above appeared brilliant blue through the filtering trees. My feet were feeling lighter and lighter, then my legs, then my chest, then my arms, then my hands. I had the astonishing thought I would be taking wing any instant. My head was filling up with what felt like thousands of butterflies.

Remember this, Shannon could have been saying.

Remember this, I was telling myself.

Remember this, the butterfly wings were whispering, remember this.

This.

This.

This.

THE DEFINITORIUM

It was a memorable moment for Stephen, though he would not be the one to remember it. That fluttering butterfly was not only the most beautiful one he would ever see in his lifetime, it was also the last.

He had seen his share of butterflies, but this one seemed to constitute a shocking revelation. Not knowing better and seeing his eyes wide open and his mouth agape, you might think a grizzly bear was running straight at him.

Today was different. Reaching for pen and paper was not an option.

Stephen was the kind of man who registered everything. He never went anywhere without a notepad, and he jotted down details along with observations about—about anything, really. A hawk sighting, a beautiful number, a tricky password, a book somebody recommended, a line of poetry, a social slight, the doctor's appointment, a song he couldn't get out of his head, a chore, anything. Also jokes. Someone who does a lot of public speaking can always use an ice breaker.

Suddenly his head jerked to the side. He seemed startled, as if someone had shouted his name. Though others were nearby, nobody had shouted anything. That was when Stephen noticed the butterfly. It was dancing on the other side of the windowpane, its orange wings framed by those blue depths of sky.

Inside the school building, a man sprawled along a weathered conference table like somebody's lost raincoat. His weary eyes could have been pleading for a wonder drug. His name was Stephen.

The summer sky looked milky blue, color of a wonder drug, and everyone was alive for now.

> A. *God made the world.*
> Q. *1. Who made the world?*

Acknowledgments

The author is thankful to:

Elizabeth Trupin-Pulli.
David Poindexter.
Sonny Brewer. Dorothy Carico Smith. Michelle Dotter.
John A. Gray. Regan McMahon.
Charles Freiberg. A certain Catholic priest.
Edwina James. Patricia James.

All for you, all for you.